The Good Fortune Bakers of Bayside Avenue

A novel by

Esta Fischer

Esta Fischer

The Good Fortune Bakers of Bayside Avenue

All the characters, places, and events in this work are fictitious or are used in a fictitious manner.

ISBN (Print): 978-1-09836-741-1
ISBN (eBook): 978-1-09836-742-8

By the same author:

Murder a la Russe

Murder by Charlotte Russe

Murder by Tea a la Russe

This book is dedicated to Susan "the Duck" Shackter, who said:

"I think there's a story here."

Chapter 1

Ida Rappaport baked sugar cookies on the day the Cheong sisters moved to her building, 388 Bayside Avenue. She happened to look out her front-facing kitchen window while she waited for the cookies to brown at the edges, just when the movers' truck pulled up and began to unload. That was when the sisters appeared. They looked like China dolls, the kind her daughter once owned as part of her Dolls of All Nations set. Ida recalled that doll dressed in pink silk pajamas. The China dolls in front of her building wore miniskirts, puffy down jackets that came only to their waists, and knee-high boots. She imagined their derrieres must be frozen in the early December chill.

She checked the cookies, removed them from the oven, and put in the next batch. Every year at the Christmas holidays she gave boxes of cookies to her building's Super and porter. Her daughter didn't approve of what she called Senior Baking (Ida was ninety-one years old), worried that Ida would forget to take the cookies from the oven and burn down the house. Ida calculated that during her lifetime she had probably baked a million cookies, one hundred thousand cupcakes, and a countless number of cakes. In her heyday she was known as the Bake Sale Queen, when school PTAs and Ladies Auxiliaries at the Jewish Centers organized those fund-raising extravaganzas. That was before Women's Lib, after which women felt they had to go to work just like men, and had no time to bake except for a quick Betty Crocker or a Duncan Hines. Ida prided herself on baking everything from scratch. That was also the time before the government got out of hand with telling people what they could eat, and deemed cupcakes and school bake sales unhealthy.

She looked out the window again at the furniture being lined up on the sidewalk and put onto dollies. Arthur Sandowsky, president of the Tenants Association, had alerted her to the new tenants' arrival.

"Two sisters," he said. "One married, one single. The married couple above you in 5C. The single below you in 3C."

"I'll be like the crème filling in a sandwich cookie," Ida thought aloud.

"Fortune cookie," Arthur said. "They're Chinese."

Now she observed the furniture: beds, chests, tables, chairs, sofas and lamps. Soon she heard the sound of unloading both below and above her. More cookies came out of the oven, more went in. She also gave a box to Arthur, or whomever was the current Tenants Association president. A few snowflakes wafted by the window and she hoped her new neighbors would survive the cold New York winter. Arthur had reported the Cheong sisters were from Hong Kong. Ida had looked up Hong Kong in her old World Atlas. Of course, as a child she had studied geography in school, was a straight-A student, but that was seventy-five years ago at least. She remembered the five continents, and the countries frequently mentioned in the television news, but the fine points such as Hong Kong had faded away.

She had always prided herself on her interest in foreign cultures, though during her childhood, the predominant foreign culture in her neighborhood was her own: Eastern European and Russian. Later, when she married and moved to the Bronx, there were Italians. Then she became acquainted with Italian cuisine: spaghetti and meatballs, and pizza.. She could still conjure up the scent of tomato sauce from the apartment of her old next door neighbor Mrs. Fratelli. Nowadays, these foods were commonplace, and Italian cooking had branched out to all kinds of interesting dishes. But when it came to China, her knowledge was limited to her Bronx neighborhood Chinese restaurant where her family would go on occasion, selecting one dish from Column A and another from Column B. In the modern multicultural world, there was more dissemination of cultural information on China. For instance, she knew the Chinese celebrated a different New Year from the Americans and Europeans, and these years were named for animals. Every year the Post Office issued a new stamp with this animal pictured on it. And there was a parade in Chinatown with firecrackers and men dancing in a dragon costume. She wondered if the Cheong sisters spoke English.

She removed the final batch of cookies from the oven, remembering to turn the oven dial to off. Then she washed her hands and neatened her hair. A glance at the kitchen clock told her the mail carrier had come and gone. Even if he hadn't, she would check the mailbox, and possibly check on the Cheong sisters as well.

Over the years, Ida had developed what she thought of as information-gathering strategies in all the apartment buildings in which she had lived. On her own floor, these consisted of pressing her ear to her apartment door, or, if necessary, taking garbage to the incinerator or compactor compartment at the end of the hallway. She always kept some throw-aways, such as old newspapers and magazines, at the ready for these situations. If an appearance in the lobby was required, there was the mail, or the laundry room. So now she put on a thick cardigan, locked her apartment door, and rang for the elevator. At the lobby, she stepped out and into an arrangement of furniture: blue upholstered couch and chair, and a coffee table. Seated side by side on the couch were the Cheong sisters.

"Hello," Ida said, beaming at them, "and welcome."

The Cheong sisters looked at each other, puzzled, and frowned. Then they exchanged several words in Chinese, and smiled back at Ida.

"Hello," they said in unison.

"I am Ida Rappaport," Ida introduced herself. "I live here."

The sisters nodded rapidly like bobble heads in comprehension.

"I am Lily," said one of the China dolls.

"I am Kitty," said the other.

Ida wondered how she would ever tell them apart. They had the same perfectly round faces, and cupid lips. They had the same straight black hair cut just below their ears. She remembered one of them was married and checked their hands for a ring, but neither wore any jewelry. She pointed to the vacant chair.

"Do you mind if I sit down?" Ida asked.

The sisters seemed startled and Ida thought they didn't understand her. She pointed at herself and then at the chair. Another rapid Chinese exchange took place.

"Please have seat," Lily smiled and waved a gracious hand toward the chair.

Ida sat.

"This not our apartment," Kitty said, waving a hand to encompass the lobby. "Just wait to move furniture."

"Yes, I understand," Ida nodded. She paused. The China dolls said nothing. "I hear you are from Hong Kong," Ida finally said.

The sisters smiled.

"Yes, Hong Kong," Lily said.

"Very far away," said Kitty.

"Why did you move to New York?" Ida asked.

Another round of Chinese echoed in the lobby.

"She marry husband," Kitty explained, nodding at Lily. "Job send him here. So we move."

"I see," Ida said.

"We are twins," Kitty continued. "Cannot separate. So two apartments."

"And your husband is American?" Ida questioned Lily.

"Not American. Swedish," Lily informed her.

Now Ida was startled. This information complicated matters. She knew Sweden was a part of Scandinavia, in Europe, and from this country Nobel prizes were awarded. But the combination of Chinese and Swedish was too much for her to contemplate on the spur of the moment. She decided to drop the Swedish and stay with Chinese. For now.

"May I invite you to my apartment for tea?" Ida asked. She had suddenly remembered the Chinese liked to drink this beverage,

The China dolls immediately perked up.

"You drink tea?" Lily asked.

"Oh, yes," Ida assured them. "I have some very good Twinings English Breakfast."

The sisters frowned.

"What is Twinings?" Kitty asked.

"It's a good brand of tea," Ida explained.

"What color?" Lily asked.

Ida tried to picture the cardboard tea box.

"I think it's blue," she told them.

Again the puzzled look and rapid Chinese.

"In China," Lily said patiently, "tea is green, white, or red. Which is yours?"

"Black," Ida said, now understanding. She thought.

More looks, more Chinese.

"Just come," Ida suggested, "and you can see for yourself."

The sisters nodded in unison.

"What floor?" Lily asked.

"Four," Ida told them.

They leaned back against the sofa cushions as if to avoid a bad smell. Ida wondered if she needed a breath mint.

"Is something wrong?" she finally asked.

"Chinese not like number four," Kitty explained. "Very bad luck. Four sound like death."

Ida was baffled. She mouthed the words "four" and "death" but could not detect the slightest similarity.

"In Chinese language, sound alike," Lily explained. She made two strange sounds, one after the other, that sounded exactly alike. "First word four, next word death," she continued, as if it were the simplest thing in the world.

"So you won't come to the fourth floor?" Ida tried to clarify. "I bake very good cookies," she informed them, hoping to tempt them past death.

"Oh, no problem, we come," Kitty assured her. "This building very lucky. Will balance fourth floor."

"Why is this building lucky?" Ida asked.

"Building number is three eight eight," Kitty explained. "Eight is very lucky number. So we come to fourth floor, no problem. Which apartment?"

"Four C," Ida said.

The Cheong sisters processed this.

"Between us," Lily finally deduced.

"Yes," Ida confirmed. "How about Saturday at three?"

"Saturday at three," the sisters confirmed. "Four C. No problem."

The elevator door opened and the movers emerged and pointed to the blue couch and chair. The Cheong sisters abruptly stood up.

"Sorry, now we go," they announced.

Ida hauled herself out of her chair.

"See you Saturday. Don't forget!" she called as the sisters and their furniture disappeared.

Chapter 2

Ida invited the Cheong sisters to come on Saturday because her cleaning girl always came on Friday. Ida's daughter Barbara didn't approve of the term "cleaning girl." She said it was sexist and demeaning, and the word "cleaner" was the correct term. But Ida insisted she did not intend to insult any of her cleaning girls, of which she had employed several over the years, both in the Bronx and in Flushing. Her late husband Irwin always felt housecleaning was not a job for his wife, especially after Barbara was born. And so a series of young women were employed to dust the furniture, scrub the floors, and push the Electrolux along the plush carpets.

In preparation for the China dolls' visit, Ida had baked three kinds of cookies: Triple Ginger, Chocolate Crackles, and Sugar cookies. It was from her Hungarian grandmother that she had most likely inherited her baking gene. As a child she had watched her grandmother make bobka, sponge cake, honey cake, and cookies. Those were the days sans electric mixer, sans food processor, sans every labor saving device that would later turn the most incompetent novice into at least a two-star pastry chef. Ida still scorned modern kitchen appliances, though her daughter had persuaded her to use an electric mixer for cakes, and she had to admit the results for her Lady Baltimore cake were excellent.

The China dolls arrived promptly at three. They were dressed in miniskirts, knee-high boots, and tight-fitting v-neck sweaters. The skirts and boots were identical, the sweaters identical in style but different in color: one purple, one green. Ida was glad of the different colored sweaters as it would be a way of telling the twins apart. Then she realized she did not know which was which to begin with.

Standing in the foyer, Lily and Kitty gazed into the living room and gasped. Ida still lived in the Bronx Rococo splendor of yesteryear, which she had taken with her to Flushing, Queens, in 1970. Two large-footed wing chairs flanked an antique sofa complete with plastic arm protectors. A large, gilt-framed mirror hung on the wall over an ancient spinet piano which had been neither tuned nor played since its arrival in Flushing. Thanks to the cleaning girl, the end tables gleamed with polish and the silk lampshades had been relieved of their coating of dust.

Lily's mouth hung open.

"Like movie set," Kitty marveled.

Ida grinned, doubling the number of wrinkles on her face.

"Come into the kitchen," she said, " and have some tea."

The kitchen table was set with lace doilies, a china tea set in a pink floral pattern, and silver flatware recently polished by the cleaning girl. The paper napkins were thick and embossed. A large pot of Twinings English Breakfast was already brewed. Ida filled the cups.

"Red tea!" Lily exclaimed.

Ida frowned. The Chinese culture was stranger than she could ever have imagined. Black was red and death sounded like four. She brought a three-tiered cut glass dish of cookies to the table and sat down.

"Please help yourselves," Ida said, gesturing at the cookies.

Two petite hands reached out and each snatched a chocolate cookie. The women ate without comment and drank their tea.

"Like fancy bakery," Lily finally declared.

"Where you buy?" Kitty asked.

"I made them," Ida said.

The sisters exchanged a look and some rapid Chinese.

"Very delicious," Kitty declared.

The hands reached out and took one of each of the other kinds of cookie. Ida helped herself. Sounds of lip-smacking and slurping filled the kitchen. The China dolls ate several more rounds of cookies and drank several cups of tea. Ida wondered how the sisters kept their slim figures with such a hearty appetite. Of course, they were young, she reminded herself, and young people could eat without gaining weight. She wistfully recalled her own youthful figure, even after pregnancy and birth. Irwin had called her "movie star material" with her long reddish brown hair, slim hips, and perky breasts. As the years passed, gray hair sprouted and body mass expanded and sagged. Now, even her respectable size twelve was a far cry from her original dimensions.

Lily patted her mouth with her napkin and sighed.

Kitty pointed to the nearly empty cookie dish.

"Is difficult to make?" she asked.

For a moment Ida didn't answer. Cookie baking was not difficult—for her. But she remembered more than a few instances when she had given recipes to friends and relatives, assuring them of success, only to be chewed out for their disastrous results. Plus she suspected the Cheong sisters could not read English.

"Have you ever baked anything?" Ida asked them.

The twins looked at each other.

"Not bake. Only cook," Lily said.

"But cook very good. Chinese dish. Not like American Chinese restaurant," Kitty said, wrinkling her nose. "Some time we cook for you."

Ida recalled the Columns A and B: chicken chow mien, beef with broccoli, and several shrimp dishes which were forbidden because shellfish were not kosher. She suspected Chinese people ate things like insects and chicken feet, and she had no intention of being subjected to such culinary delights.

"Baking is not really like cooking," Ida began, but Kitty cut her off.

"Wait! We make dumpling! Make dough with flour and water. Is like baking, yes?"

Ida had to admit it was something like baking, but only a distant cousin.

"Baking is much more complicated," Ida tried to explain. "There are more ingredients and more techniques. For instance, in some recipes you have to sift the flour three times."

"What is sift?" Lily asked.

Ida tried to think of how to explain. She got up and took a sifter from the cabinet. It was actually a double sifter. She demonstrated squeezing the handle so that the blades moved back and forth. The China dolls studied the sifter intently.

"What other?" Kitty asked.

"There's a rolling pin to roll out cookie dough," Ida said.

"Rolling pin—this we know!" Lily exclaimed. "Use to make dumpling."

"Yes, that's right," Ida agreed. "The rest is just a matter of having the right recipe, the right ingredients, the right oven temperature, and the right baking time."

"Maybe you can teach?" Kitty asked.

Ida was startled. She had never thought of teaching anyone anything, much less baking. Years ago her daughter Barbara was a Girl Scout and wanted to get her Cooking Badge. One of her assignments was to bake something for her next troop meeting. She had asked Ida for assistance. Ida suggested cupcakes, which were easily prepared from a batter, but Barbara insisted on a cookie recipe that included shredded coconut, peanuts, raisins and chocolate chips. Ida pressed her daughter to make a simple sugar cookie which she could then decorate as fancily as she liked. But, as with most things, Barbara had her way or no way. The cookies were a total disaster: there was not enough dough to hold the extraneous elements together and everything flattened and burned to a crisp. Barbara gave up on the Cooking Badge and chose the First Aid Badge instead. It was no surprise to Ida that Barbara went on to major in biology in college and went on to become a thyroid surgeon. (Irwin had voiced his displeasure by declaring that doctoring was no job for a girl, which Ida could have told him would only spur their daughter on.) Barbara's own daughter, Monica, whom Barbara hoped would go to medical school, rebelled not only against Barbara but against the world, and had become a Buddhist nun. For now. And Buddha was Chinese, Ida suddenly remembered. She wondered if the Cheong sisters were Buddhists but felt it was too early in their acquaintanceship to inquire.

"Well, I don't know," Ida demurred to Kitty's question.

"We learn fast," Kitty pressed. "Work for American Express in Hong Kong."

"Really!" Ida exclaimed.

"In back office," Lily nodded.

"Where Lily meet husband," Kitty elaborated.

"Did he also work for American Express?" Ida asked.

"No, no," Lily shook her head and giggled. "He cash traveler check. Meet on way out. Lunch time. Invite me to dim sum."

"I see," Ida said. And she could picture it: China doll Lily and a tall blond Swede, the Swede looking for a girl, the girl looking for a way out of secretarial work. "What is your husband's name?" Ida asked.

"Sven Akerblom," Lily said, but the first name came out like Sen.

"He not speak Chinese, only English and Swedish," Lily volunteered, and she giggled again.

"So what about cookie?" Kitty persisted. "You teach?"

"Well, I suppose I could," Ida nodded, mostly to herself. She was picturing her kitchen and the China dolls. They might have to stand on telephone books to get the proper leverage on the spoon to mix the dough. And the sisters might be a substitute for her own granddaughter Monica, who not only had no interest in baking but would not eat anything made with sugar.

"Well, all right," Ida agreed. "We can try it. We'll start with the chocolate cookies. They're the easiest."

"When start?" Kitty asked.

Ida paused before answering. She would need time to assemble the necessary ingredients and think about how to demonstrate and explain the cookie-making process.

"Next Saturday at three?" Ida suggested.

"Next Saturday at three," Kitty agreed.

The China dolls got up to leave.

"Thank you," they said in unison, and disappeared into the hall.

Ida went to the kitchen to tidy up, and noted an array of cookie crumbs on both the tablecloth and the floor.

Chapter 3

"That's a really bad idea!" Dr. Barbara Rappaport's voice blasted through the telephone, referring to the upcoming baking lessons.

Ida pictured her daughter wearing a white coat over her designer suit, sitting in her office in Good Samaritan Hospital in Los Angeles. She couldn't understand Barbara's objection to the Cheong sisters—she hadn't even met them! What did her daughter know of neighbors? The last time Dr. Rappaport lived in an apartment she had been interning, working long hours and hardly at home. As soon as she got her first job she had rented a house, and now owned a place. Her nearest neighbor was probably thirty feet away.

"But it will give me something to do," Ida explained.

"You know I think you should stop baking," Dr. Barbara went on. "What if you have a stroke while you're taking cookies out of the oven?"

"What if you have a heart attack while you're cutting someone's neck?" Ida countered. "You're sixty years old. Why don't you retire?"

There was a moment of silence from Barbara's end.

"I'm still an excellent surgeon," Barbara finally said. "Anyway, surgery isn't like baking and using a hot oven."

"Right," Ida agreed. "I might burn myself, but you might kill someone."

Again a silence.

"Well, be careful," Barbara backed down. "Don't let those Chinese women take advantage of you."

"I won't," Ida said, and hung up.

As usual she was annoyed at her daughter's attempt to interfere with her life, but she was used to it. Over the years Ida had occasionally wondered if Barbara herself had a thyroid problem. It would have to be overactive, considering her overly assertive behavior. Who knew, maybe that was why she had become a thyroid surgeon. And she knew Barbara was concerned about her, because they lived on opposite coasts. All the rest of the family had scattered far from the city. Ida was the only relative still a New Yorker. She had read of the burgeoning Chinese population in the city, and sometimes she wondered if one day New York would become completely Chinese and be renamed New Taiwan or New Shanghai.

She needed to look for the Chocolate Crackles cookie recipe and she located her Martha Stewart Cookies book on her kitchen bookshelf. Ida had kept up with all the new bakers: books by Martha Stewart, Maida Heatter and Dorie Greenspan were given prominent space, nestled beside the small metal recipe box that still held her grandmother's hand-written recipes, which she rarely took out because they were faded and crumbling.

Ida liked Martha Stewart's cookie recipes, though some of them had not worked out quite as they were supposed to. Personally, Ida thought Martha spread herself too thin, what with the farm and growing the herbs, milking the cows. Of course she had to have lots of hired help, but still. The Chocolate Crackles recipe was not as easy as she originally thought. But if the China dolls wanted to be bakers, they would have to plunge in. Melting chocolate, sifting flour and cocoa—it was not rocket science, as her daughter often commented about tasks people erroneously considered complicated. There was the matter of chilling the dough for two hours before baking. What would she do with the sisters for two hours? She decided to make a batch of dough on Friday, before the cleaning girl did the kitchen, so she could immediately demonstrate the baking of the cookies after the dough was made. Chefs on the Food Network always did this. Then the China dolls could take home their own dough and bake it later.

She opened the cabinet above the sink to check on her flour supply when the cabinet spoke. At least, it seemed to be speaking, in heavily accented English. Then Ida realized the voice, a man's, was coming from the apartment above her: Sven the Swede, married to Lily Cheong.

"Can't you cook anything besides Chinese?" he raised his voice, which was the deep booming kind.

"But in Hong Kong we always eat Chinese," protested Lily. "You like Chinese!"

"I'm getting tired of it. You have to learn some other dishes," Sven said, his voice moderating.

There was a pause.

"I make hamburger," Lily said hopefully.

"All right," said Sven, "for now."

"I learn baking," Lily said. "Make cookie for you."

"Oh?" Sven suddenly sounded interested.

Ida hoped he was not thinking of Swedish butter cookies, the tiny cookies that came in a round tin that people always bought at Christmastime. Ida could make these, but they were not what she planned to teach the China dolls. Sven would have to make do, just as he would have to make do with hamburger until Lily learned to make Swedish meatballs.

"Take lesson," Lily explained. "From lady downstairs."

"What lady?" asked Sven warily.

"Very old lady," Lily said. "Live downstairs. She offer teach. Kitty also."

Ida imagined Lily pointing to the floor, right over where Ida was now standing. She was tempted to shout something back up, but didn't.

Although she knew it happened all the time, she wondered how two people who barely spoke the same language could marry and think it was going to work. Especially in this case, where a sister-in-law was part of the bargain. Maybe they had threesomes in bed. She knew there were often individual agendas, mostly the acquisition of a green U.S. resident card. She shrugged it off as not her concern and checked the refrigerator for butter, eggs, and milk.

There would be an extra batch of cookies and Ida wondered what she would do with them. Ida had stopped sending her daughter cookies several years ago when Barbara informed her that she had been diagnosed with a condition called gluten intolerance and could not eat anything made with wheat. Ida suspected that a subconscious resentment of Ida's superior baking ability had manifested in this anti-baking illness. She decided she could always put the extra Chocolate Crackles in her freezer, and eat them herself later on.

Chapter 4

The next Saturday at precisely three o'clock, Ida's bell rang. The Cheong sisters stood in the hall, dressed in the same boots and miniskirts as previously, but one in a red sweater and the other in yellow. Ida wondered if she would ever be able to tell them apart. She decided she probably wouldn't, and it didn't really matter. She ushered them into her kitchen, where she had set up mixing bowls, measuring cups, and spoons along the kitchen counter. The table was covered with packages of ingredients. Ida had copied out the recipe in block print in the hope the China dolls would be able to read it.

Lily and Kitty had brought identical aprons, which they now put on. They also had pads of paper and pens.

"To write recipe and directions," Kitty explained. "In Chinese."

Ida wondered if she should tell them that this was a Martha Stewart cookie and the sisters should make note of it when they wrote down the recipe, as she herself always did.

"Do you know Martha Stewart?" Ida asked.

The sisters exchanged a look and shook their heads.

"She live in this building?" Lily asked.

"Which apartment?" said Kitty.

"Oh, no, she doesn't live here," Ida told them. "She's a famous..." She paused, not sure exactly how to describe Martha: a cook, a baker, a hostess, a homemaker? Martha's talents could not be adequately summarized with one word.

"Movie star?" Kitty suggested.

"No," Ida shook her head. "She writes cookbooks. Like this." She took the Martha Stewart Cookies book from the shelf and handed it to Lily.

The twins sat at the table, opened the book, and flipped through the pages, oohing and aahing at the color photographs of cookies.

"So many cookie!" Lily exclaimed.

"We learn all these?" Kitty asked.

Ida was speechless. She had never counted the exact number of recipes in that book but she was sure there were well over one hundred. Even if she were willing to teach them all, she might not live long enough.

"Let's just start with one cookie," Ida said.

"Like Chinese saying. Long journey begin with first step," Lily agreed. She smiled broadly, pleased with herself for this analogy.

"Lily study Chinese classic," Kitty commented. "Very smart."

Ida was happy to be in harmony with Chinese classics.

"Shall we start?" she suggested. "First, we'll melt the chocolate and then we'll sift the dry ingredients."

Ida had set up a double boiler on the stove and explained how to melt the block of chocolate. They then collected the flour, cocoa, baking powder and salt and began to measure. There was only one sifter so they took turns. While Lily sifted, Kitty took out her cell phone and snapped a photo.

"To send mother in Hong Kong," Kitty explained. Then she took over the sifter.

Ida noticed a sprinkling of flour and cocoa on the floor and realized she should have had the twins come the day before the cleaning girl, rather than the day after. At the same time she felt the China dolls were like young grandchildren who could be expected to make a mess.

"Finished!" Kitty announced, brandishing the sifter and letting another trail of flour fall to the floor.

"One time we go Wing Wah Chinese bakery on Chatham Road, have baking lesson," Lily suddenly remembered. "Really for tourist but we go anyway." She giggled.

"Yes," Kitty agreed. "Make wife cake."

"What is a wife cake?" Ida asked.

She had never ventured into a real Chinese bakery, although Flushing had several, and she was familiar with only two Chinese cookies: the crisp, cellophane wrapped fortune cookie and the large soft almond cookie. She used to enjoy an occasional almond cookie, until she discovered it was made with lard.

"Wife cake is long story," Kitty began. Then she frowned. "Story not important. Just take flour, oil, water and egg, mix, make dough. Put red bean paste in middle and fold in circle. Very famous."

Ida had never heard of red bean paste. She wondered if the red color had something to do with Communism, as in Red China, but felt it would not be a good idea to talk politics, at least until the cookie dough was made.

"It doesn't sound very tasty," Ida commented.

"This recipe happen in ancient China," Kitty explained. "No fancy food. But now we make steamed cake. Also Moon Cake. Very delicious."

"What is a Moon Cake?" Ida imagined an endless list of Chinese baked goods of which she had no knowledge, and might want to know about. She wondered if there was a Chinese Martha Stewart who had written a Chinese Cookies book.

"Moon Cake we eat at Moon festival each September," Lily explained. "Made with red or yellow bean, and fruits. Put in crust. Not make at home," she said emphatically. "Too difficult. Just buy. Next year we give you some."

"We also have Western style cake, but not like this cookie," Kitty added.

"In Hong Kong they probably don't use butter," Ida suggested.

A look and a brief exchange in Chinese took place.

"Butter," Kitty said, "we know this. But not use. Just oil and lard."

Ida knew there was nothing like butter to create a scrumptious cookie. Martha Stewart used plenty of butter in hers. And that was another of Ida's daughter Barbara's objections. Butter was high in fat and cholesterol. Though probably no worse than lard.

"You'll give yourself a heart attack from clogged arteries," Barbara had admonished.

Ida felt if cholesterol hadn't killed her yet, it was not likely to do so now. She had used butter in her baked goods for seventy-five years, long before the discovery of cholesterol and the subsequent trashing of butter. At some point, margarine was put forth as the ideal butter substitute. But Ida had never trusted its unnaturally yellow color and greasy feel. She had been proven right several years ago when margarine had been declared as bad as butter. If Barbara wanted to avoid butter, that was certainly her prerogative, but Ida refused to change her baking habits.

"Well, now it's time to cream the butter and the sugar," Ida said, pointing to the stick of butter and the box of brown sugar on the table.

Martha Stewart actually directed the use of an electric mixer in many of her recipes, but Ida preferred to do things by hand. The trick was to let the butter get so soft that it was nearly liquid. Then it could easily be mixed with sugar and egg using a wooden spoon. Also, Ida didn't know if the China dolls had ever used an electric mixer. After watching Kitty waving the sifter in the air, she had visions of cookie dough flying through the kitchen and spattering her cabinet doors. So the Cheong sisters would have to mix by hand. They were young and strong, and could easily do it.

The sisters took turns creaming, then added the egg and vanilla.

"Why use vanilla? This chocolate cookie," Kitty pointed out.

"I don't know," Ida admitted.

"Maybe you ask Cookie Book lady," Lily suggested. "Send email."

"Maybe," Ida said. She didn't use a computer.

They added the melted chocolate and the dry ingredients. Kitty looked at the bowl of dough.

"Now we bake," Kitty said.

"First the dough has to chill for two hours," Ida told them. "But I have another batch ready." She took her previously made dough from the refrigerator and put the dough made by the China dolls in its place.

Ida demonstrated shaping the cookies and rolling them in sugar, and soon with all three women working the cookies were in the oven. A chocolate aroma filled the kitchen. The sisters cleared the table and Ida made a pot of tea. When the last batch of cookies was taken from the oven, the women sat down to sample the result. Three hands reached out and each grabbed a cookie. There was silence as they tasted and chewed.

"Very delicious," declared Kitty.

"And yours will be exactly the same," Ida assured her. "You can take home the dough you just made, and bake the cookies in two hours."

"You keep dough. Tonight we practice, make our own," Lily said.

"Tonight?" Ida looked at her kitchen clock. It was just past six.

"Sure," Lily said. "Now we go to store, buy all things. Then bake after dinner. Then we bring you cookies, you tell us if okay."

"I go to sleep at ten o'clock," Ida said.

"Tomorrow morning," Kitty said. "No problem."

The sisters gathered up their aprons, pads and pens. They gave a passing glance at the flour-spattered floor.

"Sorry we make mess," said Lily, and she and Kitty hurried out the door.

Chapter 5

When Ida's bell rang the next morning, she opened the door to Kitty, who stood holding a napkin-covered plate.

"We bring you cookie," Kitty said.

Although Kitty said "we," Ida noted only one China doll was present. She ushered this one into her kitchen.

"Sorry Lily not come. Busy with husband," Kitty explained.

Ida had already deduced that Lily was busy with her husband, as she had been awakened by female shrieks and the sound of a shaking bed some hours earlier. At first she had thought to call the police; murder might be underway. But she soon realized it was that other act of passion, sex, and simply smiled. And now she realized this was the first time she was seeing only one Cheong twin, and she knew which! She scanned the woman's face, looking for a possible distinguishing feature with which to tell the twins apart, and detected a small mole on Kitty's left earlobe.

They sat at the table and Kitty whisked the napkin from the plate, revealing a dozen perfectly shaped Chocolate Crackles.

"Please try," Kitty nodded toward the plate.

"I think this calls for some tea," Ida decided, and she put up water.

After the tea was brewed and two cups poured, Ida took a cookie. She chewed thoughtfully, letting the flavor linger on her tongue.

"It's perfect," Ida said.

Kitty beamed. Then she pointed to the teapot.

"Why you always have tea in bag?" Kitty asked.

"Because that's how tea comes," Ida answered.

"Chinese not like tea in bag. Not good flavor. Just use tea leaf," Kitty commented.

Ida considered this. Her granddaughter Monica, visiting during a vacation from her nunnery, had mentioned "loose tea," in particular a roasted barley tea which the nuns drank. The nuns' diet had sounded rather Spartan: vegetables they grew in their garden, brown rice, and something called bean curd, which Ida had never heard of. She had immediately thought of lemon curd, a spread used on scones, but she suspected the two curds were not even distant cousins. Ida wondered if roasted barley tea came in tea bags, but she suspected the nuns would not use anything so convenient.

"If it doesn't come in a bag, how do you brew it?" Ida asked.

"In special teapot," Kitty said, taking her fourth cookie. "Some time I show you. You can learn many thing from us. Make tea, cook Chinese food, learn Chinese culture."

Ida smiled, but she wasn't sure she wanted to get so involved with the China dolls. Her own cooking was limited as she didn't eat a lot, and she certainly didn't need to learn the preparation of the foods she recalled from Columns A and B. Although she did still have fond memories of Chicken Chow Mein.

"Can you make Chicken Chow Mein?" she asked.

Kitty nearly choked on her mouthful of tea.

"That not Chinese food," Kitty said emphatically when she recovered. "That dish invented by American. That why American eat." She wrinkled her nose. "Chinese people not eat this."

Ida, taken aback, drank her tea. She thought again of Columns A and B. There was Moo Shu Pork and Pork Fried Rice.

"I'm kosher," Ida said. "No shrimp or pork."

"Kosher," Kitty repeated the word. "This allergy?"

"No, it's the Jewish religion. We don't eat pork or shellfish," Ida explained.

"Ah," Kitty nodded. "I understand. Like Buddhist."

"Not exactly," Ida said. "We do eat chicken, fish, and beef."

She thought of her granddaughter Monica, the alleged Buddhist, and would have liked to eavesdrop on a conversation about Buddhism between Kitty and Monica. Ida knew little of the Buddhist religion. She vaguely recalled a small statue of a fat Chinese man in the Chinese restaurant of old, and supposed that was the deity in question. And just as American Chinese food bore little resemblance to the real thing, she suspected Monica's version of that religious persuasion would not pass muster with the Cheongs.

"That why you like Chicken Chow Mein," Kitty said. "American like foods not true Chinese. Egg roll. Beef Broccoli."

"You don't eat those things in China?" Ida asked.

"We have, but not same. Next time, I make Chinese dish for you. Don't worry, I make chicken dish. No problem."

"Next time?" Ida asked.

"When you teach next cookie," Kitty said.

Ida froze with her cup midway between her mouth and the saucer. Teach next cookie? She remembered the twins' delight at the Martha Stewart Cookies book, and wondered how many cookies they expected to learn. She envisioned endless baking lessons and more messes in her kitchen. For a moment she even considered that her daughter Barbara had been right in her disapproval of the idea of giving baking lessons to the twins. But she was also flattered that the China dolls liked her enough to want her knowledge and her company.

"Which cookie do you want to learn next?" Ida asked Kitty.

"Ginger cookie," Kitty replied.

"That recipe is not too easy," Ida said, trying to sound discouraging. "You have to chop a lot of fresh ginger into tiny pieces."

"Like Chinese food!" Kitty exclaimed. "Chop into small pieces—garlic, onion, everything. No problem."

"Well, all right," Ida conceded. "But you and Lily will have to buy the supplies."

She imagined herself lugging shopping carts full of flour sacks, sugar, eggs and butter the seven blocks from the supermarket to her apartment building. Even if she had it all delivered, there was the matter of putting it away. Her kitchen cabinets were not yawning empty, waiting to be filled. Her collection of baking pans, including some that had belonged to her grandmother, took up no small amount of space. Her daughter Barbara had, of course, disapproved of the array of warped and tarnished metal.

"Why don't you just get rid of this junk," she had suggested during a visit the previous year. "Or try to sell it on eBay."

Ida had never heard of eBay and had no intention of unloading her heirlooms. She might have considered taking them with her to her grave, but Jewish cemeteries didn't allow such things.

There was also the expense of the ingredients.

"You give us list, we buy," Kitty assured her.

Ida wondered if the China dolls were both being supported by Sven the Swede. If so, he must be earning a hefty salary: two rents and two women. Ida was sure the China dolls did not come cheap.

"I'll have to take out the recipe and see what we need," Ida said.

"Recipe not in Cookie Book?" Kitty asked, puzzled.

"No, that's not a Martha Stewart cookie," Ida told her. "Is that all right?"

Kitty appeared to be stymied by this information.

"Martha Stewart isn't the only baking book writer," Ida explained. "There are dozens of baking books. Here, come and look." She led Kitty to her kitchen bookshelf. There were more than two dozen books: cookies, cakes, cupcakes. The China doll's mouth dropped open in shock.

"Don't worry, you can be a good baker without learning all these recipes," Ida said. She did not suggest Kitty browse the books. Although there were plenty of pictures, if she couldn't read English she would have no idea what was involved. "I'll look for the recipe later, and put a list under your apartment door."

"Okay," Kitty said. "When have lesson?"

"On Thursday," Ida told her.

The cleaning girl could do disaster control on Friday.

Chapter 6

Ida had not planned to discuss the Cheong sisters' baking lesson with Barbara during their weekly phone conversation, but it was a point of interest in Ida's otherwise mundane life, and she found herself going into much more detail than she'd intended.

"So I realized they should come on Thursday, so the cleaning girl can take care of the mess," Ida explained.

"Why are you still using that demeaning way of speaking?" Barbara snapped. "Doesn't the cleaning girl have a name? I don't think you've ever mentioned it."

"Charlene," Ida said. "Charlene Johnson."

Ida wondered if Barbara would now interrogate her regarding Charlene's race and age, and supposed anyone over the age of eighteen should not be called "girl." For the record, Charlene was Black (African-American, Ida mentally corrected herself) and probably in her thirties.

"And is that what you call her, Charlene?" Barbara continued. "I mean, I hope you don't call her 'girl.'"

"Of course not!" Ida declared. "But to other people, well, it's not as if she's my friend." Ida tried to think of the names of her friends, but her friends were all dead.

"And I hope you pay her Social Security tax and all that," Barbara said.

"I pay her in cash in an envelope," Ida told her daughter. "That's what she wants."

There was a brief pause in the conversation.

"So just how many lessons are you going to give these Chinese?" Barbara demanded, returning to the original subject.

Ida thought of the Martha Stewart Cookies book with its more than one hundred recipes.

"Don't just call them Chinese. They are individual women, with names: Lily and Kitty," Ida said, trying to avoid coming up with an immediate answer to Barbara's question.

"Like your cleaning girl Charlene," Barbara countered.

"I have no idea how many lessons I'm going to give them," Ida gave up on one-upping Barbara. "I had no idea I was going to give anybody any lessons about anything. But they're good students," she said thoughtfully, not having really considered this point. "The next morning they brought me a plate of cookies they'd made, so I could tell them if they did a good job. And they did."

"Why do they want to learn baking?" Barbara asked.

"Good question," Ida replied. "I have no idea. Maybe they don't have anything else to do. Like me," she added.

Barbara grunted in comprehension.

"I'm being paged," said Dr. Rappaport. "Got to go."

Ida hung up the phone. She still had old-fashioned land phones rather than the cordless type that people carried from room to room. The fact was, she was afraid she would put a cordless phone down someplace and forget where it was. Then she would have to ask a neighbor to call her so it would ring.

She went to the kitchen bookshelf to look for the Triple Ginger cookie recipe. This cookie had come to light only in the last two decades or so. Before, there were gingersnaps and gingerbread. The triple ginger must have evolved from New Age health awareness. Ginger was touted as a cure-all, in all its forms: powdered, ground, raw, and the candy-like crystallized ginger. The cookie itself was delicious, but the preparation was quite a chore. The raw ginger had to be peeled and chopped fine. The crystallized ginger also had to be chopped, a nearly impossible task as it was sticky and the little pieces insisted on being stuck together. She took up a pencil and paper and made a list of everything needed. She folded it neatly, put on a cardigan, and took the elevator down to Kitty Cheong's apartment, where she slipped the paper under the door.

Several hours later, the doorbell rang. Kitty Cheong stood on the doormat, list in hand.

"Sorry," said Kitty, "cannot read all English word. Please you read me, I write Chinese."

Ida nodded and beckoned her to come inside. She wondered if she should suggest English classes. Then she foresaw more lessons: practice speaking English. Her days would be filled with lessons. The thought gave her a headache. She motioned Kitty to sit at the kitchen table and she put on water for tea.

One by one Ida read out the list of ingredients and Kitty wrote in Chinese. Ida glanced at Kitty's piece of paper. The written Chinese looked like tiny pictures rather than letters and words.

"Chinese writing looks very different from English," Ida observed.

"Chinese language very difficult," Kitty nodded. "But I can teach you." She paused and frowned. "But take long time. Maybe not worth."

Ida could not imagine herself learning Chinese. Of what use would it be? She no longer ate in Chinese restaurants. The cleaning girl (Charlene, she reminded herself) did her laundry. She did not foresee sojourns in China, was not capable of climbing onto the Great Wall.

Kitty was scrutinizing Ida's face.

"You look same like Empress Cixi," Kitty declared.

"Who?" Ida was startled out of her not-learning-to-speak-Chinese reverie.

"You know, last Empress of China. Then came last Emperor Pu Yi," Kitty explained.

"Ah!" Ida exclaimed. "Yes. Years ago I saw a movie The Last Emperor. My daughter took me when she was in New York." She recalled the Empress, a stern-looking woman with a very wrinkled face. Like Ida's. "But I bet the Empress couldn't bake cookies!"

Kitty laughed.

"Empress not do anything," Kitty said. "Just eat, sit on throne, give order."

"Sounds kind of boring," Ida remarked.

"Anyway, I teach you Chinese. Few words. Okay?" Kitty asked.

"A very few," Ida agreed.

"First you learn easy one. All American visit China, say this: *ni hau.*"

"What?" Ida said, leaning toward Kitty as if she hadn't quite heard her.

"*Ni hau,*" repeated Kitty.

"Nee how?" said Ida.

Kitty nodded enthusiastically.

"What does it mean?" Ida demanded. "You're not teaching me a curse word, are you?"

Kitty laughed.

"Not curse word. Just mean hello," she assured Ida.

"Oh," said Ida. "Nee how," she repeated.

"Very good," Kitty told her. "I think you can speak good Chinese!"

"No," Ida said, "you can speak good Chinese. I'm terrible at foreign languages."

Ida knew that nowadays even elementary school children learned to speak foreign languages. Her daughter Barbara had studied French in Junior High, High School, and college. Ida's only experience with a language other than English was the Yiddish occasionally spoken by her parents. But her parents hadn't taught her Yiddish, because they wanted her to be American. Ida suspected the real reason was that they didn't want her to know what they were saying. She had picked up a few commonly used phrases that she still recalled: *vey is mir, nudnik, be gesunt.* She suspected her command of Chinese would consist of only a few stock phrases.

"So next time you learn one more," Kitty suggested. "Soon you can have many word."

The thought occurred to Ida that "many word" inferred "many cookie lessons."

"Why do you want to learn to bake cookies?" Ida suddenly asked.

Kitty froze with her teacup in mid-air, as if she had been caught out in something. She returned the cup to its saucer and shrugged elaborately.

"Just like bake cookie," she said. "Also Lily like bake cookie. For husband, you know?"

Yes, Ida knew about that. Irwin had loved her baking as much as he loved Ida herself. His favorite was a cookie called Thumbprint, a plain butter cookie with a dollop of raspberry jam embedded in the center. But as Irwin grew older and fatter, Ida occasionally wondered if she was showing her love or hastening his death. He did live to eighty-two, so she couldn't have done that much damage. And he died happy, keeling over from a heart attack shortly after eating a piece of Ida's dark chocolate cake with cream cheese frosting. But still.

"You'd better be careful," Ida warned Kitty. "Too many sweets can cause health problems like heart attacks and diabetes."

"Lily husband very healthy," Kitty assured her. "No problem."

"I hope not," Ida said, standing up to indicate the party was over. "See you Thursday at three."

After she closed the door, she tried to remember the Chinese words she had just learned.

"Nee who?" she said to herself, but she wasn't sure. But she was sure she would be tested on Thursday.

Chapter 7

Promptly at three on Thursday, the Cheong sisters rang Ida's bell. Laden with plastic grocery bags, they marched into the kitchen as if this was a takeover, unpacked the bags and placed the contents on the counter: a sack of flour, butter, molasses, baking soda, salt, brown sugar, ginger both ground and fresh, eggs, and a large container of beautiful crystallized ginger. They then donned their aprons, whipped out paper and pens, and stood at attention, awaiting directions.

"*Ni hau*," said Kitty.

"What?" Ida frowned.

"*Ni hau*," Kitty repeated. "Last time you learn this."

"I did?" Ida asked.

"*Ni hau*, mean hello," said Lily.

"Oh—yes," Ida admitted. "I'd forgotten. Nee how."

"Good," said Kitty. "Now we start?"

"Yes," Ida agreed. She pointed to the crystallized ginger. "Where did you get such nice ginger?"

"Korean supermarket," said Lily. "Very good quality."

Ida had passed by this store many times, but had never gone in. She'd mentioned it to Barbara, who was not enthused.

"They probably sell those strange foods, nothing you would eat," Barbara had said.

Ida looked again at the crystallized ginger.

"Well, now we have to chop some of that ginger into tiny pieces," Ida instructed.

Kitty reached into her apron pocket, removed a wrapped item, unrolled it and brandished a small knife.

"This knife chop good," Kitty explained.

Ida herself used a knife she had owned for decades. When she was a child, a knife sharpener came calling from time to time, just like the milkman and the man who collected scrap metal. Ida assumed the Cheong sisters had never heard of a milkman. Meanwhile, Kitty was chopping the crystallized ginger while Lily peeled the fresh ginger. It was sort of cheating, Ida thought, to have two sets of hands. It would make the recipe seem easier than it actually was. But maybe the China dolls did most things together. And today they seemed smaller. Then she realized they were not wearing their high heel boots. Instead, they had on dainty slippers decorated with sequins.

Kitty had made short work of chopping the fresh ginger. The twins looked at Ida expectantly.

"Next what?" Lily asked.

They quickly mixed the dough, and sat at the table while the cookies baked.

"Ginger is Chinese herb," said Kitty. "Chinese eat for health. If you eat ginger each day you can live very old. You should try. Then maybe you can be eighty year."

Ida smiled.

"That's impossible," she said. "I'm already ninety-one."

The China dolls exchanged startled looks and then some rapid Chinese. Ida waited for questions or comments, but before the women could speak, the oven timer went off. Lily jumped up and removed the cookie sheets. The aroma of ginger filled the kitchen. When the cookies had cooled, the twins packed them in a bag. They gathered up the remaining ingredients and the knife.

"Tonight we make more, bring you tomorrow," Lily said.

"Next Chinese lesson," said Kitty. "When some person say to you '*ni hau*,' you say back '*hen hau, ni ne*'?"

Ida looked at Kitty as if the China doll was out of her mind.

"Mean 'I very good, how about you?'" Lily explained.

"But what if I'm not very good?" Ida protested. "Then what do I say?"

The twins exchanged looks.

"Not polite, say not good," said Kitty.

"Next time we teach you some other word," Lily smoothed over the moment.

After they left, Ida surveyed the kitchen. There were sprinklings of flour and sugar on the floor, and bits of eggshell on the counter. How had they made such a mess? With broom and sponge she did a cursory mopping up but left the real work for—Charlene. There! She had thought of Charlene as Charlene and not as just the cleaning girl. Barbara would be pleased. But Ida had not heard from Barbara this week as she had gone to a thyroid conference in Honolulu.

"The time difference is a bit scary," Barbara had explained, "and what with the seminars and all, it will be easier if I just call when I'm back in L.A."

Ida could not imagine what a thyroid conference would entail. She supposed it was just a bunch of thyroid doctors talking about thyroids. But then she thought of another possibility: Barbara had not gone to Honolulu for a conference, she had gone to Honolulu on vacation with a man. A love interest. Her daughter never mentioned any love interests, but Ida was sure she had them, because Barbara had always had them. Starting with high school, Barbara had had a boyfriend. But it was always "a" boyfriend, not "the" boyfriend. Which was probably why Barbara and her husband had divorced. Hal must have been "a" husband rather than "the" husband, necessary to procreate children and help pay their expenses. As soon as Dr. Barbara landed a decent paying job she had ditched Hal. So now Ida had to wait to report to Barbara about her new attitude toward—Charlene! Then the phone rang. Thinking it might be Barbara (because she was practically the only person, other than Ida's doctor's secretary, who called), Ida eagerly lifted the receiver and said a bright "hello." But the voice on the other end was a stranger and not Barbara Rappaport.

"I'm calling for Charlene Johnson," said the stranger.

For a moment Ida couldn't place who Charlene Johnson was. Then she realized it was her own cleaning girl.

"She's not here," Ida said. "She only comes on Friday."

"Charlene won't be able to come tomorrow," she stranger continued. "She's ill."

"Oh," said Ida. "Well, I suppose I can get by for another week."

"She won't be able to come for several weeks," said the stranger. "She had her appendix out yesterday, she's still in the hospital. The doctor told her no heavy work for at least several weeks."

Ida was momentarily stunned. How long was several weeks? A month? She couldn't br without a cleaning girl for a month.

"She said to tell you she's sorry," the stranger added, and hung up.

Ida sat down at the table. She had to think. But she couldn't think, because she was in shock. A few minutes went by, and her head began to clear. But she didn't know what to do. Charlene had been her cleaning girl for nearly ten years. She could call Barbara on her cell phone number. Ida was not supposed to use this number except for an emergency. While this was not an immediate emergency, after another week it would become an emergency. The kitchen was already a mess. The dust would pile up on the furniture and carpets. She would run out of clean sheets. The thought of the bathroom made her shudder. She went to her phone and dialed her daughter's cell phone number.

"What happened?" Barbara spoke sharply. "Are you all right?"

"I'm fine," Ida said. "But there's a big problem. Charlene is in the hospital."

"Who's Charlene?" asked Barbara.

"My cleaning girl," said Ida. "I don't know what to do."

There was a pause on Barbara's end.

"This is why you called me? I'm on a break between presentations. I've only got a few minutes," she finally said.

Ida could hear a hubbub of voices in the background. Maybe Barbara really was at the thyroid conference and not with a love interest. Or maybe she was at a cocktail party with a love interest. Ida had no idea what time it was in Honolulu.

"I suppose you could send her flowers at the hospital," Barbara suggested, a trace of exasperation in her voice.

"That's not what I mean," Ida snapped. "Who is going to do my cleaning?"

There was another pause and an exaggerated sigh.

"Get another cleaning girl," said Barbara.

"Where?" asked Ida.

"Where did you get this one?" Barbara asked.

"She was recommended by my neighbor Mrs. Schwartz," said Ida.

"So ask Mrs. Schwartz if she knows someone else." There was marked impatience in Barbara's voice now.

"I can't ask her," Ida replied. "She's dead."

There was another long pause.

"Wait a minute—what about those Chinese women? The ones you taught to bake cookies." Barbara sounded suddenly enthused.

"How would they know of a cleaning girl? They just moved here and they barely speak English," Ida argued, annoyed at such a stupid suggestion.

"No, ask them to clean your apartment! You can pay them whatever you pay your cleaning girl," Barbara spoke rapidly. The background hubbub had died down.

"I don't know—" Ida began, but Barbara cut her off.

"I have to go, the session is starting in a minute," Barbara said. "I'll call you when I'm back in L.A." She hung up.

Barbara must definitely be at a cocktail party with a love interest, Ida decided several minutes later. She had forgotten all about not referring to Charlene as the cleaning girl.

Chapter 8

Most of the night, Ida drifted in and out of sleep, worrying about who would clean her apartment. It was all very well for Barbara to tell her to just get someone else. Her daughter had simply to ask around and find a suitable person. Ida supposed she could call an agency, but how could she trust someone totally unknown to dust her knickknacks, handed down from her own grandmother, without slipping one into their pocket. She suspected the items were not worth anything monetarily, but an uneducated person could assume a few dollars could be exchanged for a pincushion or a figurine. As far as the Cheong sisters were concerned, Ida didn't know if she should approach them. They might be insulted. Or if they were agreeable, what would she pay them? There was only one Charlene, but there were two China dolls, and Ida's income was not large.

The next morning Kitty and Lily rang her bell, a plate of triple ginger cookies in their hands. Ida motioned them inside and they settled themselves at the kitchen table. Ida reflected that this meeting of bakers could become a pleasant routine, baking and eating. Like when she played Mah Jongg in the Catskills years ago. Those were her young married days, when couples rented summer bungalows. The husbands remained in the city during the week, catching buses to the summer towns on Friday afternoon. On weekdays, the wives amused themselves with trips to the lake, and Mah Jongg. Ida's group had played on Tuesdays and Thursdays. She loved the clicking sound of the tiles. And they would drink real lemonade. She envisioned afternoons of Mah Jongg with the Cheong sisters. But they would need a fourth player. She tried to think of someone, but, as usual, most of the people she had known were dead or in nursing homes. And the China dolls probably hadn't been here long enough to have met many people.

"I'm sorry for the mess in the kitchen," Ida now told the twins. "But my cleaning girl is in the hospital, and I'm not up to any heavy work."

"Mess?" said Lily.

The twins exchanged some rapid Chinese.

"You mean kitchen dirty?" Lily clarified.

Ida nodded.

"No problem, we clean," Kitty assured her.

"Well, it's not just the kitchen," Ida said cautiously. "It's also the bathroom. And my cleaning girl also dusts and vacuums."

She realized she had reverted to referring to Charlene as "the cleaning girl," but felt under the circumstances she could be excused.

The China dolls exchanged another round of Chinese.

"We clean for you," said Lily.

"We are two," explained Kitty. "Do everything fast. Now need change clothes. Come back soon!"

The twins hurried from the table and left the apartment. Ida wondered if she had done the right thing. But it was too late now. Twenty minutes later, the sisters reappeared at her door. They were dressed in faded jeans, sneakers, and large old-looking tee-shirts that covered their entire torsos. Blue cotton scarves were tied over their heads. They were transformed from China dolls into—cleaning girls!

Lily entered the kitchen, pulled rubber gloves from her pocket and put them on. Ida showed her the cleaning supplies and hurried into the living room, where Kitty was already lifting and dusting knickknacks and carefully setting them on the sofa.

"The vacuum cleaner is in the hall closet," said Ida, pointing to a door. She stood in the foyer, somewhat disoriented by the buzz of activity. Charlene was a quiet and steady worker, going purposefully from room to room, beginning with the bedroom and finishing with the kitchen.

"Don't want to track kitchen dirt all over," Charlene explained.

Ida went into her bedroom and stretched out on the bed. Soon she heard the roar of the vacuum cleaner. She wondered how long it would take the Cheong sisters to finish the job. Her kitchen was large, the bathroom small. She dozed off and was startled awake by a loud rap on the door. Kitty peered inside.

"I clean bedroom now," said Kitty. She held a dust rag in one hand and with her other hand pulled the vacuum behind her like a dog on a leash.

Ida got out of bed and sat on the living room sofa. She glanced at the dustless end tables. Her knickknacks had been placed in their original positions. The carpet was free of lint. The only thing missing, she thought, was the scent of furniture polish, which she had not used since her younger days. She heard the sound of running water in the kitchen. Lily appeared in the doorway with a sponge mop.

"Wait floor dry," Lily called to Ida. "Then you look, see if okay. Need new mop," she added. "Get Swiff."

Ida didn't know what Swiff was but she would ask Charlene when she came back to work. If she came back. What if she didn't? Ida suddenly wondered if Charlene was really in the hospital. Maybe she had found another job and had asked a friend to call Ida with a story. Her imagination was running away with her: first thinking Barbara had gone to Honolulu with a love interest instead of for a thyroid convention, and now thinking Charlene had found another job. Ida didn't know the truth about her daughter. But Charlene was not like Dr. Barbara Rappaport, she was a steady, reliable woman. As if Charlene had picked up Ida's thoughts, the telephone rang.

"Mrs. Rappaport, it's me, Charlene," said the cleaning girl.

"Charlene!" Ida exclaimed. "Are you all right?"

"They're letting me out of the hospital tomorrow, but I can't come back to work for a while. But I'm going to send you my sister every Friday, until I can come back," Charlene explained.

"I didn't know you had a sister," Ida said.

"Her name is Sandy," said Charlene. "She's very good."

"I hope so," Ida remarked. Then she was taken aback by her own bad manners. "I hope you feel better soon," Ida said. "And thanks for calling."

By the time Ida ended the call, Lily was motioning her to the kitchen. First she looked in, then stepped inside. The counters sparkled and the floor gleamed. The stove and sink were spotless.

"It's wonderful!" Ida exclaimed. Kitty had joined them. "What can I pay you?" She looked from one China doll to the other.

The twins' eyebrows shot up and they exchanged a look.

"Pay? Not pay!" Lily said emphatically.

"You our friend, we just help you," confirmed Kitty. "No problem."

"Well, I can't thank you enough," Ida said.

"So we come next Thursday, learn next cookie," said Lily. "Three o'clock?"

For a moment Ida was speechless. She had forgotten about the baking lessons, or at least had not anticipated the next one so soon.

"What cookie do you want to learn?" Ida asked.

"You pick," said Kitty. "Put list under door."

"All right," Ida told them.

After the China dolls had gone, Ida returned to the kitchen for a closer inspection. It was as if Charlene had done her usual job. But then Ida noticed something: a gap in her kitchen bookshelf. The Martha Stewart Cookies book was missing! It seemed impossible.

She was always careful about putting her things back in their proper places. The only other people in her kitchen had been the Cheong sisters, most recently Lily. Ida did not like to think the China dolls would steal anything. And even if Lily had taken the book, where could she have hidden it? Under the oversized tee-shirt? Maybe, Ida decided, they had simply borrowed the book and had forgotten to tell her.

Chapter 9

"So did you find another cleaning girl?" Barbara asked.

She was apparently back in California in her hospital office. She always explained that it was more convenient to call from her office because of the time difference between the coasts, but Ida suspected her daughter did not want to waste her personal time speaking with her mother.

"As a matter of fact, I thought of somebody," Ida said. She did not want to give Barbara the satisfaction of knowing Ida had taken up her suggestion of asking the China dolls. "And Charlene has arranged for her sister to come in the meantime," Ida quickly added, hoping to close that subject.

"Her sister?" Dr. Rappaport said suspiciously. "Have you ever met this sister?"

"Well, no," Ida answered. "But Charlene has been with me for ten years. I think I can trust anyone she sends."

"Lock up the valuables," Barbara advised, and she hung up.

Ida sat down to ponder her next problem: which cookie to teach the China dolls. They had already done Chocolate Crackles and Triple Ginger. She decided the next cookie would be the plain sugar cookie, a good balance for the other two. She remembered the Chinese were interested in balance: yin and yang, and an exercise called Tai Chi, which had been taught at the Senior Center when she was a younger Senior and still went to lectures and classes. Ida had gone to one session of Tai Chi but had found it confusing, what with punching the air and pretending to carry a large ball that did not exist. Instead of continuing with Tai Chi, she had opted for Bingo. Now she took out her small recipe box to look for the sugar cookie recipe. Fortunately it was not a Martha Stewart recipe, since that book was currently out on loan. She hoped. The sugar cookie recipe had been handed down from her grandmother and then adapted to her own use. The original called for margarine, but Ida had found that Crisco produced a lighter, crisper product.

The sugar cookies would be more difficult than the others as they had to be rolled and cut out with a cookie cutter, and then carefully transferred to the baking sheet. And then there was the matter of decoration. Of course, the cookies could be served plain, but Ida had always frowned on naked sugar cookies. At the very least, she sprinkled them with cinnamon sugar. And when Barbara attended elementary school, Ida had made cookies for most of the holidays and sent them along to her daughter's class: heart-shaped cookies with pink frosting for Saint Valentine's Day, green-frosted shamrocks for Saint Patrick, egg-shaped cookies resplendent with nonpareils for Easter. And of course a great assortment of Christmas cookies. Which reminded her: what had happened to all those fancy cookie cutters?

The last she remembered of them was in the Bronx, in the apartment where Barbara grew up. They were kept in a plastic box, and she now assumed they had been packed and moved to Flushing with all her other possessions. She opened the kitchen cabinets above the sink and countertop and peered at the shelves, which reached to the ceiling. She had not investigated the contents of the uppermost and unreachable shelf—unreachable without a stepladder, that is—for many years. Ida had a stepladder, but Barbara had forbidden her to use it. This directive had been issued at least five years ago, possibly ten. Ida speculated on what atrocities now lived on that shelf. Powdered milk turned to sawdust, raisins turned to stone. But the cookie cutters should be fine. Or maybe they had been placed in one of the cabinets under the counter. She opened these, bent over slightly, and peered inside. Again, she could not recall what had been stored here. She used the same few pots and pans and dishes. Most of her meals consisted of barbecued chicken that she warmed in the microwave, or soup from a can, or tuna salad bought at the supermarket. The most cooking she had done in the last few months was scrambled eggs. Then an idea came to her. She would ask the China dolls to climb up the stepladder and search for the cookie cutters. And if they didn't find them on the upper shelves, they could search the lower ones. In the meantime they could use her standard round cutter.

The next item was the frosting recipe and the decorating equipment. The recipe was quickly found in her little box. It was a simple one, requiring only powdered sugar, butter, milk, and vanilla extract. And the decorating equipment—she stopped to think, and realized it was most likely in the same box as the cookie cutters. Well, the China dolls might find that too.

But then Ida's thoughts went to the rest of her cabinets' contents. She supposed she should sort everything out and dispose of what was expired or not needed. What if she suddenly died? Of course, eventually she would die, but so far she seemed to be putting it off. She imagined Barbara coming to the apartment after her mother's demise and opening the cabinets, pictured Barbara's look of dismay and consternation. Ida smiled. Sorting everything out would give her a break from the crossword puzzles she completed daily. Large books of them were sent by Barbara, who told her she needed mental exercise and this was just the thing. But Ida had become quite tired of them, and they were actually too easy. She would have to find a new interest. But getting back to the cabinets, Barbara just might send granddaughter Monica to clean the place out. Monica had once told Ida that Buddhists believed the world is an illusion and it is useless to hold on to material things. Ida imagined Monica carelessly tossing her great-grandmother's pincushion and other keepsakes into the trash, and she shuddered. Something would have to be done to prevent this.

In the meantime, she sat down at the table to make a shopping list for the China dolls. Should she have them buy food coloring to make different color frostings? She pictured small bowls (and where were her bowls?) of colored frosting lined up on the counter. This vision reminded her of Barbara's childhood paint set, little pots of paint scattered on the kitchen table, and the accompanying mess to clean up. Then Ida pictured the mess created by the bowls of frosting. But maybe the twins would take a hint and clean up after themselves. In any case, Charlene's sister would come the next day. Ida considered whether the China dolls would understand the term "food coloring." If they didn't, she was sure they would ring her bell and ask. She had used up her supply with this year's holiday baking. She completed the list and looked it over, then put on her cardigan to take the elevator down to Kitty. When the elevator door opened, to her surprise she faced Lily and Sven. They looked like a completely mismatched couple, Sven towering over Lily, he blond and blue-eyed, she petite, with dark hair and eyes.

"This cookie lady!" Lily told her husband by way of introduction to Ida.

"So you are the one helping me to get fat!" Sven said jokingly. He spoke with a slight accent.

"That's right," Ida replied. "Nice to meet you."

The elevator descended one floor and Ida got off. So they call her the cookie lady, she thought as she slipped the shopping list under Kitty's door. The cookie lady. She liked it.

Chapter 10

"Today we will make sugar cookies," Ida announced.

The Cheong sisters, aprons securely tied, pens and paper at the ready, stood at attention in Ida's kitchen.

"But before we start, I need some help," Ida continued.

Kitty looked around the kitchen, puzzled.

"Not cleaning," Ida quickly told her. "I need you to climb my stepladder and look for a big plastic box up there," and she pointed first to the broom closet where the stepladder was kept and then to the kitchen cabinets.

Kitty immediately opened the stepladder and scooted up. She began to hand down items to Lily: a double boiler, a box of packets of nonfat dry milk, and several Bundt cake pans. There was also a copper aspic mold.

"No plastic box," Kitty reported, and Lily handed the items back up.

But in the third cabinet, Kitty found it. The three women stood around the table, and Ida opened the box. The twins peered inside. Cautiously, they removed decorating tips, and the metal cutters: diamonds, hearts, Christmas trees, Easter eggs and animals. The China dolls chattered excitedly in Chinese. Lily lifted out the decorating kit, and Ida explained how it was used. Then the baking began.

By now the China dolls knew the basics and easily made the dough without assistance. Ida made tea and set the pot, cups and saucers on the table. They could all have a rest while the cookies baked.

"Now we must roll the dough," Ida said, and she removed her rolling pin from a lower cabinet.

The twins' mouths dropped open. This was no ordinary rolling pin. It had belonged to Ida's grandmother, and was an eighteen-inch dowel-shaped length of wood, with tapered ends rather than handles. Ida had taken it after her grandmother died, and felt it had given her good luck in her baking. She put a sheet of wax paper on the table and demonstrated the rolling and cutting of the dough. The China dolls quickly rolled and cut—they had four hands between them—and the cookies were put in the oven. The women sat down for tea.

"Why are you learning to bake?" Ida suddenly asked. She had assumed it was for fun. But after the disappearance of the Martha Stewart Cookies book, she began to wonder if the Cheong sisters were up to something.

"We have plan," said Lily, but then she stopped.

"Oh?" Ida looked expectantly from one China doll to the other.

Kitty was giving Lily a stern look.

"Not yet sure," Lily quickly said.

"I see," said Ida, though she didn't. "Well, if I can help you with anything, just let me know."

The sisters smiled and nodded their thanks, and drank their tea.

"Now comes the fun part," Ida told them when the cookies were out of the oven.

She instructed the twins on the making of the frosting, and set out several bowls (she had found them nestled inside a seldom-used pot). Wielding a tiny bottle of red food coloring, she made pink frosting. Then she filled the decorating tube and piped a zigzag of frosting across a round cookie. The China dolls stared in wonder, and exchanged rapid Chinese.

"May I try?" asked Kitty.

Ida handed her the tube. Kitty piped an elaborate design on a cookie.

"Is Chinese character," Lily explained. "Mean 'good fortune.'"

"You mean it's Chinese writing?" Ida tried to clarify. She knew Chinese writing consisted of lines and squiggles.

"Chinese writing called character," Kitty said. "Each character mean one thing."

"So this is good fortune," Ida nodded in comprehension. She squinted and inclined her head toward the cookie. "It's very complicated," she observed.

"Chinese writing not easy," Lily agreed.

"I write Chinese year animals," Kitty said excitedly. She frowned. "Not think right word. You know—pig, rabbit, ox, dragon."

"You mean the Chinese zodiac," Ida said. "What a marvelous idea!" In the last decade or so, due to the promotion of multiculturalism in New York City, Ida had become aware, through television and the newspapers, of the Chinese system of years and accompanying animals, though she could never keep track of which year was current.

The China dolls again exchanged rapid Chinese.

"Chinese new year very soon," said Lily. "Make many cookie, put dragon character with frosting."

While she spoke, Kitty was rapidly making pink hearts and yellow diamonds. She pointed to the diamond-shaped cookies.

"This shape like gold piece," she explained. "Bring money for new year."

Ida knew these were just superstitions, but she thought they were charming. She pictured the Cheong sisters making hundreds of cookies decorated with hundreds of Chinese characters.

"Just how many Chinese characters are there?" Ida asked.

"Educated person must know two thousand," said Lily.

Ida's mouth dropped open in shock. She could not imagine memorizing so many of the squiggly pictures.

"But have many thousand more," Lily added. "Very special word."

"Many thousand more?" Ida shook her head.

"Not worry, you not need learn," Lily assured her with a giggle.

Suddenly Lily glanced up at the kitchen clock.

"*Ay-ya*!" she exclaimed. She rushed to the sink and quickly washed her hands. "Sorry, must go. Last time, husband very angry. Come home six o'clock, no dinner waiting!"

"You go, I finish," Kitty told her, and Lily dashed out the door.

On the two other occasions when the sisters had come to bake, when they told her they would spend their evening making another batch of cookies, Ida had wondered, briefly, about Lily's husband. In Ida's day, married women were expected to put dinner on the table every night, and that was exactly what Ida had done. Fortunately for her, Irwin was a meat and potatoes man. There had been no need to fuss with fancy casserole dishes or those silly vegetable concoctions made with cheese or cream sauce, or with nuts sprinkled over them. It had been a revolving menu of pot roast, meat loaf, beef stew, and that fancy name for hamburger, Salisbury Steak, accompanied by potatoes mashed, baked, or boiled, and a simple vegetable or salad. And then there had been Barbara, a picky eater at best. Ida had read every women's magazine advice column, trying to get ideas of how to introduce Barbara to fruit and vegetables whose acquaintance she had no wish to make. Ida still recalled the meal at which her daughter had treated her serving of creamed spinach as a finger paint, and had made green designs on the kitchen table while her parents shared the details of their day.

But getting back to Lily, Ida was not surprised that Sven had voiced his objections. Ida had observed over the years that despite the Feminist movement, in the vernacular referred to as Women's Lib, men still expected their women to provide services, particularly of the culinary sort. Ida remembered the argument she had heard from upstairs regarding Sven's tiring of Chinese food. She supposed he wanted something familiar. The only Scandinavian food Ida could think of was Swedish meatballs. Surely those were not terribly difficult to learn?

"Sorry," said Kitty, interrupting Ida's thoughts. "This why I not marry," she confided. "Not want to be house maid. But Lily," Kitty shrugged, "she fall in love."

"I understand," Ida replied.

The cookies were packed up and the kitchen tidied

"So will you come next Thursday to learn another cookie?" Ida asked.

"Next week not come. Very busy. Prepare for Chinese New Year," Kitty explained. "Prepare special dish. I bring some for you."

Ida frowned. She suspected "special dish" meant something exotic beyond her own tolerance: chicken feet, jelly fish, tree molds and other items described on a television program.

"Not worry, I bring you long life noodle. Very delicious," Kitty promised. She paused. "You already have long life, but maybe have more."

Ida walked Kitty to the door.

"Now you learn next Chinese word," Kitty said. "*Dzai jian.* Mean see you again."

"Zai jean," said Ida.

"Very good," said Kitty. "Bye bye."

Chapter 11

When Ida's doorbell rang the next morning, she expected to see the China dolls holding a plate of cookies. Instead, a strange African-American woman stood in the doorway. At first Ida thought it must be one of those Jehovah Witness people. They had not come around for a long time. But they usually came in pairs. And then she took in the woman's bleach blond afro and realized a Jehovah's Witness would probably not wear such a hair style.

"I'm Sandy, Charlene's sister," said the woman. "I'm here to clean your apartment."

Ida had completely forgotten that Charlene was sending her sister to clean. She attributed her lapse in memory to the change in routine and the excitement of the previous day's cookie lesson. Barbara had sent her numerous articles on the memory of the elderly, especially short-term memory and the lack of it. But the phone call from Charlene had been a week ago, Ida now recalled. She didn't think this counted as short-term memory, although it certainly was shorter than the memory of something from fifty years ago. Was there such a thing as a mid-term memory? She would have to ask Barbara about that, if she remembered. Meanwhile she ushered Sandy into the apartment and showed her where to put her coat and purse.

"Where do you want me to start?" Sandy asked.

For a moment Ida just stared at Charlene's sister. In the ten years that Charlene had been with her, Ida had never told her cleaner what to do. Maybe when Charlene had first started on the job she had given instructions, but now she couldn't remember. (That memory thing again!)

"Well," Ida finally said, "Charlene usually starts in the bedroom, and works her way around the kitchen. Dust and vacuum," she added with a wave toward the other rooms. "And you'll find what you need in that hall closet."

"Okay," said Sandy. "I'll just get to work."

Ida sat at the kitchen table for a few moments. Then she got one of her crossword puzzle books. There were still a few unfinished puzzles to be done. Soon she heard the roar of the vacuum cleaner. It was during a brief pause in the noise that she realized someone was pounding on her apartment door. Kitty and Lily stood in the doorway holding a plate heaped with cookies. Ida immediately thought of a rainbow: frosting of all colors shone in the hallway's fluorescent glow. The China dolls entered and went straight to the kitchen, oblivious to the vigorous vacuuming going on in the living room. They sat at the table and waited expectantly.

"Goodness, I've forgotten to make tea!" Ida exclaimed and she set the kettle on the stove. Discombobulated by the arrival of Sandy, she had entirely forgotten the previous day's baking and the expected arrival of the Cheong sisters.

"We make you special New Year cookie," Lily said proudly.

"Many design," Kitty added.

Ida scrutinized the cookies. Each one was frosted with a different color, and then decorated with those Chinese squiggles. In all her years of baking and bake sales she had never seen anything like it. The kettle whistled and soon the women were sipping tea and eating cookies. Suddenly Sandy entered the kitchen.

"Oh! Sorry to disturb you," Sandy said. "I was just going to… didn't realize you had company."

Ida paused, her teacup in the air. Her childhood training in good manners raced through her mind. Fortunately, these were long-term memories and remained fairly intact. She felt the polite thing to do would be to invite Sandy to join the party. On the other hand, Sandy was the hired help. Ida knew that if Charlene were here, she would decline any offer of socialization. Long ago, she had told Ida that she was a professional cleaner, there in Ida's apartment to do a job, period. Which was fine with Ida. But perhaps Sandy was not a professional, just filling in for her sister. And then how would the China dolls feel if Ida asked Sandy to join them? Ida looked at the plate of cookies and then at Sandy. She knew her daughter Barbara would be scandalized if she were here, but she wasn't here.

"Why don't you take a break and join us?" Ida said to Sandy.

"Don't mind if I do," Sandy said, and she took the remaining empty seat.

"These are my neighbors Lily and Kitty," Ida introduced the China dolls. "And this is Sandy, my..."

"Cleaning lady's sister," Sandy furnished between sips of tea. "These cookies are wonderful. Who made them?"

"We did," said Ida, Lily and Kitty simultaneously. Then they all laughed, and Ida explained about the baking lessons.

"I wish I could learn to bake," Sandy sighed. "But I just don't have the time."

"Ida very good teacher," Kitty declared. "She our *bin gan shr.* Mean cookie master."

Ida decided she preferred the title "cookie master" to "cookie lady." She sat up straighter in her chair. Then she had what she could only think of as a brainstorm. She suspected Dr. Barbara Rappaport would say it was not possible for someone past ninety to have such a thing, but Dr. Rappaport was wrong.

"I have a very good recipe book for cookies," Ida said to Sandy. "It's by Martha Stewart. I'd be happy to show it to you, but I can't seem to find it." She quickly lifted her cup and took a long sip of tea.

As she returned the cup to its saucer she smiled and looked from one China doll to the other.

The twins' faces were inscrutable, their smiles frozen on their lips.

"After I finish cleaning, I'll help you look for it," Sandy offered, demolishing another cookie.

Still the twins' expressions remained fixed. No rapid exchange of Chinese took place. Ida wondered if perhaps she actually had misplaced the book. She could always ask Barbara to send her another one. But then she would have to either confess that she had misplaced it, and suffer through a lecture about declining mental faculties, or confide her suspicions about the China dolls, and suffer through a lecture on the inadvisability of inviting unknown neighbors into your home. Ida reflected that it was a good thing her daughter had become a thyroid surgeon rather than an attorney.

"That would be very nice," Ida said pointedly to Sandy, again glancing at the China dolls.

The sisters simultaneously put down their teacups and wiped their mouths daintily with their napkins.

"Sorry, must go," said Lily.

"Prepare Chinese New Year," said Kitty. "Shop. Cook. Clean. Very busy."

"I guess so," said Ida.

She stood and walked them to the door. After they had gone, she realized neither she nor they had mentioned the next baking lesson. She supposed they would not have time the following week. And she was feeling somewhat ambivalent herself, since the disappearance of her book. She was feeling less charmed by the China dolls. But maybe Sandy would find the book. Back at the table, Sandy was clearing the dishes.

"Shall I wrap up these cookies and put them away?" Sandy asked.

"Yes, and pack up some for yourself to take home," Ida told her. "I can't possibly eat them all by myself."

"Thanks," Sandy said. "I'll just clean the kitchen and then we'll try to locate your book."

Ida went to the living room with her crossword puzzles and resumed work on the puzzle she had been doing earlier. There was only one more left. She could ask Barbara to send a new book, or she could find another hobby. She thought of the writer Agatha Christie's character Miss Marple, the elderly woman who solved murder mysteries. Ida had read all of Agatha Christie's books years ago. While the disappearance of a cookbook was a far cry from a murder, it was still something to investigate. And that, she decided, would become her new hobby.

Chapter 12

For several days Ida contemplated how to go about tracking down the Martha Stewart Cookies book. Sandy had done a thorough search of the kitchen, even going so far as to climb up to the high cabinets and remove many of the same items Lily and Kitty had unearthed during their search for the plastic box. Sandy had encouraged Ida to dispose of many of these things.

"When was the last time you made aspic?" Sandy asked, holding up the copper mold.

"Never," Ida admitted after a moment's pause.

"And when is the next time you're going to make aspic?" Sandy asked.

"In my next lifetime?" Ida suggested.

Sandy handed down several expired food products to be thrown away: powdered milk, Ovaltine (did they still make it?) and a large tin of black pepper.

"The next time I come, we'll go through more," Sandy promised. She had peered into every shelf and cabinet but the book had not been found.

If the book was not in her own apartment, Ida knew, there were only two other possible places it could be: apartment 5C above her, or 3C below. Since she had access to neither apartment, she would have to think of a reason to visit. She decided she would bake some complicated cookies made with browned butter and sandwiched with jam, and take a plateful to one of the Cheong sisters. She felt Kitty, below her, was more likely to be the mastermind behind whatever was going on. Lily had that husband to attend to. Although Ida had seen Sven only twice, she suspected he was very demanding. Only the day before, she had overheard another argument between Sven and Lily. She supposed "overheard" was not quite the accurate term. The couple had been shouting at the top of their lungs and even if neighbors were not interested they couldn't help hearing it.

"Stop this stupid baking and make me some food!" Sven had demanded.

"Baking not stupid!" Lily had shouted back. "I make many dish for you! You too fussy! I am not restaurant! Not make all dish you like to order!"

"Maybe I'll just go to a restaurant!" Sven had shouted back.

Ida heard a door slam, but she couldn't tell if it was the apartment door, or the door to the bedroom.

Now she checked her supplies and decided to go to the supermarket for a few necessities. She put on her boots, her cardigan sweater, and her ancient ranch mink coat. The mink had been a gift from Irwin for their thirty-fifth wedding anniversary. It was showing its age, with tiny gaps in the fur at the shoulders, but it still kept her warm. The only problem was that the coat was as heavy as a Mack truck and she could barely support it. Barbara had suggested her mother buy a down coat, which she claimed was warm and light. Ida always saw people wearing such coats, and she thought they looked very tacky. Of course, the Cheong sisters had those puffy little jackets that looked so cute, but Ida wanted something that covered her behind.

She took her shopping cart and left her apartment. As she walked through the lobby, the China dolls entered, each pushing a shopping cart filled to the top with grocery bags.

"*Ni hau*," said Kitty and Lily together.

"What?" Ida frowned, wondering if there was something wrong with her hearing.

"You forget we teach you this!" admonished Kitty. "*Ni hau* mean hello."

"Oh, right," Ida said, only half-remembering. "Where have you girls been? I've not seen you for ages!"

"Very busy. Bake cookie. Now make more." Lily pointed to the bags in the twins' carts.

Ida bent over and looked at the thin plastic grocery bags. She could see sacks of flour, boxes of confectioner sugar, and cartons of eggs.

"What are you going to do with all those cookies?" Ida asked.

"Chinese lady club," said Kitty. "We join. Drink tea. Eat cookie."

"Many lady, many cookie," Lily elaborated.

Ida pictured a few dozen China dolls seated at round tables, all drinking tea and eating Martha Stewart cookies. She wondered if they used Lazy Susans like the Chinese restaurants, with the teapot and plates of each kind of cookie going round and round. She was reminded of her own women's club days, the meetings at the Parent Teachers Association and the Jewish Center's Ladies Auxiliary. She supposed every religious and ethnic group had their version of a Women's Club. And it was a smart idea for the Cheong sisters to join such an organization. How else would they meet other Chinese women? But then she thought they might be a bit young for such a gathering. Most women the age of the twins would either be working or at home with young children. Instead of several dozen China dolls, Ida now pictured older ladies in their fifties and more, with dyed black hair, sagging chins, decked out in jade bracelets and pearl necklaces.

"Soon we need learn next cookie," Kitty interrupted Ida's train of thought.

"Cannot bring same same all time," explained Lily.

"Is okay?" Kitty asked.

"Another baking lesson? Of course," Ida replied. "By the way, I'm going to make some very fancy cookies. I'll bring you a plate, if that's all right."

"Fancy cookie? We can learn?" Lily immediately asked.

Ida pictured the dozens of Chinese ladies eating the brown butter jam-filled cookies. Then she imagined the hours of work needed to make them.

"I think we should talk about it. I'll bring the cookies to your apartment tomorrow afternoon at three, if that's all right," Ida said to Kitty.

"Tomorrow at three," the China dolls agreed.

"We serve you Chinese tea," said Kitty. "Not in bag."

Ida knew the Chinese did things differently, but what could be different about making tea? There was tea and there was boiling water. You put them together and had tea. Even the English, with their fuss of milk, cream, sugar, and lemon, and tiered dishes holding sandwiches and cakes, made tea in a pot with boiling water. Maybe the Chinese used different tea—that must be it! But didn't all tea come from China?

"Chinese tea not like Western," Lily explained, as if reading Ida's mind. "Different tea. Several kind. We show you."

"More complicate," Kitty added. "Not like just put water in pot with tea."

Ida supposed she would have to see for herself. She reminded herself that her main purpose in visiting the China dolls was to look for her book.

The twins exchanged some rapid Chinese.

"We serve you Chinese snack, very delicious," said Lily.

"Sounds like a regular tea party," Ida remarked.

The Cheong sisters giggled.

"Must go now," said Lily, pointing to the grocery bags. "Must bake many cookie."

"See you tomorrow," Ida told them.

After the elevator door closed and the twins had gone, Ida wondered if there was any real food—meat, chicken, vegetables—in the sisters' grocery bags. She thought of Lily's husband, demanding a meal.

Poor Sven, Ida thought. Poor Sven.

Chapter 13

"I feel like I'm going to a foreign country, visiting the Cheong sisters," Ida confided to Sandy the next day as her substitute cleaning girl polished the living room end tables.

"I don't know about that visit," said Sandy as she gave one of the table tops a spray of Pledge.

"It's not like they're going to kidnap me and hold me for ransom," Ida laughed.

Ida didn't want to feel disloyal to Charlene, but she was enjoying Sandy's personal attention, almost as if Sandy was her daughter or granddaughter. Ida knew her real daughter Dr. Barbara Rappaport would be scandalized to hear her mother thought of her Black, bleach blond cleaning girl as a close relative. In her most recent phone call, Barbara had asked how the new cleaner was working out.

"Oh, she's fine," Ida had said vaguely, not anxious to go into detail. She especially didn't want to tell Barbara that Sandy had helped her discard things from the cabinets. On the one hand, Barbara would be glad that was already done when Ida passed away. On the other hand, she would chide Ida for letting a stranger go through her things.

But in her usual bulldog way, Dr. Barbara had not let the subject go so easily.

"Make sure nothing's missing," she had advised. "How long will your regular cleaner be away?"

"I don't know," Ida said. "But I'm lucky to have this one."

"I suppose," Barbara had sort of agreed. "What about the Chinese women?"

"What about them?" Ida parried.

That was another subject she didn't want to pursue. She certainly didn't want Barbara to know she would be visiting their apartment. Any time Barbara called and Ida wasn't at home, Barbara demanded to know where she'd been. Sometimes Ida felt like a teenager reporting to a parent. Ida should be the one asking the questions. Such as whether her daughter had really gone to Honolulu for a thyroid conference.

"Are they still baking cookies?" Barbara asked.

"Yes," Ida had answered. "Shall we send you some?"

"No, I don't eat refined carbs," Barbara had quickly answered, and had hung up.

Sandy finished the end tables and stood back to admire the shine.

"I've packed up some cookies for you," Ida told her. "Brown butter raspberry sandwich cookies. I'm bringing some to the China dolls."

"Sounds like a regular party," Sandy commented as she took her coat from the closet.

"More like a spy mission," Ida said.

"Well, have fun and be careful," Sandy told her. "See you next Friday." She took her cookies and left.

Ida arrived at Kitty's apartment a few minutes past three. She had intended to be there promptly on the hour but upon leaving her apartment she had run into trouble holding the cookie plate in one hand and locking the door with the other. Even though the cookies and plate were swathed in plastic wrap, she couldn't tuck the parcel under her arm to free both hands. Finally, she had gone back inside for a plastic grocery bag for the cookies, hooked the bag over her arm and locked the door. In the elevator, she had decided the bag looked tacky, removed the cookies, and stuffed the bag into a pocket of her cardigan.

Kitty snatched the cookies from Ida, as she motioned the cookie master to come in. The small round kitchen table was set for tea, but this tea party was definitely not English. A large tray held a small clay teapot, three tiny cups with saucers, a large ceramic bowl, and two cylindrical containers, one with a lid and the other filled with wooden utensils.

"Gung Fu Tea Ceremony," announced Kitty. "Please sit down." She indicated a chair.

Ida sat. Lily stood at the stove in front of a steaming kettle. She brought the kettle to the table, placed it on a trivet, and handed the pot holder to Kitty. Then the China dolls took their seats.

"Kitty study tea in Hong Kong," Lily explained. "Now expert."

Kitty proceeded to fill the tea pot with hot water and poured the water out into the bowl. She then placed the pot in the bowl and poured hot water over it.

"Need warm pot for hot tea," Kitty explained. She then took large wooden tweezers from the container. "Also warm cup," she said, and went through the same procedure with each cup, holding them by the rim with the tweezers. "Now tea," she said.

But when she opened the tea container, instead of putting tea in the pot, she handed the tea to Ida.

"Please smell and admire tea," Kitty instructed.

Ida looked dubiously into the tea container. There was tea in it, but she didn't know what to say. Her only experience with this sort of tea happened several decades ago at a friend's birthday party, where a woman dressed as a gypsy had read tea leaves in everyone's cup. She had warned Ida to be careful.

"I see death by fire, but possibly a narrow escape," the gypsy had said.

That had been nearly seventy years ago. So much for reading tea leaves, Ida thought. Now she squinted at the tea.

"Well, it's green," she finally said. She had heard of green tea but had never tried it. "It's actually a bright green," she added, hoping she was making the correct comment.

"Now, please smell," Kitty said.

Ida put her nose to the container and sniffed, hoping she wouldn't sneeze.

"You like?" Lily asked hopefully.

It was not exactly Chanel Number Five, Ida thought but did not say.

"Very nice," she said, nodding vigorously.

"Now we make tea," said Kitty, and she placed some of the tea into the teapot.

Lily poured hot water into the pot. There was a silence. The China dolls seemed to be counting in their heads. Then they nodded to each other. Kitty immediately poured tea into the three cups. Ida suddenly felt very thirsty. But instead of passing the cups, Kitty took up the large wooden tweezers and emptied each cup into the bowl. Kitty saw her guest's look of dismay.

"Always throw away first cup," the China doll explained. Then she emptied the teapot of the remaining tea, and added hot water to the pot. The sisters appeared to silently count, then nodded to each other. Kitty poured tea into the cups again, and passed one to Ida.

Ida lifted the cup and saucer and was about to blow on the tea to cool it.

"Not drink!" Kitty commanded. "First smell."

Ida sniffed the steam rising from the cup. Again it was not Chanel Number Five.

"Lovely," she said enthusiastically.

The three women sipped tea.

"When do we eat the cookies?" Ida asked.

Lily and Kitty looked as if they were about to exchange some rapid Chinese, but then Lily spoke in English.

"Not eat at Kung Fu Tea Ceremony," Lily said. "But because you are foreigner, we eat cookie." She went to the kitchen counter and brought the plate of cookies to the table.

Ida thought to protest that they were in the United States and the Cheong sisters were the foreigners, but she let it pass.

For several moments the women munched cookies.

"Very delicious," Kitty declared. "We can learn?"

"Maybe later on," Ida said. "They are quite complicated."

"When next cookie lesson?" Lily asked.

"Next Thursday," Ida told her. "What cookie do you want to learn?"

"You pick," said Kitty. "Leave list."

"You really should look through my Martha Stewart's Cookies book to get some ideas," Ida said, and she looked intently from one twin to the other. "But I can't seem to find it."

She scanned the kitchen but there was no bookcase, no open shelf on which a book might rest. The China dolls stared back at Ida, politely inscrutable.

"Well," Ida said after a few moments, "I think you should learn Peanut Butter cookies. It's a good winter cookie." She glanced out the window at the late February snow sifting down.

"Peanut butter cookie," Lily repeated. She and Kitty exchanged rapid Chinese.

"Okay, see you next Thursday," Kitty announced, indicating the tea party was over.

Chapter 14

Although the missing Martha Stewart Cookies book did not present a major problem in the matter of finding a peanut butter cookie recipe, it was a minor annoyance. Ida went through several other baking books until she found a suitable recipe and wrote out a shopping list. She decided she might as well plan the next cookie. Oatmeal raisin it would be, another good winter cookie. By the time they made those, the winter would be over. As far as cookies suitable for spring, Ida decided she wouldn't trouble herself now. Maybe the China dolls would stop baking. Or maybe Ida herself would leave the planet, as her granddaughter Monica would phrase it. She put on her cardigan and was nearly out the door to give Kitty her shopping list when the telephone rang.

"It's me, Sandy," the substitute cleaning girl announced herself. "I was a bit concerned about your Chinese tea party, so I thought I'd just check back."

"Oh, the tea party was lovely," Ida informed her. "That is, if you like pouring hot water over crockery." She went on to briefly explain the events of the tea. "But then we ate my cookies, so in the end it was fine," she concluded.

"They didn't serve any strange snacks? Fried snake skin, or beetles in soy sauce?" Sandy asked.

"Certainly not!" Ida declared. "Do the Chinese really eat those things?"

"I don't know," Sandy admitted, "but I've heard they do eat some things we Americans would consider very strange. I used to date a guy who worked in a Chinese restaurant, and he told me stories. Some time I'll tell you about it," Sandy said. "Anyway, see you next Friday."

"Thanks for calling," Ida told her.

Ida again took up the shopping list and left her apartment. When the elevator door opened, Arthur Sandusky, president of the Tenants Association, smiled out at her.

"Off to do some snooping?" Arthur joked in greeting, though Ida knew he was only half joking.

Arthur was about the same age as Dr. Barbara. He had grown up in the building, so Ida had known him nearly his whole life. At one time, when Barbara and Arthur were teenagers, they had gone on a date. But afterwards, Barbara had declared him a "total jerk" and refused to date him again. Arthur had become a real estate lawyer but continued to live with his parents. When his father died, he stayed with his widowed mother and now lived alone in the two-bedroom apartment. He had never married, but often mentioned his "latest girlfriend."

His joke about Ida snooping referred to her information-gathering techniques. After he became president of the Tenants Association, Arthur occasionally asked Ida to "gather information," as he politely put it. He had not rung her bell for quite a while, so Ida assumed nothing unusual was going on in the building.

"He should look in on you at least once a week," Dr. Barbara had declared. "You and his mother were good friends for decades. But of course he's a total jerk and wouldn't even think of it."

But Ida really didn't want Arthur to come around that often. His conversation consisted of real estate deals and tax avoidance and bored her nearly to death.

"I haven't seen you in a long time," Ida commented as she stepped into the elevator. "Not since the Chinese sisters moved in." She reached out and pushed the button for the third floor.

"Where are you going?" Arthur asked.

"Oh, just leaving someone a note," Ida told him.

"Speaking of the Chinese sisters, I ran into the couple who live in the apartment above one of them, in 6C," Arthur said. "Seems there's been a bit of noise."

"There's a bit of noise everywhere," Ida remarked, thinking of Lily and Sven, in their bedroom and kitchen.

The elevator arrived at the third floor and Ida got off, but Arthur held the Door Open button so he could continue his conversation. This was an annoying habit some tenants had, annoying to anyone else waiting for the elevator. But Arthur seemed oblivious to the possibility that he was detaining others. Ida suspected he thought his position as president of the Tenants Association exempted him from the rules.

"Sounds like there's a lot of fighting going on," he continued. "Do you hear anything?"

"My hearing isn't what it used to be," Ida said. She didn't think her hearing was bad, but certainly at age ninety-one it couldn't still be what it was at age thirty, so she wasn't lying.

"Well, let me know if you hear any disturbances," Arthur said, and he released the Door Open button.

Ida waited until the door had fully closed and the elevator was on its way. She didn't want Arthur to see which end of the hall she was headed for. She slipped the list under Kitty's door and went back to the elevator, but hesitated to press the Up button. She would not put it past Arthur to come back up on the pretext of having something he forgot to tell her, just to try to find out whose apartment she had gone to. And she was sure it would not be a good idea to tell him she was socializing with the Cheong sisters, even though giving baking lessons was not exactly socializing. But finally she pushed the button and returned to her floor.

As she approached her door, she heard her telephone begin to ring. She unlocked the door, locked it behind her, and hurried into the kitchen to grab the telephone extension on the wall.

"Hello?" she said breathlessly into the receiver. She pulled the long cord and sat down at the table.

"Why are you out of breath?" demanded Dr. Barbara. "Are you having a heart attack? Should I call 911?"

"I'm fine," Ida assured her. "I was just coming in the door and rushed for the phone." She didn't see how calling 911 in Los Angeles would result in an ambulance coming to Bayside Avenue.

"Where were you?" Barbara demanded again.

"Just checking the mail," Ida said, hoping to end her daughter's questioning.

"Well, I have some news," Barbara announced. "I'm engaged."

"Engaged?" Ida repeated, not sure of her daughter's meaning. "Engaged in what?"

"Engaged to be married!" Barbara nearly shouted into the phone.

There was a moment of silence while Ida took this in.

"You're getting married?" Ida asked, dumbfounded.

"Is there something wrong with your hearing?" Barbara asked.

"No, I'm just surprised," Ida replied. Then she remembered the supposed thyroid conference in Honolulu. "Who is it?" she asked. "The man you're marrying."

"He's a doctor here at the hospital," Barbara explained. "We'll get married next Christmas. And when we retire, we'll move to Hawaii."

"I see," Ida said.

This news seemed almost positive proof that Ida's suspicions about her daughter's trip to Honolulu were correct. But maybe this doctor had also been at that conference and they both had liked Hawaii.

"What kind of doctor is your fiancé?" Ida asked.

"Ear, nose and throat," said Barbara.

"Well, I wish you the best," Ida told her.

"Thank you," said Dr. Barbara. "We'll talk more next time."

Ida hung up the phone and sat for several minutes at the table. Would she be invited to the wedding? Would she still be alive? If still alive, could she travel to Los Angeles? And if the answer to all these questions was yes, would Barbara ask her mother to bake the wedding cake?

No, Ida decided. Even if Barbara asked her, she would not bake the wedding cake. It would be asking too much.

Chapter 15

The China dolls reported promptly on Thursday at three. Ida immediately noticed that Lily had dark circles under her eyes. Even her usual eyeliner and lipstick could not disguise her tired face.

"Lily, why do you look so tired?" Ida asked as she took items from the grocery bag the twins had brought.

"Work too hard!" Lily exclaimed. "Stay up half night clean apartment. Iron husband shirt. His shirt so big! Like tablecloth! Must iron seven!"

Ida pictured Sven the tall Swede. She could imagine tiny Lily at the ironing board, struggling with the huge garments.

"Why don't you just send his shirts to the Chinese laundry? It's only a few blocks away. And they deliver," she added, picturing Lily lugging the shirts along Bayside Avenue.

As soon as the words were out of her mouth, Ida wondered if she had just committed a grave ethnic faux pas by telling Chinese to go to the Chinese laundry. For most of her life, all the laundries she had encountered had been owned by Chinese. She supposed that in China laundries were just called laundries, as everyone was Chinese. But Lily and Kitty seemed not to have taken any offense.

"Husband too cheap," Lily explained. "Say I spend too much money make cookie."

Kitty stood by while Ida made tsk tsk sounds.

"Husband like slave master," Kitty finally said. "I not want get married."

"Not all husbands are like that," Ida said quickly. "My own husband treated me very well. I never felt like a slave! Maybe Lily just married the wrong man."

"We bake cookie now," said Lily, indicating she wanted to drop the subject of husbands.

"Let's get started," Ida agreed, and she consulted her recipe. Soon the twins were measuring and mixing.

For the last several days, Ida had been preoccupied with her daughter Barbara's engagement, and the talk of husbands brought that situation to the forefront of her mind. Barbara had said that her fiancé was a doctor, but this fact shed no light on the man's personal character. Not that Dr. Barbara Rappaport was ideal wife material. She was self-centered and career oriented. But maybe—just maybe—if Barbara was thinking of retirement, she might be looking for a companion. And what better companion than another doctor? Together they could read medical journals, just to keep abreast of things, and could discuss former cases and patients.

"We finish mix butter and sugar," Kitty startled Ida back to the kitchen. "Can put egg?"

"Yes, go ahead," Ida said.

Lily was busy mixing the flour, baking soda and salt together. Cookie-making was certainly easier when two people joined forces, Ida reflected. Soon the dough was made, the cookies shaped and placed on the cookie sheets. Then Ida demonstrated flattening the cookies with a fork and pressing a few peanuts into the tops. The women sat at the table to await the finished cookies. The aroma of peanuts filled the kitchen.

"Doesn't that smell wonderful!" Ida commented. "Will your Chinese ladies like them?"

"Must taste," said Lily, "but sure they like."

"Soon have Mah Jongg contest," said Kitty. "Many day play Mah Jongg. Eat many cookie," she added. "You know this game?"

"I used to play Mah Jongg!" Ida exclaimed.

It was during several summers long ago, when Dr. Barbara was a child, that Ida played that curious game. She had been taught by one of her fellow bungalow renters, Gloria Rosenfeld. Ida could still picture Gloria with her auburn curls and crisp cotton dresses. After Ida had got the hang of the game, she and Gloria played with two other women at a card table set up in the shade. The provision of refreshments was rotated among the women. It was usually too hot to light the oven, but Ida would bake late at night and always made something that required only half an hour of baking. Lemon chiffon pie, light with beaten egg whites, was one of her favorites. Occasionally she would make a pudding pie with a graham cracker crust and instant pudding, with whipped cream piled on top.

"Chinese Mah Jongg, American Mah Jongg not same," said Lily.

"How can it not be the same?" Ida asked, startled. "Don't you use the same set? Ours came from Chinatown," she insisted.

"Use almost same set but play different," said Kitty.

"Different how?" Ida persisted.

There was a rapid exchange of Chinese between the China dolls.

"Our English not so good to explain," Kitty finally said.

"Different rule," said Lily.

"Don't you get a card every year with the winning combinations?" Ida asked. From what she remembered, this card was a kind of Bible of every Mah Jongg player.

The twins looked at each other, puzzled, and shook their heads.

"No card," they said.

The oven timer rang, putting a temporary halt to the Mah Jongg discussion. The first batch of cookies was removed and the second put in.

"There's another way to make these cookies," Ida told the twins, suddenly remembering. "Instead of putting peanuts on top, you press a Hershey's Chocolate Kiss in the center."

"Hershey Chocolate Kiss?" Kitty repeated. She handed Ida her little notebook in which she transcribed recipes into Chinese, and her pen. "Please write."

Ida printed out the words, reflecting that the afternoon had veered into cross-cultural stumbling blocks. First Mah Jongg, now Chocolate Kisses.

"It's a candy," Ida explained. She drew a small picture of a chocolate kiss. "It's wrapped in foil and they come in a bag."

"Is kiss this?" Kitty asked, puckering her lips and kissing the air.

"Yes," Ida said.

"Why call candy kiss?" asked Lily.

"I have no idea," Ida said after a moment's thought. "It's an American thing." One of those things that could not be explained, she decided. "So you press the Chocolate Kiss in the center of the peanut butter cookie, and the chocolate melts, and it's delicious. Chocolate and peanut butter."

The China dolls looked at each other and shrugged.

"I'll make some one of these days, and you'll see," Ida told them.

Ida hadn't made those cookies in years. They had been her granddaughter Monica's favorite, until she had joined the nuns and stopped eating anything delicious. But she didn't have to worry about what to do with excess cookies. The twins would have some, and she would give a few to Sandy. And she would bring some to Arthur Sandowsky. Even though she didn't really like him, he was president of the Tenants Association. Some day she might need his help.

Ida wondered if Sven and the China dolls knew about the Tenants Association. Back when it was formed, the tenants had decided to give every new tenant a Welcome to our Building letter outlining basic manners and unacceptable behavior. She imagined most tenants threw this away without reading it.

"When you moved in, did you get a letter?" Ida asked the twins.

"Oh yes," Kitty said, brightening. "Our mother send good luck card for Chinese New Year, we put by Lily apartment door. But then it disappear." She frowned. "Maybe American not like."

"I didn't mean that kind of letter," Ida explained. "This one would have been put under your door. Just a piece of paper, no envelope."

The China dolls looked at each other.

"Not see," said Lily. "Maybe Sen take, but maybe throw away."

"Maybe have," Kitty said, "but I not read English, so maybe throw away."

"Is important?" asked Lily.

"Not really," said Ida as the oven timer went off. "Let's get that batch of cookies out."

Chapter 16

"We need to talk," said Sandy as she put her coat in the closet.

Ida had heard this line many times, mostly while watching television soap operas years ago. It was usually what one member of a couple said to the other when they wanted to end the relationship. Ida and Sandy sat down at the kitchen table.

"Are you going to quit?" Ida immediately asked.

"Oh, no, not at all," Sandy assured her. She paused. "The thing is," she continued, "Charlene probably won't be coming back to work."

"Is she all right?" Ida demanded.

"She's fine," Sandy said. "She's getting married."

"Married!" Ida's mouth dropped open. It was an epidemic—first Barbara, now Charlene.

"When she was in the hospital with her appendix," Sandy explained, "she met this orderly who works there. After she was discharged, they started seeing each other. And now she's pretty sure she's pregnant."

"That was fast!" Ida reacted without thinking.

This was just like a soap opera. It couldn't have been more than six or seven weeks since Charlene's surgery. But as her own mother used to tell her, all it took was one instance of intercourse.

"I mean, that's wonderful!" Ida tried to correct herself. Then she thought: what if Charlene didn't want the baby and was getting married just to avoid an abortion or an illegitimate birth? "If that's what she wants," she concluded her confused reaction.

"Well, they want to have the baby," Sandy said. "They're getting married and going on a honeymoon. And the doctor told her what with the pregnancy and the appendix, he doesn't want her to do any heavy work."

There was silence while Ida took this in.

"So you'll keep on cleaning for me?" Ida asked.

"Sure," Sandy grinned. "If that's okay with you."

"Of course! That's fine!" Ida told her. She paused. "Will you want more money?"

"Not right now," said Sandy.

"That's settled, then." Ida smiled.

Sandy got up and got to work. Ida felt happy. Then she wondered if her happiness was disloyal to Charlene. And then she wondered how Dr. Barbara would react to this news, as the subject of the cleaning girl would inevitably be discussed. Finally, the doorbell rang.

"*Ni hau*!" said Kitty, holding a napkin-covered plate.

Lily stood beside her sister, looking, to Ida's relief, much less tired than previously.

The twins went to the kitchen and Kitty ceremoniously whipped off the napkin covering the cookies.

"We give you surprise," giggled Lily.

Ida peered down at the plate. The cookies looked like peanut butter cookies, but instead of peanuts pressed into the top, there were what looked like tiny seed pearls.

"What are they?" Ida asked.

"Sesame seed," said Kitty.

Ida wracked her brain but the only sesame she could think of was the phrase "open sesame" spoken by Ali Baba. Then an image of seeded rolls popped into her mind.

"We think American peanut butter too strong for Chinese lady," said Lily apologetically. "So we change recipe. Use sesame butter. Like peanut butter. Please try." She held her hand out to the plate of cookies.

Ida reached out and gingerly took a cookie. She pretended to be inspecting it while she attempted to sort out the thoughts running through her head. On the one hand, she was upset that her students had gone behind her back and made their own cookie. On the other hand, she should be proud of them for their initiative. Did Martha Stewart have a sesame cookie recipe? She would have to check. Then she remembered she didn't have the book. She took a bite and slowly chewed.

"Very subtle," said Ida.

The China dolls looked at each other.

"Sorry," said Kitty, "not know this word."

"It means...," Ida tried to explain after swallowing her morsel of cookie, "that the taste is not overpowering." She looked at the twins' blank expressions. "The cookies are just right."

"You like?" asked Lily hesitantly.

"Delicious," Ida said. "I'll make tea. But the real test," she pointed out, "will be whether the Chinese ladies like them. Asians and Americans tend to like different things, especially when it comes to food."

The China dolls smiled and nodded as Sandy entered the kitchen.

"They sure do," Sandy agreed.

"Try these cookies," Ida told her.

Sandy seated herself and took a cookie. She savored it as Ida poured tea.

"This is an interesting cookie," Sandy finally said. "Sesame is sort of like peanut butter, but not exactly."

"You know sesame?" Kitty asked.

"I used to have a boyfriend who worked in a Chinese restaurant," Sandy explained. "I learned a lot about Chinese food. If you just go to an American Chinese restaurant, you're not really eating Chinese food."

"You eat real Chinese food?" Kitty asked. "Chicken feet? Cow stomach? Jellyfish?"

"Well, I wouldn't order them," Sandy admitted, "but if they turned up at a meal, I could eat them."

Ida felt her stomach churn. She decided to change the subject.

"Guess what!" she announced. "My daughter is getting married!"

The twins frowned and exchanged some rapid Chinese.

"Daughter is old?" asked Kitty, but it was not exactly a question.

Ida was startled. She never thought of her daughter as being old. But she supposed to someone in their twenties, age sixty or more was…old.

"She's in her early sixties," Ida told the twins. "But many people that age and older get married. Don't they do that in Hong Kong?"

"Some time," Kitty admitted.

"She have big wedding, wear white dress?" asked Lily.

"I don't know, but I don't think so," Ida said. She could not picture Dr. Barbara in a white dress. She would probably wear something red.

Everyone took another cookie.

"My sister is getting married," Sandy told the China dolls.

"Sound like everybody get marry," commented Kitty. "Hope they have good luck."

"Maybe Kitty get marry," Lily suddenly said. "She have date."

"Kitty is getting married?" Ida exclaimed. "To who? When?"

"Just have date to see man," Lily corrected herself.

Kitty gave her sister a disapproving look.

"You mean like a romantic date?" Sandy clarified.

"Not romantic," Kitty said firmly. "Too old. Just friend date."

"Did you meet him through the Ladies Association?" Ida asked.

"No," said Kitty. "Meet here in lobby."

Ida could not imagine how a China doll could meet a man in the lobby of their building. She tried to do a fast run-through of all the male tenants in the building, but came up blank.

"He make joke, say he president," said Kitty. "I tell him I know he not tell truth. But he say is true. How can be?"

Suddenly Ida realized who the man must be: Arthur Sandowsky, president of the Tenants Association. And she could just picture it, Arthur thinking he was still a dapper gent of thirty salivating over the petite China doll in her tight short skirt and high heel boots.

"I know who this man is," Ida said, "and it's true. But he's not president of the United States. He's president of the Tenants Association."

Sandy laughed long and loud, but the Cheong sisters only looked puzzled.

Ida gave them a brief description of the Tenants Association, which seemed only to cause more confusion.

"We must join?" asked Lily.

"We pay money?" asked Kitty.

Ida sighed.

"Don't worry about it," she told the twins. "You'll probably never have to have anything to do with it."

Chapter 17

During their next phone conversation, Ida reported to Dr. Barbara on the change in the cleaning situation, or rather the new permanence of Charlene's sister Sandy. She did not go into the details of Charlene's pregnancy, as that would only give her daughter the opportunity to sound off about how the "lower classes" would never pull themselves out of servitude unless they got a good education and stopped having babies willy-nilly. Ida had once pointed out to Barbara that if the serving classes all bettered themselves, there would be nobody to help people clean their homes. But of course Dr. Barbara had an answer to that.

"Robots will take over domestic chores," Barbara had declared. "There's already a robotic vacuum cleaner. It's called Roomba or something like that. You turn it on and it goes around the room by itself."

Well, Ida thought, Barbara had an answer for everything.

"How are the wedding plans coming along?" Ida asked, trying to change the subject to avoid a political discussion of housecleaning.

"I think we've picked a place," Barbara said. "It's on the beach. You'll love it."

Ida already knew she would not love it.

"Will I have to wear a bathing suit?" she asked.

Dr. Barbara laughed, a rare event. Ida suspected she was laughing at the image of her ninety-one year old mother in a bathing suit.

"Of course not," Barbara finally said.

"Are you sure?" Ida persisted. "I've still got a two-piece from nineteen sixty something."

This time Barbara did not laugh.

"It will be semi-formal," the bride-to-be informed her. "You won't have to wear a gown."

Ida wondered if her daughter had considered the possibility that her mother might have died by then, or might not be physically able to make the six-hour flight. In any case she would have to consult with Dr. Schwartz. Dr. Barbara did not approve of Dr. Schwartz.

"Too laissez-faire," she had summed him up. "You should be taking more meds at your age."

"If there's nothing else new, I've got to bake some cookies," Ida said, immediately realizing this remark was a mistake.

"You shouldn't be baking at your age," Barbara scolded.

"I'll think about it," said Ida, and she hung up.

She had decided to make the peanut butter cookies with the Hershey's Kisses, and had called Sandy to ask her to pick up the peanut butter and chocolates on her way to Ida's apartment. Sandy had gone from being a substitute cleaning girl to a cleaner, personal assistant, and confidante. In fact, it was Sandy who had given her the most brilliant idea.

"Why don't you have the next baking lesson in one of the twins' apartments instead of here," she had suggested. "That way you can snoop around their kitchen and look for your book."

Ida and Sandy had agreed that the book was most likely in the hands of Kitty. Since Lily's husband disapproved of the excess baking, the lesson would of necessity be arranged for Kitty's apartment.

"And less clean-up for me," Sandy had chuckled.

Ida's plan for the peanut butter chocolate kiss cookies was to bring a plate of them to Arthur Sandowsky, and to have a chat with him. Kitty Cheong had not said when her date was to take place. And while Ida was sure Kitty could take care of herself, she was also sure that Arthur would do his best to present himself as the perfect American man. Dr. Barbara might call her mother a meddler, but Ida had a vested interest in her Chinese protégé, having become somewhat addicted to the congeniality of the baking lessons. Suppose Arthur was totally charming to Kitty? Suppose there were more dates? Suppose Kitty decided to bake cookies for him? Ida had a sudden image of Kitty and Arthur on a double date with Lily and Sven. The couples would be seated across from each other in a booth in a Chinese restaurant. A real Chinese restaurant. A plate of jellyfish would be placed in the center of the table.

Ida banished this scene from her mind and creamed the butter, peanut butter and brown sugar. When the dough was made, she shaped the cookies and unwrapped the chocolate kisses. It was a time-consuming job, and she wished the China dolls were there with their two sets of hands to help her. Finally, the cookies went into the oven. Ida sat at the kitchen table and soon wonderful smells of peanut butter and chocolate filled the room. When the cookies were done, she would call Arthur and arrange for a visit. She hoped he was at home. She hated those message machines that made her feel as if she were talking to empty space. But as soon as the cookies were done and cooling, the telephone rang.

"Grandma, it's me, Monica," said the voice at the other end.

At first Ida panicked. Calls from Monica were rare (maybe nuns weren't allowed to use telephones?), plus she sounded as if she was crying. Could something have happened to Barbara?

"Monica, what's wrong?" Ida managed to get out.

Monica stifled a sob.

"Oh, Grandma, I've been expelled from the Buddhist nunnery," Monica said, and she broke into a string of sobs.

"Monica, I'm so sorry," Ida said.

Of course she was not really sorry, she was actually relieved that Monica would have to move herself back into real life, get a paying job and grow up. On the other hand, what job could she get with a college degree, a keen interest in macramé, and a couple of years of nun experience? But not to worry, Monica's mother Dr. Barbara had plenty of money. Monica wouldn't starve. Of course Monica would have to deal with her mother's "I told you this wouldn't work out."

"Monica, why did they expel you?" Ida asked.

There was another sob.

"I went into town with two other nuns to buy supplies. We split up, each of us with a list. When I finished my list, I passed a fast-food stand and they had hot dogs. The smell was so wonderful, and I hadn't had a hot dog in years...I couldn't help it, I bought a hot dog with the nunnery money. And one of the other nuns saw me eating it." Monica sobbed again.

"That doesn't sound like enough of a reason to expel you," Ida commented. "I would think they would give you extra kitchen work or something."

There was silence on Monica's end. Then she finally spoke.

"That's not the only thing I did," said Monica.

"Oh?" Ida looked at her cookies, which were cooling nicely.

"I talked about sex. I said I missed it," said Monica. "I hope I'm not shocking you, Grandma."

"Oh, no, not at all," Ida assured her. But she wanted to deliver the cookies while they were fresh. "So I suppose the nuns weren't pleased about that," she said, hoping to hurry the conversation along.

"They said they felt I would never achieve the correct mind-set to become a nun. But all I did was talk about it. It wasn't as if I said I wanted to find a man and have sex," Monica protested.

"But they did see you eating the hot dog," Ida pointed out. "So maybe they thought if you acted on that forbidden impulse you would act on all of them."

"Maybe," Monica sighed.

"When you get back to Los Angeles, call me and I'll send you some cookies. What kind would you like?" Ida asked.

"Oatmeal chocolate chip," Monica told her. "Thanks, Grandma."

They said goodbye and hung up. Ida suddenly wondered if Monica knew about Barbara's engagement. Barbara's getting married could present a problem. But it was not Ida's problem. She picked up the phone and dialed Arthur's number.

"Arthur Sandowsky here," he answered.

"It's Ida. I've got some cookies for you," Ida said.

"Come right over," Arthur told her.

Chapter 18

Arthur Sandowsky lived on the sixth floor in the large two-bedroom apartment in which he had grown up. After the deaths of his parents he had gotten rid of the ancient wing chairs and doily-draped sofa, the lamps, wooden sideboard and everything else in the living room, and had replaced those items with leather sofas and steel and glass accessories. A large flat-screen television was mounted on one wall. Arthur referred to the room as his "man-cave" but Ida thought it looked like a furniture showroom.

"You're just the person I want to see," Arthur greeted Ida at the door. He thanked her for the cookies and deposited them in his kitchen, in which he had installed a microwave oven and an espresso machine.

He motioned Ida into the living room and she sat gingerly on one of the leather sofas. Arthur had also gotten rid of his parents' lovely old Persian carpet and now there was a modern rug with a pattern of squares in shades of beige and brown.

"I take it you're friendly with the Chinese twins," Arthur plunged right in.

"Well, I wouldn't exactly say friendly," Ida said cautiously. "I do know them slightly."

"The one called Kitty said you've been giving them baking lessons. I met her in the lobby—she had a shopping cart full of home-made cookies she was bringing somewhere,"Arthur continued.

"That's true," Ida confirmed. "But we're hardly bosom buddies. Their English isn't all that fluent, you know, and sometimes it's difficult to communicate."

Arthur pursed his lips, obviously not pleased with Ida's reply.

"The thing is, I'm going on a date with Kitty, and I was hoping to get your advice," he finally said.

"A date?" said Ida, feigning complete ignorance of this development. She frowned. "I think those twins are only in their twenties."

"It's just a date," Arthur said defensively. "It's not like I'm proposing marriage."

Ida pictured Arthur's mother turning in her grave, for several reasons. The first was that Arthur had deprived his mother of grandchildren by never marrying, and Ida doubted he had any illegitimate offspring, either. Although Dr. Barbara had dismissed him as nerdy, Ida suspected there was more to that dismissal than Barbara had wanted to go into. Ida herself never thought of Arthur as "attractive" or "sexy." He was pleasant looking, even now in his early sixties, but not a face or figure that would inspire passion. The next reason was that Arthur never brought a girl home to meet his parents. Of course, this was because he never intended to become serious with any of them, but his mother had been insulted by this behavior.

"Is he embarrassed by us? Is our home not good enough?" Mrs. Sandowsky had once asked Ida years ago, when Arthur was of prime marriageable age.

And the last reason was something Arthur did, and never told his parents about, which was possibly why he never brought a girl home: Arthur dated only women of races other than his own. Ida knew this because Barbara had reported seeing him with such women while she was still living on Bayside Avenue and hanging around the neighborhood. Ida suspected Mrs. Sandowsky had figured this out, but had never said anything. For a woman of her time and ethnic background, a son dating anyone other than a white Jewish woman was a slap in the face. Since Arthur was not Ida's son, she didn't care what he did, and if he wanted to make a fool of himself by dating a woman thirty-five years younger than he was, she certainly wouldn't try to stop him.

"So what advice are you looking for?" Ida asked. "Surely a man of your age and experience doesn't need dating advice."

Arthur smiled and Ida imagined his ego artificially inflating.

"True, true," said Arthur. He was never humble. "But the thing is, Kitty Cheong hasn't been in the U.S. very long. I don't know what the dating customs are in Hong Kong, and I thought you might have a clue. Or if you don't," he added slyly, "maybe you can find out for me."

Ida had never been of the matchmaking persuasion, and she didn't intend to start now. She remembered the time her late older sister Sarah tried to fix her up during her junior year of high school. Sarah had been sure that this boy, Norman Shapiro, was a perfect match for Ida. She neglected to mention that his face was peppered with pimples ("In a few years they will have cleared up," Sarah had later defended herself.). Ida towered over him in her high heels ("He's still growing," Sarah had declared). But it was his personality that was the worst thing about him. He held neither a door nor a chair, nor did he take her arm and walk beside her. Instead, he rushed down the street while Ida tottered after him in her high heels, trying to keep up. When they finally arrived at their destination, Moe's Coffee and Donut Shop, and were seated at a table drinking coffee and eating French crullers, Norman had informed Ida that he planned to become a lawyer, and he would need a wife to do his housework and have his children. Was she interested? Ida had pretended to be thinking about her answer long enough to finish her coffee and pastry. Then she had politely told him "no thank you" and had walked out of the coffee shop and gone home.

However, it was not as if Arthur and Kitty didn't know each other, and Kitty had already agreed to a date. Also, Arthur was the president of the Tenants Association and it could come in handy for Ida to be owed a favor. There was the time, several years ago, when the tenant then living in apartment 3C (now occupied by Kitty Cheong) complained about noise coming from Ida's apartment. The only noise Ida could think of making was one instance of a rolling pin rolling from her kitchen table to the floor when she paused while rolling cookie dough to answer the telephone. Arthur, in the role of mediator, had come to Ida's apartment to discuss the matter. While they sat at her kitchen table they heard a loud noise from the kitchen below. Arthur had immediately gone downstairs to investigate. He later told Ida the outcome: the husband was in the couple's living room when he heard repeated loud noises coming from his kitchen where his wife was preparing dinner. When he went to the kitchen to see what was going on, his wife had insisted the noise was coming from upstairs. But when Arthur confronted the wife, she admitted she was dropping pots herself, due to unsteadiness from too many afternoon cocktails.

"Well," Ida finally said, "it just so happens that I'll be giving the Cheong sisters a baking lesson later this week."

Arthur immediately sat up straighter on his leather sofa and beamed.

"So you think you can help me out?" he asked.

"What I can do," Ida replied, "is try to find out what Kitty Cheong considers a good date, so you can be better prepared to make a good impression. But there's no guarantee that it will lead to a successful date."

"I know," said Arthur. "There's that thing called chemistry."

Ida remembered chemistry as one of her more annoying high school subjects. She had heard it used in discussions of personal relationships, and supposed it meant a good mix of ingredients, like a good cookie recipe.

"I'll do my best," Ida promised. She hauled herself out of the leather chair, which made a great squeaking noise, and Arthur saw her to the door.

Chapter 19

As Ida walked down the third floor hallway to Kitty Cheong's apartment for the next baking lesson, she tried to remember all the tasks to be done. The first, and of course most important, was the making of oatmeal raisin cookies. When she gave Kitty the shopping list, she had suggested that the raisins be soaked in advance in rum or some sort of liquor. She was now having a bit of trepidation about the possible outcome of this instruction, imagining they had used a strange Chinese brew. The next task was to get the information Arthur had requested. And lastly, she would try to look for her Martha Stewart Cookies book.

"I'd love to be a fly on the wall," Sandy had remarked when Ida told her about the next lesson. "Too bad we can't drill a little spy hole in your kitchen floor, so I can see and hear what's going on."

"Sometimes you can listen at the radiator," Ida had advised her.

Now that was another thing to remember: give Sandy a full report of the conversation. Ida hoped her memory was up to it.

The ingredients for the cookies were neatly arranged on Kitty's round kitchen table. A bowl of raisins soaking in a brownish liquid gave off an alcoholic aroma that Ida could not quite place as she took a sniff.

"We use Xiaoxing wine," explained Kitty. "To give Chinese flavor for Mah Jongg lady."

As the China dolls mixed the cookie dough under Ida's supervision, Ida scanned the kitchen, looking for a possible hiding place for a book. But the cabinet doors were all shut tight, and there was no bookcase, not even a shelf.

"Do you have any cookbooks?" Ida asked casually.

"Not bring," said Lily. "Too heavy in luggage. But really not need. We already know most dish. Just write down cookie recipe."

Ida could not imagine living without cookbooks. Even now, though she hadn't cooked much in years, she had an occasional urge for something that had been a family favorite. Italian-style meatloaf was a dish even Barbara, the picky eater, enjoyed. Ida had served it with mashed potatoes and peas, both side dishes topped with a pat of butter. Those were the days before cholesterol was discovered. People had heart attacks and died. Now they lived more food-deprived years. She didn't know any of her recipes by heart, or, now remembering the memory thing, maybe she just didn't remember them.

"Now we add raisin?" Lily asked.

Ida peered into the mixing bowl and nodded. Kitty drained the alcohol-soaked fruit and tossed it into the bowl while Lily stirred. Then the twins put spoonfuls of dough on their cookie sheets and the cookies were put into the oven.

Kitty had made a pot of tea (fortunately not the crockery-washing kind) in preparation for the cookie tasting. When the cookies were cool enough to eat, the women munched and drank. Ida thought the raisins had an interesting taste, fairly pleasant.

"So when is your date with the president?" Ida asked Kitty.

Lily giggled.

"On Sunday," Kitty said. "We will go Manhattan, see parade."

"Parade? What parade?" Ida asked, and then she remembered. Sunday was St. Patrick's Day!

Ida imagined Arthur and Kitty squashed in the crowd, surrounded by beer can-wielding teenagers. It was not a pretty picture.

"Then we go to restaurant, eat special food. He tell me, but I not understand. Maybe corn?" Kitty continued. She looked at Ida for help.

"Corned beef and cabbage," said Ida. "It's a sort of preserved meat. And cabbage is a green vegetable."

Ida had to admit that this was a smart choice on Arthur's part. Sandy had told her that the Chinese liked to eat preserved meats, so Kitty might not find this concoction strange.

"And drink beer," Kitty added with a grin.

Lily giggled again.

"Do you drink beer?" Ida asked.

Lily and Kitty laughed.

"Kitty like drink beer," Lily reported. "Can drink many beer."

"Is that so?" Ida commented.

Ida could not recall Arthur's drinking habits. At one time the Tenants Association had a yearly Christmas party in the lobby, until the landlord put a stop to it due to complaints of drunkenness. Ida remembered a table set up with a punch bowl and paper cups, and plates of cookies, one batch made by Ida herself (gingerbread, her standard Christmas cookie). She had a vague memory of Arthur with a cup in his hand and a stupid grin on his face. But he often had a stupid grin on his face, so it was not proof of inebriation.

"Have iron stomach," Kitty assured her, patting her tiny abdomen.

Ida recalled Sandy telling her that most Asians couldn't drink much alcohol, that it was a genetic predisposition. But of course there were always exceptions.

"Will you bring Arthur some cookies?" Ida asked.

"Not think," Kitty said. She had a puzzled look. "He ask for green cookie. What cookie that?"

For a moment Ida was stymied. Then she realized Arthur meant a green cookie for Saint Patrick's Day. She explained it to the twins.

"You can make the sugar cookies, and put green food coloring in the dough. And then you can frost them with green frosting," Ida suggested. "There's a picture of such cookies in my Martha Stewart Cookies book," she suddenly thought to say, "and I could show you, but unfortunately the book is missing."

As usual, the China dolls gave Ida their inscrutable look. But she now realized that their lack of response was in itself a response. If they truly did not have the book, wouldn't they have responded with suitable dismay? Offered to help her look for it? Ida again scanned the kitchen. So many possible hiding places: cabinets both above and below the sink and counter, and four large drawers in which the book could easily be stashed. She would have to give this matter much more thought. She would go to the library and read all of Agatha Christie's Miss Marple mysteries. And all of Sherlock Holmes. Ida visualized herself becoming a female Sherlock, with Sandy as her Dr. Watson.

"Can see design on Internet," Kitty was saying, "copy on cookie."

Lily giggled.

"Just fun," Kitty said firmly.

"Maybe president want marry you," Lily persisted.

"Not marry old man," Kitty insisted.

"Old man best," Lily said. "Soon die, then you can get all money!"

Ida thought this was a good point, but Arthur was not exactly old. He could easily live another twenty or thirty years. But she was sure he did have money. He still worked part-time as a lawyer, and his rent-stabilized apartment must be costing him as little as the rent on her own place. She imagined Kitty marrying Arthur and moving into his apartment. But would he let Kitty and Lily use his kitchen to bake their dozens of cookies for the Mah Jongg ladies? She suspected he would be like Lily's husband Sven, and not want his kitchen turned into a cookie factory. Then she had a terrible thought: the twins would descend on her own kitchen and bake cookies day and night.

"I make green cookie tomorrow," Kitty decided. She turned to Ida. "Can bring you some, okay?"

"I'd love to have some," Ida said.

"But not tell president," Kitty warned. "Must be surprise."

"Don't worry," Ida assured her. "I won't tell him."

After Ida left Kitty's apartment she remembered she had promised to report to Arthur. She decided she would simply write him a note telling him she thought the date would be fine, and slip it under his door.

Chapter 20

Dr. Barbara was on the phone and she was not happy. Not that she ever was. In fact, thinking back to Barbara's childhood and young adult years, Ida would say that Barbara was never happy or unhappy. She was satisfied or dissatisfied. And at the moment she was very dissatisfied.

"Monica's back," Barbara announced. "I don't know what to do."

"Don't know what to do about what?" Ida asked.

"What am I going to do with her? She has no job and no money," Barbara snapped.

"You have a house," Ida pointed out. "Surely there's enough room. And you must have enough money to feed her, at least temporarily."

Ida had never been to Barbara's house, but most houses had more than one bedroom.

"Of course there's enough room," Barbara said. "That's not the problem. The problem is that I have a fiancé. He spends a lot of time at my house, and we're used to our privacy."

Ida knew what this meant: sex. It seemed as if there had been a recent outbreak of sex drive: Monica, Barbara, Kitty, Arthur. Perhaps it was the onset of Spring, stirring up everyone's juices.

"Why don't you just go to your fiance's house?" Ida suggested.

"His son lives with him," said Dr. Barbara.

"You could introduce Monica to his son," Ida said, "and if they hit it off, they could live in one house and you and your fiancé could live in the other one."

"That won't work," Barbara immediately explained. "His son is gay."

"They could be housemates," Ida suggested.

"Actually," said Barbara, "I was thinking of sending her to you. At least for a while."

For a moment Ida was stunned. Not that she didn't love Monica. But it had been decades since anyone had lived with her.

"Well, I don't know where she would sleep," Ida told her daughter. "I got rid of the old sofa bed after you moved to California."

Before Barbara moved to California to begin her college and medical career and was still in residence on Bayside Avenue, Ida and Irwin slept in the living room on the sofa bed, giving Barbara the bedroom. Many couples did this back then, wanting to save money on rent so they would be able to afford college tuition.

Barbara grunted.

"Maybe Monica will find a job and get her own apartment," said Ida.

"Maybe," said Barbara after a pause. "I've got to go." She hung up.

Ida heard a key turn in the door. Sandy had arrived. Ida had decided to give Sandy a set of keys, in case of emergency. Sandy had protested that someone in the building should have them, perhaps the Cheong sisters or even Arthur, but Ida would have none of that.

"I trust you," she told Sandy. "Arthur would drive me crazy checking up on me. And if the Cheong sisters took my Martha Stewart Cookies book, what else might they take?"

"Your rolling pin?" Sandy had asked slyly.

They had both burst out laughing.

Now Sandy hurried out of her coat and into the kitchen, where Ida was making tea.

"So tell me what happened!" Sandy demanded. "Did you find the book?"

"No," Ida said, "but I'm sure they have it." She explained her theory.

"You're right," Sandy agreed, "but we can't give up."

"But where could they be hiding it?" Ida asked.

Sandy smacked herself lightly in the head.

"We're idiots," she announced. "The twins knew you were coming to Kitty's apartment, so of course they stashed it somewhere, because they knew you'd be looking for it."

Ida nodded in comprehension.

"So what you have to do," Sandy mused, "is to visit Kitty Cheong unexpectedly. Then maybe the book will be out in the open."

Ida nodded.

"I could drop by Sunday evening, to see how the date with Arthur went," Ida decided, pleased with her idea. "I could bring her some brownies."

"Good idea," said Sandy as she got to work on the oven.

Suddenly Ida had a thought: what if the date went so well that Kitty invited Arthur to her apartment after they returned to Bayside Avenue? What if they were kissing and snuggling? What if they were having sex? She realized that if they were having sex, Kitty wouldn't answer the door. Or maybe they would go to Arthur's man cave. He could serve espresso from his machine. They might need it after a St. Patrick's Day of drinking. Brownies were a good accompaniment to espresso. Martha Stewart's recipe was the best. But of course the book was missing. Well, if Kitty Cheong didn't get the best brownies, it was her own fault. Then reality entered her mind. Arthur was just past sixty. Even with Viagra, would Kitty, in her twenties, consider sex with Arthur? Probably not.

While Sandy was busy scrubbing, Ida went downstairs to get her mail. She was glad the lobby was empty, as she was too preoccupied with the current events to make small talk. She reached into her mailbox and withdrew a handful of envelopes. It was the usual assortment: one bill, several charities asking for money, a few advertisements. In the middle of these was a thick cream-colored envelope, addressed in fancy hand lettering. It was unmistakably an invitation. But to what? An idea crossed her mind. Could Barbara have pushed up her wedding date due to Monica's unexpected return? Maybe Dr. Barbara had decided to marry in haste and honeymoon in Hawaii, hoping that Monica would get her life together in the meantime. Ida turned the envelope over to check the return address. Charlene Johnson, her former cleaning girl! Ida had been invited to her wedding.

On her way up in the elevator, Ida tried to sort out her thoughts. It was lovely of Charlene to invite her, but should she go? She supposed after ten years with Charlene, she was not quite family, but close enough. She imagined Dr. Barbara's annoyance, her mother attending a cleaning girl's wedding, when it was doubtful Ida could attend her own daughter's nuptials. But could she go to Charlene's wedding? Ida hadn't left her neighborhood in several years. She would have to take a taxi. And what would she wear? She mentally flipped through the contents of her closets. Impossible! When she returned to her apartment, Sandy was cleaning the refrigerator. Ida waved the thick envelope at her.

"Oh, so you got it!" Sandy exclaimed.

"I don't know about this," Ida said, seating herself at the kitchen table. She was exhausted just thinking about it.

"Of course you'll go," Sandy said firmly, hands on hips.

"How will I get there and back?" Ida asked. "And what will I wear?"

"I'll come and get you in a taxi," Sandy told her. "And I'll go shopping for an outfit. And you'll need shoes," she continued, glancing at Ida's feet in their house slippers that she wore at all times in the building. "Think of it as a practice for your daughter's wedding," Sandy suggested.

Ida pointed to the silver topknot of hair on her head.

"Will I have to go to the beauty parlor?" she asked.

"I've got a friend who does great hair," Sandy assured her. "She'll come to your apartment the morning of the wedding. Just leave everything to me."

Ida supposed she could leave everything to Sandy. Maybe when Barbara got married she would take Sandy with her to California.

Chapter 21

Ida had always found baking to be the antidote when she felt out of sorts, so she decided to make a double batch of brownies. The recent events—Barbara's engagement, Monica's dismissal from the nunnery, Kitty and Arthur's date, and now Charlene's wedding—had given her too much stress. Even though these events did not have to do with her personally, they all did impact on her in one way or another. Beating eggs and sugar together, melting chocolate: these simple tasks soothed her. She did wish she had Martha's Double Chocolate Brownie recipe. She would make do with her other recipes. She was tempted to buy another copy of the book. She would not have to ask Dr. Barbara and go through a lengthy explanation, as Sandy had offered to get one for her. But if she acquired a new copy of the book she would have to hide it from the China dolls. If they saw she had a new one they might think it was all right to keep her original copy. She put the pans of brownie batter into the oven, and soon the aroma of chocolate filled the kitchen.

It was three o'clock and Kitty and Arthur should soon be returning to Bayside Avenue. Unless they were having such fun that they stayed in Manhattan long after the parade. As soon as the brownies had cooled she would cut them in squares and bring half a batch to Kitty. Half a batch would go in the freezer, to be saved for Sandy, who had gone to the store for eggs and baking chocolate. And the second batch, well, she might just eat the entire pan herself.

Ida remembered the time when she was a child and her grandmother had made two chocolate Babkas, those aromatic yeasty cakes. The cakes had just cooled, and Grandma had poured a sugar glaze over them.

"If you're careful, you can cut yourself a slice," she'd told Ida.

And Ida had cut herself one slice, and then another slice, until she had eaten half the cake!

She didn't really think she could eat an entire pan of brownies. She cut one pan into squares, piled half on a plate, and left her apartment to deliver them to Kitty. As she walked down the hall, the elevator door opened and Kitty stepped out, carrying a plate of what appeared to be green cookies.

"*Ni hau*," said Kitty.

The two women stood and stared at each other for a moment.

"I was just going to bring you some brownies," Ida said.

"I bring you green cookie," said Kitty. "I make for president, but have very many."

"Well," said Ida, "let's have tea."

She returned to her apartment, followed by Kitty, and boiled water for the tea. Now she would have a good excuse to eat not only brownies but also cookies. Soon the women were stuffing their mouths.

"Very delicious," Kitty declared after consuming her third brownie.

Ida, knowing she had more brownies tucked away, had focused on the cookies. They were clearly the sugar cookies she had taught the China dolls, but these were shamrock shaped. They were frosted with green icing and then dipped in green decorating sugar.

"Did Arthur like your cookies?" Ida asked.

"He like," said Kitty. "He ask me come to his apartment this night, drink coffee, eat cookie."

"Will you go?" Ida asked.

"I say too tired," Kitty told her.

"And how was the date?" Ida pursued.

"Date is fun," said Kitty. "But I think not go again."

"Oh?" Ida wanted to say more but her mouth was full of brownie. Anyway, she didn't want to seem too nosy.

"President too old," Kitty said matter-of-factly. She studied one of her green cookies. "He not think, but I think."

"Most men think they're still attractive, whatever their age," Ida commented. Even her own husband Irwin had been of this philosophy. But what Ida really thought was that men never grew up, so they went on thinking they could attract very young women.

"Old men look like grandfather," Kitty stated. "Not want date grandfather."

The women laughed. The plates of brownies and cookies contained only leftover crumbs.

"So maybe you want to find a young man," Ida suggested.

Kitty paused before answering.

"In Hong Kong I have many boyfriend," she finally said. "Give me many gift, take me many place. Very nice. But later," she continued, "I am like concubine. You know this meaning?"

"Yes," Ida said. "I know what you mean."

"Always tell me I cannot go some place, cannot see some person. Just do they tell me what. So I break up. Find one more. But always same. Then we leave Hong Kong, come here."

"But Lily found Sven," Ida pointed out.

Kitty rolled her eyes.

"Sven just same," Kitty said. "In Hong Kong very nice. Then his job move here. He want Lily come. She say if get marry and can take me, she come."

"I suppose twins really are inseparable," Ida mused out loud.

"Not so true," said Kitty. "Lily say that to Sven. But I think real reason she say I must come, she afraid of Sven. Want me close by."

Ida's hand froze with her teacup in midair.

"Really?" she asked. Then she remembered the overheard arguments. But all couples argued. "Then why did she marry him?"

"Lily say come to U.S. is good chance," Kitty explained. "Take chance to have better life."

"But it's not better," Ida concluded.

Kitty nodded.

"Some night Lily sleep on my sofa," Kitty admitted. "Very tired. All day cook, clean, wash clothes. Then at night husband want sex. Lily too tired. Husband angry." She shook her head.

Kitty's confession threw a whole new light on the China dolls. Ida had heard stories of marital mistreatment, read about it in the newspaper. But she had never actually known a victim.

"Why don't you go back to Hong Kong?" Ida asked.

"Not have enough cash for air ticket two people," Kitty said. "U.S. allow only small amount money bring in. We use some buy baking supply, other thing."

"You could ask your family to wire you the money," Ida suggested.

"Lily not want admit make mistake," Kitty explained. "Not want lose face. In Chinese life, face very important. So she not ask for help."

"So you'll just stay here and suffer?" Ida was appalled both at the situation and at the China dolls' lack of initiative to correct it.

"We have plan," said Kitty. "But not do yet."

Several moments of silence passed. Then Kitty drained her teacup.

"Sorry tell you trouble," Kitty said. "Now I go."

"I wish I could help you," Ida told her as she saw her out the door.

Ida sat at the kitchen table contemplating Kitty's conversation when the telephone rang.

"Arthur Sandowsky here," announced the voice. "How are you, Ida?"

Arthur sounded happy, upbeat, on a wave of what he doubtless thought had been a successful date. This did not bode well, as the wave would soon crash and fizzle on the beach.

"Fine," Ida said. "How are you, Arthur?" she asked, even though she already knew.

"I'm great," Arthur said. "If you're not busy, I was wondering if you could come to my apartment for a little while. I need your advice. Again."

Ida knew he wanted advice about Kitty Cheong, and she knew the advice she would have to give him would not go over well. She also knew that Arthur would not leave her alone until the subject had been discussed. Might as well get it over with now.

"I can come up in half an hour," she said. "Is that all right?"

"Perfect," said Arthur. "See you then."

It would not be perfect, Ida thought. But the situation might be a tiny bit improved by a gift of some fresh-baked brownies. She thought regretfully of the extra batch she had made. She would part with half of it. If she ate more sweets this afternoon, she would be sick.

Chapter 22

Ida marched down the hall to Arthur's apartment carrying that day's second plate of brownies that day. But this time she felt like the wooden horse in the Greek myth, in which the Greeks brought a huge wooden horse as a gift to their enemies. When the gates were shut and the horse inside the enemy's compound, soldiers poured out of the horse and the enemy was slaughtered.

Then she paused a few feet from Arthur's door. There was actually no reason for her to be totally discouraging to Arthur. Kitty had said she didn't want to date him again, but after some time went by, she might change her mind. Ida knew Kitty wouldn't change her mind. But Arthur had no way of knowing what Kitty had said. And Ida had no obligation to tell him. Feeling some relief about the forthcoming discussion, Ida rang Arthur's bell. She heard his footsteps approaching.

"Ida, come in, come in!" Arthur beamed when he saw the plate of brownies. "How did you know that brownies are my favorite dessert?"

Ida handed him the plate, went into his man cave living room, and seated herself in the squeaky leather chair.

"I bet you can guess what I want to talk about," Arthur said as he plopped onto the sofa.

"I have no idea," Ida demurred.

Arthur's face fell momentarily. Then he beamed and plunged in.

"Today was my date with Kitty Cheong," he reminded her.

"Oh, that's right," Ida said. "How did it go?"

"I actually believe it went swimmingly," Arthur said. "The parade was great. And then we went to an Irish pub and had corned beef and cabbage. And several beers." He frowned. "That girl can certainly put away her beer."

"Really," Ida remarked. She was glad that Kitty had at least gotten a good bit of drinking out of the date. But Arthur was notoriously cheap. He would not be pleased by Kitty's alcohol consumption.

"And she made me some wonderful green cookies," Arthur went on. "I've got them in the kitchen. I invited her up here for espresso and cookies when we got back, but she said she was tired. Too bad, she could have had some of your brownies as well."

"Too bad," Ida agreed. She smiled to herself, thinking of all the cookies and brownies she and Kitty had just eaten.

"Well, I wanted to get your advice as to how I should proceed," Arthur said.

"That seems obvious," Ida replied. "You ask her for another date."

Ida knew what Arthur was getting at, but she wanted him to just say it.

"What I mean is, maybe you could speak to Kitty. Ask her how the date went. From her point of view. And then let me know, so I can move ahead." He paused. "You didn't happen to speak to her this afternoon, by any chance?"

Ida was startled. She wondered if Arthur had been lurking in the hallway on Kitty's floor, and had seen the China doll get into the elevator with her plate of cookies. This sort of behavior was considered stalking. Ida shivered. She had read about such people in the newspapers, men, and sometimes women, following their object of unrequited love everywhere, making not only a nuisance of themselves, but also a menace. She asked herself whether she thought Arthur could become such a person. The answer was yes.

If he had been in the hall and had seen Kitty get on the elevator, he could then have watched the indicator and seen on which floor she got off: Ida's. But Ida decided to play innocent.

"How could I have spoken to her if you just got back a short while ago?" Ida asked with a puzzled look.

Arthur glanced at his watch.

"It's been at least two hours," he said. "I just thought she might have given you a call. Being as how you're friends and all."

Ida now realized she had fallen into a black hole. No matter how long she could string Arthur along, he would be a perpetual pest, first asking, then demanding her help in the wooing of Kitty Cheong. This was really a job for Dr. Barbara to figure out. She had always made short shrift of unsuitable men. Of course, this method was more difficult when you lived in the same building as your pursuer. But Ida was tempted to call her daughter and describe the circumstances. She was sure Dr. Barbara would be satisfied to take a pot shot at her former neighbor. Arthur was looking at Ida expectantly.

"Kitty Cheong and I are not friends," Ida said firmly. "We're simply neighbors who like to bake. And I could hardly be a friend to a woman the age of my granddaughter and who does not speak fluent English," Ida added.

"Well, maybe you're not her friend," Arthur admitted. "But you're probably the closest thing to a friend that she has, besides her sister."

Ida could not argue this point. It was possible that Kitty had made friends with some of the Mah Jongg ladies, but she didn't know. And now a new avenue of discourse had been opened.

"Maybe you could chat up Kitty's sister. You know, ask her how Kitty's date went." Arthur seemed pleased with his new idea. "Maybe it would be better not to confront Kitty directly."

"What do you think I am, the Bayside Avenue gossip?" Ida finally burst out. "Or your personal private investigator?"

Arthur's mouth dropped open.

"For God's sake, you're a grown man, not some pimply adolescent," Ida went on. "If you want another date with the woman, just ask her! I'm an old woman, not your errand girl!"

Arthur leaned back against the leather cushions of the man couch, his face pale. Then he abruptly leaned forward.

"Ida, I am terribly sorry," Arthur said. "I don't know what I was thinking."

Arthur put his head in his hands. Ida was tempted to feel sorry for him. But she remembered fifty years of Arthur Sandowsky. He had been given every advantage as an only son. And here he was, half a century later, chasing after a Chinese girl. She stifled a laugh. The problem was, he was still her long-time neighbor and the president of the Tenants Association. She needed to tread carefully.

"Look, Arthur," she said, "I can understand your attraction to Kitty. She's young and pretty. But I have to tell you that I really don't approve of May-December romances. So I'm not going to get involved in this business. You are certainly free to pursue Kitty, and I wish you luck. But please don't try to involve me again."

Arthur nodded.

"I'm sorry to have bothered you, Ida," he said.

Ida heaved herself out of the leather chair, left the man cave and went back to her apartment. For several minutes she sat quietly, thinking about her conversation with Arthur. She didn't know what had come over her to speak her mind. But she felt relieved. She couldn't resist the temptation to call Barbara and tell her what had happened, and she dialed her daughter's number. The voicemail came on, informing her that Dr. Rappaport was not available and gave another number for a medical emergency. Ida left a brief message of "just calling to say hello" and hung up. She wondered if thyroid surgery patients had medical emergencies. She imagined that they were rare, which was probably one of the reasons Barbara had chosen that specialty. Her daughter disapproved of emergencies.

There was a loud bang on the kitchen ceiling, as if a pot had been dropped, or thrown.

"I cook all day! I am not restaurant!" she heard Lily Cheong shout.

A door slammed. Ida imagined Lily was headed for Kitty's sofa.

It was all too much. Then she remembered the second batch of brownies. She put up water for tea, took the brownie pan from the refrigerator, and cut herself a large piece.

Chapter 23

Over the next few days, Ida gave much thought to the Saint Patrick's Day weekend and events. She was most disturbed by Kitty's revelation about Lily and Sven. Still annoyed over the disappearance of the Martha Stewart Cookies book, Ida was now inclined to make less of an issue about it. The China dolls had more serious things on their minds. Kitty had said they had a plan, but hadn't revealed any details.

"I hope they're not going to work illegally in a Chinese restaurant," Sandy commented when Ida told her what she had learned.

"I doubt it," Ida said, recalling Lily's "I am not restaurant!" shout.

"Or in some kind of nightclub," Sandy continued. "They're young and cute, and they look good in miniskirts."

"Sven wouldn't allow Lily to go out at night," Ida assured her.

"Maybe Kitty will marry Arthur, get hold of some of his money, and take off with Lily," Sandy mused.

"Fat chance," Ida said. "I don't think they're that desperate."

"Yet," said Sandy. "You never know."

But Ida could not dwell on the fate of the China dolls for long.

"I'm mailing you a photo of the place where I'll be married," Dr. Barbara informed Ida on her next phone call. "I wish you had a computer," she said. "It's so much easier."

Ida's lack of a computer had been a sore point with Barbara, who had offered to buy one for her mother. But Ida was adamant: she did not want one. She didn't see what was so difficult about putting a stamp on an envelope and dropping the envelope into a mail box. And why did she need to see Barbara's wedding location now? Ida would see it when she attended, and if she couldn't go, she was sure she would be subjected to extensive photographs of the occasion.

"How is Monica?" Ida asked, hoping to divert the conversation from both the wedding and computer.

"Monica will be my maid of honor," Barbara informed her. “"We're negotiating a dress."

"That's nice," Ida said.

She could imagine the shopping trips. Barbara had always gone in for the latest fashions, while Monica preferred the long skirts and Granny dresses of the 1960's hippie movement.

"And she's got a job,' Barbara continued. "At an Arts and Crafts store, doing craft demonstrations."

"That sounds right up her alley," Ida said approvingly. She remembered Monica's long-ago gifts of necklaces made of beads and seashells. Of course, Ida wouldn't be caught dead wearing such things, but some people liked them.

"It may be right up her alley, but it's not making a living," Barbara snapped.

"Well, it's probably temporary," Ida tried to smooth things over. "Has she been sending out her resume?"

"What resume? She's spent the last couple of years in a nunnery. Before that, she worked on a farm co-op baking fruit pies," Barbara answered. "If she ever had any skills, she's forgotten them."

Ida's immediate thought was that Monica had inherited the family baking gene and she felt proud of her granddaughter. But she knew this would cut no mustard with Barbara.

"Maybe she could go back to school and learn a new skill," Ida suggested. "Something useful."

"You know, that's a good idea," Barbara said after a pause. "I'll tell her it was your idea."

"Good," Ida agreed.

"I've got to go," said Dr. Barbara, as she always did as soon as she had accomplished her purpose for the call. The line went dead.

Then the doorbell rang. The ringing of Ida's doorbell was a rare occurrence. There had been Charlene's ring every Friday, but that, of course, no longer occurred. And the China dolls were not due for a lesson.

"I'll get it," Sandy called out.

A moment later Kitty entered the kitchen carrying a napkin-covered plate, which she set on the table.

"I make you cookie," Kitty announced, and she dramatically whisked away the napkin.

Ida stared. They were unmistakably Martha Stewart's lemon-poppy seed cookies.

"Please try," Kitty encouraged.

Ida reached out and took a cookie. She gave it a sniff: definitely lemon. The poppy seeds looked not quite like poppy seeds. She took a bite. Yes, they were definitely the Martha Stewart lemon-poppy seeds, or rather lemon-not-quite-poppy seeds. Further proof of the whereabouts of Ida's book! She was tempted to ask Kitty where she got the recipe. But by now Ida knew the inscrutability of the China dolls and decided not to waste her breath.

"Delicious," Ida pronounced.

Sandy had entered the kitchen and put up water for tea.

"I have question," said Kitty. She reached into her pocket and took out a folded piece of paper. "I find this under apartment door. I think must be from president. But my English not good. Please you tell me say what." She held out the paper to Ida.

After a moment's pause, while she put the rest of the cookie into her mouth and brushed the crumbs from her fingers, Ida took the paper and opened it. It was indeed from Arthur Sandowsky.

"'Dear Kitty,'" Ida read aloud, "'will you do me the honor of accompanying me to the movies next Saturday?' signed Arthur Sandowsky, President, Bayside Avenue Tenants Association."

Sandy, pouring the tea water into the teapot, snickered.

Kitty looked puzzled.

"He's asking you for another date," Ida told Kitty. "Next Saturday. To go to the movies."

Kitty seemed to be taking this in.

"Movie?" she asked. "Movie is English? I not understand. Anyway, not go to movie with old man. Is dark, too many hands," she said emphatically. "What I can do?"

"You can write him a note back," Sandy suggested.

"Say what?" asked Kitty.

Ida and Sandy exchanged a look.

"You can tell him you don't understand enough English to go to a movie," Ida said.

"No, that's no good," Sandy disagreed. She poured each of them a cup of tea and sat down. "He'll just think of something else for the two of you to do on Saturday. We have to come up with something better."

Ida noted Sandy's use of the word "we." She had resolved not to become involved in the Arthur-Kitty non-romance, but apparently she did not have a choice.

"There's always the classic not feeling well," Ida suggested.

"No, no, no," Sandy immediately scrapped that idea. "That's been used so much, the men are on to it. Anyway, in Arthur's case, it might make him try harder. He might leave flowers on her doorstep."

"Well, she has to answer the note," Ida insisted. "If she doesn't answer, he might try knocking on her door. And then he might invite himself in."

"Not want!" declared Kitty.

"Right," Sandy nodded. "And if you manage to keep him out, he'll just try again, and then you'll have to develop a whole secret knocking system with everyone so you know when it's safe to answer the door."

Ida envisioned a system of one knock for Lily and two knocks for herself, and any number of knocks for other known visitors, on the order of Paul Revere's one if by land, two if by sea.

"The fact is," Ida stated, "Arthur will not be deterred. The best we can do right now is a stalling tactic. By written note. To avoid direct contact."

"Agreed," said Sandy. She took a cookie and munched it thoughtfully. "Wait a minute—I've got it!" she exclaimed. "Kitty will write him a note—in Chinese!"

There was a moment of stunned silence.

"President read Chinese?" Kitty asked dubiously.

"Of course not! And that's the point," Sandy explained. "You can write a note just saying you're sorry but you can't see him on Saturday."

Ida pictured Arthur receiving this missive. No doubt, he would go to every Chinese restaurant in Flushing until he found someone to translate for him.

"Maybe president angry," Kitty said.

"How can he be angry? You can't read or write English," Sandy said.

Ida went to a kitchen drawer and brought a small pad of paper and a pen to the table.

"Now, we'll tell you what to say," Sandy instructed Kitty, "and you just put it down in Chinese."

Chapter 24

When Sandy arrived the following Friday, she carried several large shopping bags.

"These duds are for you," she announced, depositing the bags on the floor.

Ida stared at the bags. She hadn't heard anyone use the word "duds" in ages.

"Duds?" she repeated questioningly.

"Your outfit for Charlene's wedding," Sandy elaborated, rummaging in a bag. She pulled out and held up a two-piece outfit, the top on a hanger in one hand and the skirt in her other hand. "What do you think?"

The costume was made of a silky peach fabric shot with gold thread. The skirt was gathered with an elastic waist. The top, which was obviously worn as an over-blouse, had three-quarter length sleeves and a deep cowl neckline. Ida reached out and gingerly fingered the material.

"You like it?" Sandy asked.

"I think I do," Ida admitted. She could picture herself wearing the outfit not only to Charlene's wedding, but also to Dr. Barbara's ceremony. "It's not an old lady dress," Ida said.

"And look what else." Sandy reached into another bag and pulled out a shoe box. She opened it and revealed a pair of beige satin sandals. "And this," she said, and held up a small satin purse. "Go try everything on," Sandy instructed. "I'll put it all on the bed."

Ida went to the bedroom and put on the top and skirt, and the shoes. Then she looked in her full-length mirror. She liked what she saw. But she needed accessories. Out of a drawer she took her pearl necklace, a long-ago gift from her husband. She clipped pearl earrings onto her earlobes and went to the living room, where Sandy was dusting, and held out the pearl necklace.

"Wow," said Sandy, looking Ida up and down. "You look like the mother of the bride."

"I need some help with this," Ida told her, handing her the pearl necklace.

Sandy fastened the necklace.

"I think I'm ready to party," Ida announced.

"I'll say," Sandy agreed.

Ida couldn't remember the last time she had gotten dressed up. It might have been fourteen years ago for Monica's Sweet Sixteen party. Ida had been only seventy-seven then, and Barbara had arranged for her to fly to California and to stay at a posh hotel. On that trip, Ida had brought three outfits, one to wear on the airplane going and coming back, one for the party, and one for the extra day on which Barbara had arranged a half-day tour of a movie studio as a special treat. She didn't know what had happened to those clothes—probably given away after they'd gone out of style, or she might have gained a bit of weight. Or maybe, the thought now occurred to her, she had loaned them to Arthur's mother for some occasion.

Now she could really see herself in California, as mother of the bride. Dr. Barbara would not be embarrassed by her mother.

"You'll need some lipstick and eye shadow," Sandy decided, scrutinizing Ida's face. "I'll tell my friend Betty, the one who's going to do your hair, to do some make-up, too."

"Now, I don't want to be all tarted up," Ida insisted. "It's not like I'm looking for a husband."

"Well, you never know," Sandy countered. "But I'll tell her to go easy."

Ida returned to her bedroom, changed back into her housedress, and put the new items away. She checked to see if she had a new pair of stockings. Would she need a pedicure? A manicure? Charlene's wedding was getting complicated.

"So when is the next baking lesson?" Sandy asked. "I'm ready for a new cookie."

Ida thought for a moment.

"You know, I haven't seen or heard from the twins all week," she said. "Maybe they're busy baking. They have quite a repertoire."

"What are they doing with all the cookies? They can't be eating them all," Sandy said.

"They go to some Chinese Ladies Association," Ida recalled. "The ladies play Mah Jongg and the twins bring cookies."

"Interesting," commented Sandy.

"Maybe I'll ring Kitty's bell," Ida decided. "I'll try a new recipe. Maybe some bar cookies. I saw an interesting recipe in Cooking Light."

Ida had subscriptions to three cooking magazines, although she rarely prepared anything that required more than three or four ingredients. And she hadn't made bar cookies in ages. She wondered if her desire to make bar cookies was a sign that she was getting old. They were less work than individual cookies. Where was her latest issue of Cooking Light? She had no idea—the memory thing again. She took her Maida Heatter's Cookies book down from the bookshelf and studied the list of bar cookies. She wavered between Dark Rocky Road and Light Rocky Road, both chock full of nuts and marshmallows, and finally opted for the Dark. A few ingredients were needed and, as the weather was fine, she decided to go to the store herself. After she changed into street clothes, she grabbed her shopping cart and set off. Ida left the elevator in the lobby and saw two women enter the front door. One of them was Kitty. The other was…Lily? Lily's head was covered with a large scarf tied under her chin, and she wore large, very dark sunglasses. The three women converged in the center of the lobby.

"Lily?" Ida asked, assuming it was the China doll behind the disguise.

"Lily have problem, we go Chinese doctor," Kitty said nervously.

"What problem?" Ida asked.

Lily hurried into the elevator and its doors slid closed.

"Lily and Sen have fight," Kitty told Ida, keeping her voice low. "Sen hit Lily, give her black eye. We go to Chinese herbal store, get medicine."

"You should call the police!" Ida exclaimed. "That's domestic violence!" Then she realized the twins might not have called because their English was not adequate. "I'll call for you," Ida offered.

"No, no, not call," said Kitty.

"Why not?" Ida asked, taken aback.

"We have only visitor visa, we already stay too long. If must go back to Hong Kong, family will know Lily marriage not good. Lily not want."

"Everybody makes mistakes," Ida said. "It's nothing to be ashamed of."

But Ida knew there were some people who would never admit to a mistake. Dr. Barbara was such a person. When she got divorced, she said she had married only for convenience, and the marriage was no longer convenient. But when Barbara was married she'd seemed really in love with her husband. Or maybe she was just in love with marriage, and discovered that for her, marriage was a mistake.

Kitty rang for the elevator and Ida left for the supermarket. By the time she returned home, Sandy had left. Which was probably a good thing, Ida decided, because she had a strong urge to talk to someone about Lily and she knew she shouldn't. She certainly could not tell Dr. Barbara. Ida knew exactly what her daughter would say: she should never have gotten involved with those foreigners and now she should have nothing more to do with them.

So she decided to apply herself to making Dark Rocky Road. She removed bags of pecans and marshmallows from her shopping cart and deposited them on the table. Soon she had the chocolate bottom layer of the bars spread in the pan and in the oven. She cut the marshmallows in half and melted more chocolate and butter. When the baked layer was ready she quickly assembled the topping and returned the pan to the oven. There was half a marshmallow left over and she popped it into her mouth.

The bars would have to sit overnight before she could cut them.

The telephone rang. The caller was Arthur, and he was not happy.

"Ida, you've got to help me!" Arthur exclaimed. "Kitty left me a note, but it's in Chinese!"

"Arthur, you know I can't read Chinese," Ida told him. "Why don't you go to one of the neighborhood Chinese restaurants and ask them?"

"I've been to all of them," Arthur tersely informed her, "and they all just looked at the note, looked at me, shrugged, and handed the note back."

Ida realized the situation called for a face to face conversation, but she didn't want Arthur in her apartment with the aroma of Dark Rocky Road in the air.

"Arthur, can we talk tomorrow? I'm really quite tired," Ida said.

"All right," Arthur conceded, but from his voice Ida knew it wasn't. "Shall I come to you at ten in the morning?"

"I'll come to you," Ida said, and she firmly replaced the phone receiver into its cradle.

Chapter 25

Ida took the elevator up to the man cave at ten before ten. She didn't want Arthur to get impatient and ring her bell. She carried no gifts. The Dark Rocky Road bars were sliced, wrapped, and waiting on her kitchen counter to be delivered to Lily. She had resolved not to become further involved in the Arthur-Kitty business, yet here she was, on her way to another session with the lovelorn president. She was tempted to blame Sandy for this. It had been Sandy's idea for Kitty to leave a Chinese note. If she had written in plain English, Ida would not at this moment be marching down the sixth floor hallway. She reached Arthur's apartment and rang the bell.

"Ida, come in," Arthur said.

He held the door open and Ida paused in the foyer. She peered into Arthur's kitchen and saw that he still had his mother's maple kitchen table with its four chairs.

"Arthur, do you mind if we sit in the kitchen?" Ida asked. "Your leather furniture is a bit difficult for me to negotiate."

Arthur seemed surprised but led Ida into the kitchen. Considering what he had done to the living room, it was astonishing that he had left the kitchen nearly unchanged. Ida thought he might have installed a breakfast bar with stools to perch on while gobbling a quick meal. She couldn't understand how anyone could eat while balancing precariously on those high seats, and was sure such furniture was a great contributor to indigestion. She wondered if Dr. Barbara had them in her house.

"Look at this!" Arthur indignantly slapped Kitty's note on the table.

Ida glanced at the note and carefully and deliberately pushed it back toward Arthur.

"I've already told you I can't read Chinese," Ida said patiently, "so there's no point in showing it to me."

"Well, what am I supposed to do?" Arthur whined. "No one will tell me what it says."

"What do you mean?" Ida asked, completely forgetting their previous conversation.

"Don't you remember? I told you last night! I took this to every restaurant in the neighborhood and not one of them will translate it!" He shook the note at Ida for emphasis.

"The solution is obvious," Ida told him. "Ask Kitty what the note says."

There was a long stretch of silence. Arthur stared at Ida, and then at the note.

"Why didn't I think of that?" the president asked himself out loud.

"Look, Arthur, I've got to be going," Ida declared. She stood up and walked toward the door.

"Wait! Should I just ring her bell?" Arthur cried.

Ida paused.

"You could write her a note telling her you don't understand her note, and put it under her door," she suggested.

"In English?" Arthur asked.

"Well, do you write Chinese?" Ida snapped.

"But I don't think Kitty can read English," Arthur persisted. "Wait—maybe you'll explain it to her?"

"Of course I will," Ida assured him. "Of course."

"Great!" Arthur rubbed his hands together.

"'Romeo, wherefore art thou?'" Ida thought as she hurried out his door.

Her next task was to deliver Dark Rocky Road to Lily. But did she dare go to Lily's apartment? Suppose Sven was at home? She knew he would not welcome the woman who was responsible for his wife's cookie extravaganza, especially if she appeared with yet another recipe. So she headed for 3C: Kitty. She rang the bell but there was no response.

"Kitty, it's Ida," she shouted as loudly as she could, which was not terribly loud, and she rapped on the door several times. "*Ni hau*," she shouted, suddenly remembering the Chinese phrase.

Just when she was about to give up and leave, she heard the lock click and the door opened. Kitty motioned her inside.

"I made these for Lily," Ida explained, handing over the Dark Rocky Road bars, "but I don't know if I should ring her bell."

"Lily here," said Kitty. "Take rest. Soon get up. We drink tea, eat cookie. Please sit." She indicated a chair at her kitchen table.

Kitty put up water and placed a stack of napkins on the table, and three Chinese teacups. Ida hoped this would not be the ceramic-washing tea. Kitty unwrapped the Dark Rocky Road bars and placed them on a plate.

"Is new cookie?" she asked.

"New to you," Ida said. She tried to think if the Martha Stewart Cookies book had a recipe resembling Dark or Light Rocky Road, but it had been so long since she had browsed the book's contents that she couldn't remember. "Try one," she told Kitty.

Kitty reached out and snatched a bar. She inspected it carefully, turning it this way and that. Then she took a bite and chewed thoughtfully.

"Very delicious," she declared. Then she poured tea, which was green in color. "Dragon Well tea," said Kitty. "Very famous. Very expensive."

Ida looked at the steam rising from her cup and decided to wait for the tea to cool.

"I saw the president this morning," Ida told Kitty. "He was very upset about your note. He said he went to several Chinese restaurants but no one would translate it."

Kitty giggled, covering her mouth with her hand.

"Kitty, what did you write in that note?" Ida asked.

"I just write I not want date grandfather, it not proper," Kitty said, and she giggled again.

Ida didn't know whether to believe the China doll.

"Well, the president is going to write you a note back," Ida advised her.

"I not read English," said Kitty. She covered her mouth and giggled.

Ida pictured a succession of notes being sent back and forth, Kitty's in Chinese, Arthur's in English, and absolutely no communication taking place. Which was the idea. Then Lily entered the kitchen. She looked much better than she had when Ida encountered the twins in the lobby. The black eye was nearly gone.

"Ida bake cookie for you," Kitty told Lily, pointing to the plate. She poured tea into Lily's cup.

Lily sat down and took a Rocky Road bar. And then Ida saw it: the Martha Stewart Cookies book. It was laying flat in the corner of the kitchen counter. With her ancient farsighted vision, she could make out the dark brown of the binding, the turquoise print of the author's name, and in large white lettering: COOKIES. For a moment the room seemed to go silent and dark. Then she realized someone was speaking to her.

"Very delicious," Lily declared. "What name this cookie?"

"Dark Rocky Road," said Ida. She picked up her teacup and drank slowly, buying time to think what to do. Should she mention the book? Or should she, when ready to leave, simply take the book and say she would just take her book back now?

"May have recipe?" Lily asked.

"Of course," Ida said. "I'll have to copy it out, and explain it to you." She wondered how to say marshmallow in Chinese.

"Chinese lady like this cookie," Kitty said thoughtfully. "Is American. Want more American cookie."

"So you're doing more baking for the Mah Jongg ladies?" Ida asked.

Lily nodded.

"Sen not like," Lily confided. "Say I waste time, waste money. Say I must have baby."

Ida tried to picture their baby: it would be a girl with a tiny body, and Asian face, and blond hair, or a dark-haired Asian-looking beanpole of a boy with blue eyes. And poor Lily would be chained to domestic slavery for another twenty years.

"Not want baby," said Lily firmly.

"I fully agree," said Ida.

Ida looked wistfully in the direction of the kitchen counter. Then she thought of the China dolls, trapped on Bayside Avenue, Lily with an abusive husband. She couldn't just walk off with her book. Now that she had proof that the twins had it, she would have to think of a tactful way to get it back. She drained her teacup.

"I have to go," Ida said, and she left Kitty's apartment.

Chapter 26

"I can't believe you walked out without that book!" Sandy exclaimed. She stood facing Ida, hands on hips.

Ida had not been able to resist telling Sandy about the sighting of the Cookies book, and now she struggled with herself, trying to decide if she would tell her cleaner about Lily's domestic situation. Finally she made a decision.

"This is confidential," she said, and she related her lobby meeting with the twins.

Sandy was quiet for several moments.

"Shouldn't we do something?" she finally asked.

"They don't want anything done," Ida explained.

Sandy shook her head.

Trying to get away from the depressing subject, Ida told Sandy about the outcome of Kitty's Chinese note to Arthur.

"But I'm not getting involved from now on," Ida insisted.

"Right," said Sandy sarcastically. She chuckled and headed for the vacuum cleaner.

It was Dr. Barbara's usual day and time to call Ida, and the phone rang right on schedule. Barbara had once explained that early Friday morning, California time, was best for her to talk. The week was winding down and there were no surgeries scheduled.

"Monica is going back to school," Barbara announced.

Ida thought her daughter might have added "thanks to you" as it had been her idea, but she knew better than to voice this opinion.

"That's wonderful!" Ida exclaimed. "What is she going to study?"

"She's going to become a medical assistant," Dr. Barbara reported triumphantly.

"Oh," said Ida. She was tempted to say "and whose idea was this?" but bit her tongue.

Ida couldn't think of a less suitable occupation for her granddaughter. For one thing, there was the obvious problem of Dr. Barbara. Although Monica's mother could be a convenient resource for information, there was also the fact that Barbara liked telling people what to do. Ida could already imagine the arguments that would take place: the proper way to take temperature and blood pressure, how to speak to a patient. But beside all that, there was Monica's lifelong squeamishness about bodily fluids and functions. She fainted at the sight of someone else's blood and could not stand the smell of vomit. Ida didn't know how Monica had been persuaded to go into this field but she wouldn't be surprised if her granddaughter was soon out of it. Another failed enterprise.

"And the school is costing me a fortune," Dr. Barbara went on. "I told Monica when she gets a job she can pay me back."

"How did she get accepted so quickly?" Ida asked.

"My fiancé knew someone at the admissions office and he pulled a few strings," Barbara explained.

"That was very nice of him," said Ida.

"He owed me," said Barbara.

Ida decided not to ask what he owed Barbara for. She wondered about her daughter's upcoming marriage.

"I've got an outfit for your wedding," Ida told Barbara. "It's quite lovely. I'm sure you'll be pleased."

"Isn't it a bit early to get a dress? We don't even have the date," said Barbara.

"Well, something came up, and I needed clothes, and as it turned out, the dress is just right for both occasions," Ida explained.

Ida had completely forgotten she had decided not to tell Barbara about Charlene's wedding—the memory thing again—and now it was too late.

"Are you going somewhere? What's the occasion?" Barbara demanded.

"Charlene is getting married and I'm invited to the wedding," Ida said.

"Who is Charlene?" Barbara asked.

"My former cleaning girl," said Ida.

There was silence on Barbara's end of the line.

"After all, she worked for me for ten years," Ida said defensively.

"Oh, I can understand that you've been invited," said Barbara. "What I don't understand is why you're going."

Now Ida was speechless.

"Why shouldn't I go?" Ida finally got out.

"It's not that you shouldn't," Barbara said. "I just don't see why you would want to."

Ida knew there was no acceptable answer. Yet she felt the need to explain her gratitude and loyalty to Charlene for staying with her for so many years, and Charlene's sending Sandy in her place when she couldn't come herself. But she would be wasting her breath.

"You wouldn't understand," Ida said with a sigh.

"And you'll have to buy a gift," Barbara continued as if Ida hadn't spoken.

"I hadn't thought of that," Ida admitted.

"And how will you get to the wedding? You can't take the subway," Barbara pointed out.

"That's been arranged," Ida told her emphatically. "I'm taking a taxi."

"And how are you getting home?" Barbara continued.

Ida actually had no idea how she was getting home from Charlene's wedding but decided to end the discussion.

"Sandy's running the vacuum cleaner and it's hard for me to hear," Ida said. "We'll talk next week." She hung up.

She marched into the living room, where Sandy was wielding a dust rag, not a vacuum.

"Sandy, what can I get Charlene for her wedding present?" Ida asked.

Sandy stopped dusting.

"That's the one thing we haven't thought of," Sandy said. She thought for a moment. "She's got a registry."

Ida had heard of such things, where a bride-to-be registered at Bloomingdale's for the things she wanted, like blenders and chafing dishes. She wondered if people still used these items. More important, would Barbara have a wedding registry? She already had a house full of worldly goods. But maybe Barbara and her fiancé would sell their houses and set up together in Hawaii, and want all new things.

"The registry is on the computer," Sandy said. "I'll look it up for you and pick a few possible items. Then you can decide, and give me the money and I'll take care of it."

"That was easy," Ida said. "I don't know how to thank you for all your help."

"Brownies would be nice," Sandy said with a grin, and she resumed dusting.

Back in the kitchen, Ida contemplated her own daughter's wedding, or future wedding, as Dr. Barbara had pointed out. All of the issues brought up pertaining to Charlene's wedding were the same as those for Barbara's. Obviously, Ida would go by plane and would be taken around by car or taxi. She already had a dress, but what about other clothing? Housedresses and what Ida considered street clothes were out of the question. She would have to send Sandy to shop. And she would need a suitcase. She had no idea what had happened to the one she'd used fourteen years ago. And then there was the gift.

Dr. Barbara was not easy to buy for, nor was she a gracious recipient. As a child, she opened birthday gifts carelessly and made no bones about her likes and dislikes. If an item of clothing was the wrong color, the comment "ugh" was announced with abandon. This was in contrast with Ida, who had been taught to give equal graciousness to an impossibly large and hairy sweater and to a coveted piece of jewelry. Maybe the invitation would specify "no gifts." Ida had heard of this phrase and thought it rather cheeky of the honoree, as "no gifts" conveyed the assumption that there would be gifts, and who wouldn't want them? And would any invitee take it seriously and come giftless? She doubted it.

But all this was in the future. At age ninety-one, Ida considered anything more than a week away to be the far future, and she might not be around to have to face it. Dr. Schwartz always told her she was good for another decade, but what did he know? Meanwhile, she decided to make brownies for Sandy and oatmeal chocolate chip cookies for Monica. That would keep her busy for a couple of days.

Chapter 27

As Ida rolled her empty shopping cart out of the elevator the Cheong sisters rolled their full shopping carts in from the service entrance ramp. Ida stood in place until the twins were next to her.

"*Ni hau,*" said Lily and Kitty together.

"*Ni hau,*" said Ida. She looked at their carts filled to overflowing with grocery bags. "You certainly have done a lot of shopping," she commented.

Lily giggled.

"Must make many cookie," Kitty explained. "Buy many flour, sugar."

"Egg," Lily added. "Five box."

"Butter, chocolick, nut, ginger, everything," Kitty said proudly.

"You must be making hundreds of cookies," Ida said, peering again at the shopping carts. "What are you going to do with so many cookies?"

Kitty and Lily exchanged a look, as though deciding whether to answer Ida's question.

"Now we have business," Kitty explained. She reached into her tiny purse, took out a business card and handed it to Ida.

Ida looked at the card, which was printed in Chinese.

"I can't read Chinese," Ida said, returning the card to Kitty.

"Oh, sorry," said Lily. "Is Good Fortune Cookie Company. Mean me and Kitty. We make cookie, sell to Chinese lady. They play Mah Jongg and eat cookie. Some lady have private party, we bake cookie for them."

Kitty looked around the empty lobby, as if checking to be sure no one was listening. She lowered her voice.

"This our plan," she explained. "We use Lily housekeep money, buy these," she indicated the filled shopping carts. "Keep my apartment, not want Sen know. Make cookie. Sell cookie. Put back housekeep money, keep extra. We sell cookie, save money. Then we buy ticket, go Hong Kong. When Sen at work, just leave."

"Ah," Ida nodded. "I understand." She paused. "You're going to have to sell a lot of cookies to make that much money," she said. "I'm sure plane tickets to Hong Kong aren't cheap."

Kitty nodded.

"We have more plan," said Lily. "Take cookie to Chinese store, ask they sell."

Ida wondered about the legality of all this, but said nothing. She had heard on the news of all kinds of illegal doings in immigrant communities: unlicensed bus service, knock-off designer handbags sold to tourists in Chinatown, and restaurants that "changed owners" every time the Health Department gave them a bad rating. While she didn't condone illegal activities, she could understand that immigrants who couldn't read or speak English had to get by in whatever way they could. She remembered how her own mother sold stockings door to door in their Bronx neighborhood when she was a child.

"Well, I wish you good luck," Ida told them. She paused. "I guess you won't need any more baking lessons," she said sadly.

"Not need," agreed Lily.

"But need help," Kitty said. Again she scanned the lobby, as if to be sure no one was in earshot. She lowered her voice. "President send me letter. But I not read English. Please you tell me letter say what."

Lily giggled.

"Of course I'll help you," Ida assured Kitty. "Can you bring the letter tomorrow? I'm quite busy today."

"Tomorrow okay," agreed Kitty. "Not one letter. Have many."

"Many?" Ida asked, puzzled. "How many?"

"Five letter," said Kitty. She held up one hand, palm facing Ida, and wiggled the five fingers as if to be sure she was making her point.

Ida's mouth dropped open.

"Five?" she repeated.

Kitty nodded.

Ida tried to remember when her last meeting with Arthur had taken place. It couldn't have been more than a week. Five letters? Arthur had become obsessed with Kitty, and this was not good. She knew she should reserve judgment until she saw the actual letters. But she knew she was just trying to avoid the inevitable.

"Well, bring them all tomorrow, and I'll take a look," Ida said.

The women said their goodbyes and Ida pushed her shopping cart down Bayside Avenue. Her thoughts returned to the China dolls and Sven. She wondered how closely he monitored Lily's use of the housekeeping money. And how would the twins ever earn enough for their tickets to Hong Kong? It would take months, possibly a year. Ida steered her cart into the supermarket, still immersed in the plight of Lily and Kitty. She was looking over some bananas when she felt a tap on her arm.

"Ida, you're just the person I need to talk to," said Arthur.

Ida had never imagined Arthur doing grocery shopping. She had always assumed that as a single man he took his meals in restaurants, or had frozen dinners warmed in a microwave. Her own Uncle Isaac, a confirmed bachelor, had eaten dinner every night either with Ida's family or at a small kosher restaurant on Southern Boulevard. But here stood the president with a cart full of food: chicken drumsticks, mushrooms, cans of tomatoes, onions, and breakfast cereal and milk.

"Arthur, I had no idea you could cook," said Ida.

Arthur beamed.

"I'll have you know I make an excellent Chicken Marengo," the president declared proudly.

Ida wasn't sure she'd heard of this dish. Or maybe she once had, and had forgotten.

"Really!" she exclaimed.

"Oh yes," Arthur confirmed. "In fact, I'm hoping to make it for Kitty Cheong." He frowned. "I've left her several invitations, but I haven't heard back. Hasn't she asked you what the notes say?"

So that explained Arthur's five notes, Ida thought. She felt her obsession theory had fallen flat. On the other hand, the president had apparently expected an immediate reply. And when he hadn't gotten one, he'd behaved as if...obsessed.

"I actually haven't seen the Cheong sisters for quite a while," Ida told him, almost truthfully. "Seeing" wasn't the same as a chance encounter in the lobby. "I've been quite busy," she went on, "and I'm sure the twins have been busy, too."

"Busy with what?" Arthur asked.

Ida stared at him, dumbfounded.

"Well, Kitty doesn't go to a job, so what does she do all day?" demanded Arthur.

"I have no idea," said Ida, although she knew perfectly well what Kitty was doing, at least some of the time.

"And what about you?" Arthur went on. "What could you be busy with?"

Ida was tempted to tell him that what she and Kitty did was certainly not his business, but he would only become angry, and she didn't want to have a fight in the middle of the supermarket.

"Just because people aren't busy doesn't mean they're going to ring each other's doorbell for a visit," Ida said.

"But if Kitty wanted to know what my notes said, wouldn't she have asked you? I put one under her door every day this week!" said Arthur.

"Arthur, why didn't you just give her a chance to answer you?" Ida asked him. "Maybe she hasn't been feeling well. And maybe now you've scared her off by bombarding her with notes. Since she can't read them, who knows what she might think."

"But they're just dinner invitations," Arthur whined.

"But Kitty doesn't know that!" Ida exclaimed, exasperated. She had the urge to grab a large spaghetti squash from the vegetable display and hit Arthur over the head with it.

"Oh," Arthur said. He paused. "So what should I do?"

"Give her a chance to get back to you," Ida told him. She remembered Kitty was bringing his notes the next day. "I'm sure you'll hear from her soon."

"Do you really think so?" Arthur said anxiously.

For a moment Ida was tempted to feel sorry for him. But then she pictured how he apeared to Kitty: thinning gray hair, liver spots on his hands, wearing a golf jacket that had gone out of style twenty years ago. Kitty was young, pretty, and full of life. Arthur would get no sympathy.

"Look, Arthur, I have to do my shopping," Ida said, and she began to push her cart. "I'm sure things will work out."

Things always worked out, Ida reflected as she hurried away, but not always the way you wanted.

Chapter 28

It was not until her phone rang the next morning that Ida realized Dr. Barbara had not called as usual on Friday.

"I couldn't call you yesterday because I was in conference," Barbara explained. "I hope you weren't worried."

"I assumed Monica would have called me if anything had happened," Ida said, not wanting to admit her lapse of memory. Or maybe it was not a lapse of memory but a preoccupation with the Arthur-Kitty non-romance. But she would never admit this to her daughter. "And I know you don't like to be disturbed when you're busy," Ida added.

"Right," said Dr. Barbara. She sounded almost disappointed at Ida's lack of concern.

"And how is Monica?" Ida asked, trying to move the subject away from Barbara's not calling. "Did she start her classes?"

"The semester begins in a few weeks," said Barbara. "But she's already studying her textbooks."

Ida tried to imagine Monica reading books on anatomy. She predicted to herself that her granddaughter would not last until the semester's end.

"Maybe she'll meet a doctor and get married." The thought popped out of Ida's mouth before she could stop it.

Ida hated the cliché of the Jewish grandmother trying to marry everyone off, but in Monica's case it was the obvious solution. Because if Monica couldn't hack it in medical assistant school, what would she do? Most young women without burning desires to "be something" succeeded at being wives and mothers. Ida realized this was an out-of-date idea, but someone had to raise the children and clean the house. Then she remembered that nowadays children were sent to daycare or had nannies, and paid workers did the housekeeping. But surely there was a young man somewhere who would be happy to have a more traditional wife who already knew how to bake bread. Not that Monica could be called traditional. Her stints on the commune and her time at the nunnery were not in the normal range, even in these modern times. And what exactly did Monica do at the nunnery, Ida wondered. Pray, she supposed.

"Well, I wish her the best," said Ida, cutting off whatever reply Dr. Barbara was preparing to deliver. "I'm sure she'll have a lovely bedside manner."

"It takes more than a bedside manner," Barbara snapped.

Ida did not have to imagine what her daughter's bedside manner was like. At least her patients were unconscious during their surgeries.

"I have to get moving on my baking here," Ida said. "We'll talk next week."

"You know I don't approve of your baking," said Barbara.

"Brownies and oatmeal chocolate-chip cookies," said Ida, and she hung up.

By the time the China dolls arrived promptly at three, both the brownies and the cookies had cooled, were packed and stored in the freezer. Ida had decided that Sandy did not need the entire pan of brownies, nor Monica five dozen cookies. So she had prepared a plate of brownies and cookies for herself and the twins. The tea water had just started to boil when the doorbell rang.

"*Ni hau*," said the twins in unison.

"*Ni hau*," said Ida. She felt she was getting the hang of speaking Chinese.

Kitty clutched a wad of papers in one hand, presumably Arthur's dinner invitations.

"Let's all have some tea and brownies while I look at those notes," Ida suggested. She held out her hand and Kitty gave her the pieces of paper.

Ida shuffled through the notes and put them in order. Arthur had dated each one at the top. She scanned the first one, and then slowly read it aloud.

" 'Kitty, I really enjoyed our day at the parade, and I'd love to have you over for a dinner of Chicken Marengo and chocolate mousse,'" Ida read, wondering where Arthur would buy chocolate mousse—or would he actually make it himself? "Did you understand that?" she asked Kitty.

Kitty nodded but looked puzzled.

"He invite me eat dinner. Cook chicken, but what chicken that? Moose is meat? But say chocolate," said Kitty.

"Ah, yes—the chicken. It's a special dish with mushrooms and tomatoes. And the mousse isn't an animal, it's a French word for a dessert," Ida explained.

Kitty nodded.

"Which day he ask I come?" said Kitty.

Ida scanned the note.

"That's interesting," Ida said. "He actually doesn't say when you should come."

"How can eat dinner if not know which day?" Lily pointed out.

"Well, let's read the next letter," Ida suggested. "Maybe he forgot and that's why he left another note." She scanned the second note and read aloud. "'The invitation is for Saturday at seven o'clock, so please let me know if you can make it. We can drink beer, too."

"Saturday," said Kitty, "is today."

"Yes," said Ida.

"I not read English, so how can answer?" Kitty asked.

"Not matter, you not want go," Lily pointed out.

"Let's read the next one," said Ida, shuffling the pieces of paper. "Please let me know by Friday night if you're coming. I have to buy the ingredients and everything and the beer. Is a six-pack enough?"

Ida was tempted to laugh out loud, although she knew the situation was not really funny.

"What is six pack?" Lily asked.

"He means cans of beer. They come in sets of six cans," Ida explained.

"I not like beer in can," said Kitty. "Not taste good."

"There are two more notes," Ida said, smoothing out the next one. She was taken aback as she skimmed it, but read it aloud anyway. "You could at least have the decency to give me an answer one way or the other. Please ring my bell immediately."

The twins looked at each other, obviously not understanding the language.

"He's a little angry that you didn't answer him," Ida explained to Kitty.

Kitty shrugged.

"How can answer if not read English," she said.

"Let's just read the last note," Ida decided, wanting to get the entire business over with. She read the note to herself and blanched. Arthur had written "you fucking cunt, you are just a stupid useless bitch. Cook your own dinner." Ida stared at the piece of paper, speechless.

"Note say what?" Kitty asked.

"He's rather angry," Ida said. "He's taken back his invitation."

"Stupid man," said Lily.

"Anyway I not want go," said Kitty. "Now finish. Okay."

Each of the three women reached out and took a cookie, as if this would end the subject of Arthur's pursuit. But Ida knew this was not the end. The president wanted to be the one doing the dumping, and now he thought he'd been dumped. Ida suspected he would do everything he could to make Kitty's life miserable.

"I'm going to write him a note," Ida decided, "to explain that he is greatly mistaken to think you just didn't answer and he shouldn't be angry."

"But I not want see him!" Kitty protested.

"Yes, but you don't want him to be angry with you either. He's president of the Tenants Association, and he could try to make trouble for you," Ida said.

"What trouble? Each month Sen pay rent," said Lily. "Pay two apartment."

"I not make noise," said Kitty.

"Even so," Ida said, "he's clever and he's a lawyer. He'll think of something."

"Okay, you do," Lily agreed. "We finish. Thank you."

After the China dolls left, Ida sat at the table and stared at the brownie and cookie crumbs, as if they could give her a solution. She didn't want Arthur to be angry with Kitty. At the same time she wanted to be clear that he had to stop his pursuit. It was like walking a tightrope, she thought. For a moment she imagined how Dr. Barbara would have said Ida had to be insane to have gotten involved in this. It was a rare instance in which Ida had to admit Barbara would have been right.

Chapter 29

For several days Ida thought about writing to Arthur, but she couldn't decide on precisely what tone to use. The fact was, after reading his last note to Kitty, she was a little afraid of him. She had never thought him capable of such anger. But in the meantime, Charlene's wedding day arrived.

Precisely at ten a.m. the doorbell rang, just as Sandy had promised. When Ida had asked Sandy what sort of person to expect, she'd described Betty as a "redhead bombshell." Sandy had given Ida a mysterious smile when she said this. When Ida opened the door there was no mistaking the person standing there. Betty was nearly six feet tall and quite slender. Her head was crowned with a mass of curly red hair, matched by red lipstick and red nail polish. She was dressed in a red shimmery pants outfit with a thigh-length tunic. A huge carry-all bag was slung over her shoulder.

"You must be Betty," said Ida and she opened the door wide, noting that Betty was probably as tall as Lily's husband Sven.

"I sure am," said Betty in a deep, throaty voice. She glanced in all directions and nodded at the kitchen. "I suppose we'll do you in there."

Ida watched as Betty emptied the contents of her bag onto the table: hair spray, plastic curlers, bobby pins, several jars of cosmetics, a lipstick, nail polish, cotton balls. It made Ida think of the ingredients for a complicated cake.

"Would you like some tea before we start?" Ida inquired. At Sandy's suggestion she had made a batch of Dark Rocky Road to serve.

"Tea?" Betty looked at Ida as if she had spoken a foreign language. "Honey, I only take tea if I'm deathly ill. Now, let's get started. I need to know what kind of neckline your outfit has."

"It's a cowl neck," Ida told her. "There's a big opening to go over my head."

"That's good," said Betty, "because you're going to have a bigger head." She rummaged in her seemingly bottomless bag.

"I washed my hair this morning, like Sandy told me to," Ida said anxiously.

"That's good," said Betty. "You got paper towels? And then you can sit in that chair."

Soon Betty was combing lotion through Ida's hair and wrapping sections of hair around large plastic rollers. It reminded Ida of her younger days, when she and her sister went to the beauty school on Southern Boulevard to have their hair perm'd. They didn't have much money, and at the school a student would do their hair for a small fee. Of course, they were taking a chance at coming out looking like Clarabell the Clown, but they had been lucky and always looked well-groomed and stylish afterwards.

"What style do you have in mind for me?" Ida asked.

"I'm doing a fall," said Betty as she wrapped more hair around plastic and pinned it in place.

Ida winced.

"Too tight?" Betty asked. "Speak up! This is not a torture session. Anyway," she went on, "I'm doing a cascade of big curls. By the way, what do you have for earrings?"

"Pearls," said Ida.

"Perfect!" Betty exclaimed. "I've got a clip with pearls. Fake, of course," she quickly added, "but nobody will notice."

Ida thought to say her earrings were real, but stopped herself. She watched Betty's hand reach for another roller. The woman's hand seemed unusually large, but with a six-foot frame, it made sense.

"Well, that's done!" Betty announced. "Now let's see those fingernails."

Ida held out one hand and Betty made tsk tsk noises. Ida noted that Betty's own nails were filed almost to points, her hands resembling claws. She glanced at the floor; the woman's enormous feet were encased in men's sneakers. Betty noticed Ida's expression of surprise.

"You're on your feet all day in the beauty industry," Betty explained. "Basketball sneakers are just the thing." She looked down at Ida's feet in their house slippers. "We'll need a basin to soak your tootsies. And a bowl for your fingers."

Ida got up and produced these items, which Betty filled with hot water from the sink.

"If you're hungry, I've got some Dark Rocky Road bars," Ida offered.

"Say what?" said Betty.

"They're chocolate bar cookies with pecans and marshmallows," Ida explained. She realized it was wrong to assume a professional hairdresser would know the term. It would be like asking Ida if she wanted her hair to be frosted, although Ida had heard of frosted hair and knew it did not consist of butter and sugar mixed and applied to the head.

"I love pecans," Betty declared.

Betty devoured half a dozen Dark Rocky Road bars while Ida's hands and feet soaked. Ida marveled at the woman's appetite. She again attributed it to Betty's height.

"Now I thought we'd go conservative on the nails," said Betty. She held up a bottle of pink pearl nail polish. "I guess we've got a pearl theme going here. We'll need a towel."

Ida directed her to the linen closet. She was beginning to enjoy what she thought of as her beauty makeover. She sometimes watched the morning television shows, which often featured makeovers for ordinary women, and while in doctors' waiting rooms she leafed through magazines showing "before" and "after" pictures. The "before" were frowsy and unkempt, the "after" were chic and perfectly groomed. Ida was certain her pre-Betty self fit into the "before" category.

"Now keep those hands flat on the table until the polish dries," Betty instructed. She lifted one of Ida's legs and balanced the foot on what felt like a substantial thigh.

Again Ida watched the large hands cut cuticles and apply polish.

"On to make-up," said Betty when Ida's toenails were done.

Betty studied Ida's face for a moment. She reached into her bag, brought out an eyebrow pencil and made sketching motions along the lines of sparse hair.

"For a bit of definition," Betty explained. She studied Ida's face and frowned. "Honey, I think you've got too many wrinkles for a heavy foundation. We'll go for powder and blusher. Close your eyes."

Ida closed her eyes and felt a flurry of brushes and puffs on her face.

"Now, let's finish the hair," said Betty. She whisked the rollers from Ida's head and Ida felt her hair bouncing down.

Betty whipped a large pearl-encrusted hair clip from her bag. With one large hand she gathered Ida's new curls and clipped them high on her head. Finally, Betty held out a lipstick.

"You're to put this on yourself, after you've dressed," she instructed. "And put this on before that cowl top goes over your head." She handed Ida a short face veil on an elastic band. "It will keep your clothes clean and your face intact. And remember to be downstairs at three for the taxi."

Betty scooped her equipment into her bag.

"Nice to meet you," she said, and she was out the door.

Ida was afraid to move or eat. She sipped a cup of tea while sitting on her sofa and watched television until it was time to dress. When her outfit was complete, she looked in the full-length mirror. It was definitely an "after" reflection.

It was not until she was speeding along in the taxi that she realized Betty was a man.

Chapter 30

The taxi brought Ida to the Villa Barone Manor, an ornate building along an expressway in the Bronx. Inside, there were the standard chandeliers and glitz. The place reminded her of Dr. Barbara's wedding. Despite her daughter's unemotional attitude toward life, she had insisted on a traditional wedding, complete with white gown, bridesmaids in yellow chiffon, and a three-tiered wedding cake which Ida had thought dry and tasteless. Of course, the purpose of a wedding was to see people married, not eat cake, but Ida always felt a wedding cake should be special. She hoped Charlene's cake would be up to snuff.

An usher led her to a chapel for the ceremony and she took a seat near the back. The room filled quickly. Ida wondered if she should have worn a hat. But Sandy hadn't suggested it; in any case, a hat would never have fit over her hairdo.

Strains of "Here Comes the Bride" shushed the murmuring chit-chat and Charlene appeared in the aisle, flanked by her parents. She wore an a-line gown that nearly concealed what was now referred to as "the baby bump." The groom stood at the chapel's front, the best man beside him. Ida was glad she did not have to watch a circus parade of bridal attendants and small children dressed in party clothes who hadn't a clue as to what was going on.

After the "I do's" were spoken, the couple walked up the aisle and a receiving line formed at the door to the reception area. Ida hung back, waiting for everyone else to leave the chapel. She didn't like crowds and felt she wasn't steady enough on her feet to risk being jostled. Not long ago, Dr. Barbara had suggested she get a cane.

"I don't want to look like an old lady," Ida had protested.

"But you are an old lady," Barbara had pointed out.

Ida was also intimidated by the sea of Black faces. She spotted one other white person, a middle-aged man who also seemed to be waiting for the crowd to disperse. When they finally joined the end of the receiving line, they smiled at each other.

"Oh, Mrs. Rappaport, I'm so glad you're here!" Charlene exclaimed when Ida finally reached her.

"And I'm glad to see you so happy," said Ida.

She entered the reception room. Two waiters carrying trays approached her, one with glasses of wine, the other with canapés. She selected what appeared to be puff pastry filled with smoked salmon. As she popped it in her mouth, she recalled Dr. Barbara's reception. It was the style then to serve tiny hot dogs wrapped in pastry, referred to as "pigs in blankets," before people became more health conscious. She actually had loved the tiny hot dogs, and she wondered if anyone still served them.

"Ida, you look fantastic!" Sandy appeared in front of her. "I just love that hair."

Ida smiled.

"Your friend Betty is very interesting," she remarked.

Sandy grinned.

"I've got to circulate," Sandy said. "Enjoy yourself."

The guests were shepherded into a dining room. Ida found her name card, and then her table. She was seated beside the middle-aged white man, Mr. Diamond.

"Are you the bride's side or the groom's?" he inquired.

"Bride," said Ida. "Charlene was my cleaning girl for ten years. Until her appendicitis." She immediately realized she should not have used the term "cleaning girl," but it was too late. "And you?" she quickly asked.

"Groom," said Mr. Diamond. "I'm his supervisor at the hospital."

"Isn't it amazing," Ida remarked as a waiter placed a roll on her bread plate, "how a bit of bad luck can result in something wonderful."

"It certainly is," Mr. Diamond agreed. "You know, Charles wasn't actually assigned to Charlene's floor. He was filling in for someone who was out sick."

"Really?" Ida remarked.

Once again, the fantasy of granddaughter Monica meeting Mr. Right at Physician's Assistant school went through Ida's mind. Mr. Right might be a doctor, even a surgeon. Although she had to admit she could not quite see Monica being attracted to this sort of man. An organic farmer, yes. A doctor, no. Unless he was one of those doctors without borders who went to the third world to save people. But then Monica would go to the third world with him and be eaten by a crocodile. A waiter put a Fruit Cup in front of her and she attacked it, having eaten nothing since breakfast to preserve her make-up.

"They always serve so much food at these things," Mr. Diamond commented.

Ida nodded in agreement. She wondered what Dr. Barbara would serve at her wedding reception. There was Barbara's gluten intolerance, which would rule out bread and pasta unless they were of the gluten-free variety. She envisioned a brown rice casserole. Or perhaps Barbara would go for a California-style buffet with vegetarian dishes and fresh fruit.

Charlene and her new husband were making the rounds of the tables. Ida noted that Charlene looked a bit flushed as she approached Ida.

"Charlene, are you feeling all right?" Ida whispered in her ear.

"Not really," Charlene murmured to Ida. "This pregnancy hasn't really gone smoothly."

Ida looked worriedly after her as the couple moved to the next table. Then she reminded herself that Charlene's husband Charles was an orderly and Mr. Diamond was a hospital supervisor and if medical attention was required they could provide it or summon it. She was distracted by the arrival of her main course, a chicken and mushroom concoction. Finally, the dishes were cleared and the wedding cake was wheeled in on a cart. The guests gasped.

The cake was five tiers high with white icing and decorated with what looked like yellow swags of buttercream. The traditional bride and groom statues stood on the topmost layer. Charlene and Charles stood beside the cake. Charlene cut a slice and fed it to Charles. The room echoed with loud applause. Coffee was served. Soon the cake was distributed and Ida eyed her slice.

Under the white icing was a white cake. She picked up her fork and put a small bite into her mouth. The cake was light and tender, with a hint of lemon. But best of all, the yellow swags were a mix of creamy frosting and lemon curd. Ida closed her eyes and smiled.

Suddenly there was the sound of silverware tapping on glasses and the room became quiet. Several toasts were made. Finally, Charlene and Charles stood up to make a speech. Charles thanked the guests for being there. Charlene smiled and seemed about to speak. But then she grimaced and clutched her abdomen. And then she sank to the floor. For a moment the dining room was silent, followed by gasps of horror. Charles knelt beside his bride. Someone shouted for an ambulance.

After a few minutes, it became apparent that the party was over, and people began to leave. Once again, Ida waited for the crowd to disperse, but this time Mr. Diamond was not waiting, as he was attending to Charlene. Alone at the table, Ida noticed he had not touched his slice of cake. She glanced around the room to see if anyone was watching. Then she swiftly scooped the slice into her napkin and dropped it into her purse.

Chapter 31

That night, Ida tossed and turned, unable to sleep. For one thing, she was worried about Charlene, primarily that her former cleaning girl was all right. But other thoughts nagged at her. Suppose Sandy had to take care of her sister? Who would come to help Ida? There were the China dolls, but they were now busy with their cookie business. Or what if—God forbid—Charlene had miscarried? What if she decided to resume her cleaning jobs and displaced Sandy? Of course, Ida would be happy to have Charlene back; she would never tell her she would rather have Sandy. But it was Sunday night, and Sandy wasn't due to come back until Friday. Maybe things would work themselves out in the interim. She finally fell into a troubled sleep.

She dreamed she was baking peanut butter cookies with her grandmother, and a wonderful nutty smell filled her grandmother's kitchen. But Ida was confused. Her grandmother had never made peanut butter cookies. She woke up, still confused. There actually was a smell of peanut butter cookies in the bedroom. She remembered she had left her bedroom window open when she went to bed, as the weather was warm and she wanted fresh air. Her clock showed the time as three a.m. She heaved herself out of bed and padded to the window. Breathing deeply, she determined that the peanut butter smell was coming from outside. Someone nearby was baking those cookies. In her bare feet, she went as quietly as she could into her kitchen and sat at her table in the dark, listening. Sure enough, she soon heard sounds from the kitchen below hers: an oven door banging shut, a clatter of pans. The China dolls must be baking.

Ida was surprised they were using Lily's apartment. Where was Sven? Satisfied that she had solved the mystery of the smell, she crept back into bed. But again she couldn't sleep. She knew the China dolls were just home bakers trying to make a bit of money, no different from mothers who baked cakes to raise money for their children's schools. But the twins had shown her their business card. And Ida was sure that running a food business out of an apartment required a license. Of course, it was not illegal on the order of illegal drug factories which were detailed on the evening news. In fact, she realized with a start, most of the illegal drug factories reported on television were in her own borough of Queens, though not near Bayside Avenue. Fortunately, Arthur Sandowsky's windows faced the opposite direction and he would not be aware of the nighttime baking. Given his current attitude toward Kitty Cheong, the smell of peanut butter cookies in the middle of the night might enrage him further. But now the baking must have finished, as a whoosh of fresh clear air came into the bedroom, and Ida fell asleep.

She was awakened the next morning by the telephone.

"Goodness, Ida, your telephone rang so long I thought you might not have made it home from the wedding," said Sandy.

"I was asleep," said Ida, looking at the clock: ten a.m. She didn't think she'd slept this late since before giving birth to Dr. Barbara. "How is Charlene?"

Sandy sighed.

"She lost the baby. But she'll be all right. They're keeping her in the hospital for a couple of days," she reported. "That pregnancy wasn't going well since day one."

"I'm terribly sorry about the baby," Ida told her. "It must be quite a blow."

"It is," said Sandy, "but they'll deal with it. Anyway, I'll see you on Friday."

Ida got up and made herself a breakfast of tea and toast. She knew there was nothing she could do for Charlene and Charles except to write a note of sympathy. Then she realized she had forgotten the obvious: she could bake something for them, freeze it, and ask Sandy to deliver it when she left on Friday. She went to her bookcase to get her Martha Stewart Cookies book to browse possibilities. The book was not there. She had forgotten—always the memory thing—that it had disappeared into the hands of the China dolls. And when she remembered, she again felt consternation at the theft and then sympathy at the plight of Lily. She took her copy of Maida Heatter Cookies off the shelf and thumbed through it, indecisive. Suddenly the choice became obvious. She had recently made Dark Rocky Road, and now she would make Light Rocky Road. She immediately perked up.

The difference between Dark and Light Rocky Road was simple: Dark had chocolate in the bottom cookie layer and used pecans, whereas Light Rocky Road had chocolate only in the marshmallow topping and used walnuts. Ida made a shopping list. She had four days in which to do the baking. As she sat, she leafed again through the Maida Heatter book. She had bought it long before the Martha Stewart book and had made many of its treats: Moonrocks, Blind Date Cookies, Coconut Washboards. Maida Heatter had a flair for naming cookies, making them sound exotic and exciting. Martha Stewart's cookie names were more mundane but were accompanied by glossy color photographs of the finished products. Ida could understand that book's attraction for the China dolls. But she missed it and she wanted it back. She would have to think of another plan.

She reviewed all of her sleuthing techniques. She knew for certain where the book was located. Of course, it could have been moved to Lily's apartment, but given Sven's attitude, this was unlikely. She would simply have to get herself invited into Kitty's kitchen again. Ida hardly saw the twins these days. She would have to run into them coming and going. Which meant she herself would have to do more coming and going.

It was two in the afternoon, and the mail had probably arrived, so Ida decided to begin her coming and going. Her keys were lying on the table beside her purse, rather than in her purse where she always kept them, a sign of her probable discombobulation on returning from the wedding. She took the elevator downstairs and walked across the lobby to the mailbox area, hoping to run into the China dolls. But to her dismay, the person at the mailboxes was Arthur Sandowsky, flipping through a handful of envelopes. He looked up, hearing Ida's footsteps.

"Hi, Ida," Arthur said absently, returning to his mail.

"Hello, Arthur," Ida said cautiously. She reminded herself that it was Kitty with whom Arthur was angry. But the venom in his last note to Kitty now put her on her guard.

Suddenly Arthur looked up from his mail and gave Ida a piercing stare.

"By any chance have you seen the Cheong sisters recently?" he asked.

"I actually haven't," Ida said truthfully.

"I left Kitty several notes, but she never responded. Do you think they might have gone back to Hong Kong?" Arthur asked.

"I really don't know," Ida said. She opened her mailbox and took out her mail. "Isn't it a shame, all this junk mail," she commented, hoping to drop the subject of Kitty.

"Maybe that's why she didn't answer me," Arthur mused out loud. He scrutinized Ida. "Maybe I should try again."

On the one hand, Ida felt, it would be better if Arthur was not angry with Kitty. On the other hand, more unwanted invitations would only prolong the unwanted courtship.

"Kitty Cheong cannot read English," Ida said emphatically. "You can't expect her to respond to something she can't understand."

Arthur seemed to think about this.

"Well," he finally said, "then I'll just have to keep a lookout for her, and ask her in person." He turned and whistled as he left the lobby and exited the building.

Ida went upstairs with a feeling of trepidation. There was nothing she could do to stop Arthur, but she could warn Kitty. And there was the perfect excuse to visit Kitty's apartment. When she deposited her keys in her purse, she saw the napkin she had put there before leaving the wedding. Puzzled, she removed and opened it: the extra piece of wedding cake! She made herself a cup of tea and happily ate the slice. It was still delicious.

Chapter 32

"How was the wedding?" Dr. Barbara asked. It was her Friday morning phone call.

"Wedding?" For a moment Ida was lost.

"Your cleaner's wedding. Last Sunday?" Barbara prompted.

"Oh, you mean Charlene's wedding," Ida said, realizing this was what Barbara was talking about. "The wedding was very nice. But towards the end of the reception, Charlene had a miscarriage and everyone left."

There was silence on Barbara's end.

"I see," Dr. Barbara finally commented.

Ida realized she had never told Barbara Charlene's entire story—meeting Charles, getting pregnant—but she was sure her daughter could put two and two together.

"The wedding cake was excellent," Ida said. "I couldn't have made a better one myself."

"I'm glad to hear that," said Barbara.

"And how is Monica? Did she begin her classes?" Ida asked.

"She did," Barbara reported. "She's already worried that she's going to faint when she has to draw blood."

And Monica probably would faint, Ida thought to herself.

"I don't understand that girl," Barbara went on. "Everyone has body fluids. Everyone has blood. Monica has been menstruating for ten years. She doesn't faint from that."

"Maybe it's different when the blood is coming from someone else," Ida said. She didn't really know, as she personally had no experience with other peoples' blood. Thank goodness.

"But blood is blood," Dr. Barbara insisted. "You know, I think you should see Dr. Schwartz," Barbara continued. "Your memory might be getting worse. It could be an early warning of future dementia. You should get yourself checked out."

Ida wondered what future dementia could be like if she was already ninety-one. She knew she was muddled by the previous week's mix of events: Betty, Charlene, Arthur, Kitty. Which reminded her that she had completely forgotten there were Light Rocky Road bars in her freezer to be given to Sandy for Charlene. She needed to get off the phone quickly and take them out before she forgot.

"My cleaner needs me for something," Ida said. We'll talk next week."

"Don't forget to talk to Dr. Schwartz," said Barbara, and she hung up.

Ida went to the freezer, removed the Rocky Road bars and set them on the table. She tried the recall the date of her last visit to Dr. Schwartz. She had seen him just before Thanksgiving, just before the China dolls had moved to Bayside Avenue. If she remembered when the China dolls moved to Bayside Avenue, her memory could not be that bad. She would not call Dr. Schwartz. She most likely already had a six-month appointment set up for the end of May or early June. Dr. Schwartz's secretary always called a week ahead to remind her.

"Sandy, do you think I'm getting more forgetful?" Ida asked as her cleaner came into the kitchen.

"Not that I've noticed," Sandy replied, looking at the Light Rocky Road bars. "What do we have here?"

"They're just something I made for Charlene," Ida explained. "I was hoping you would bring them to her."

"Of course I will," Sandy assured her.

"And I need your advice," Ida said. "Sit down for a minute."

Briefly, she described her latest encounter with Arthur. Sandy let out a long whistle.

"That creep never gives up, does he," Sandy shook her head.

"Do you think I should warn Kitty? I keep telling myself I should bow out of the situation. What do you think?" Ida asked.

Sandy was silent for a few seconds. Suddenly she half stood up and dug into her jeans pocket.

"Speaking of Kitty, I found this on the floor in your lobby on my way in. I almost forgot about it." Sandy fished out a crumpled business card and handed it to Ida. "I can't read Chinese, but I bet this belongs to your friends."

Ida took the card and glanced at it.

"I'm sure it does," she agreed. "They showed me such a card a while ago. They've started a cookie business."

"A cookie business?" Sandy seemed surprised. Then her expression changed. "I guess I shouldn't be surprised. They're always baking. Did they rent a shop?"

"I don't think so," Ida told her. She explained seeing the twins carting home large supplies of ingredients, and the Mah Jongg ladies who had been plied with cookies as an incentive to buy.

Sandy mulled over this information.

"To run a food business out of your home, you need a license," Sandy finally said. "You have to have the right equipment, and pass inspection with the health department."

"I'm sure they don't know about all that," Ida said. "Or any of that. Anyway, it's just selling to the other Chinese ladies. The twins need money for plane fare back to Hong Kong."

"Let's hope there isn't any trouble," Sandy said.

Ida could not imagine what trouble there could be. The China dolls kept to themselves and were busy baking. If they limited their business to the Mah Jongg ladies, who would find out? Ida pictured a government agent ringing Kitty's or Lily's doorbell, sent to investigate an illegal cookie business. The China dolls would not understand anything. An interpreter would have to be brought in. The twins would have to engage a lawyer, Chinese and English-speaking. They would have to appear in court. And if they had already overstayed their visitor visas, which was likely, they would end up at Immigration and be deported back to Hong Kong. Which was what they wanted. It was a win-win situation.

"I think you should forget they ever told you about a cookie business," Sandy advised her. "Just in case there's legal trouble later on."

"Good idea," Ida agreed. Then she remembered what she had started telling Sandy about: Arthur.

"So what should I do about Arthur?" Ida asked.

"Arthur!" Sandy made a face. "Try to avoid him. He's not going to give up on Kitty, and he'll drive you crazy. And no matter how tactful you are, he won't get the message."

Ida nodded. She remembered Barbara's youthful assessment of Arthur, and marveled at how her daughter had been so insightful so long ago. To Ida, Arthur had seemed like a nice boy. She wished she could tell Barbara about his latest behavior; Barbara would have a well-earned chance to say "I told you so." But Ida knew telling her daughter would result in Barbara berating her mother for getting involved in the situation, and rightly so.

"I'm too old to have to deal with this," Ida declared.

Sandy burst out laughing.

"You certainly are," Sandy said. "You should just ignore that idiot. Stay home and bake cookies."

"But I do have to warn Kitty," Ida said. "She's my friend and I want to look out for her."

"You can warn her, but that's it," Sandy told Ida. "No more writing Chinese notes. That really backfired."

Ida refrained from telling Sandy that the Chinese note had been her own idea. And she herself couldn't think of any strategy other than trying to avoid him.

"Yes, definitely talk to Kitty," Sandy continued. She sighed. "Back to work," she said, and she left the kitchen.

Ida sat at the table. She felt depressed. Even the thought of baking didn't cheer her up. She knew she ought to browse through her baking books for an untried recipe. But that idea only made her think longingly of her Martha Stewart Cookies book. Maybe she would just confront Kitty and ask for it back. In the meantime, she made do with Maida Heatter.

That night, with her bedroom window open, she dreamed she was baking ginger cookies. The smell of ginger filled the room, but didn't wake her up.

Chapter 33

Several days went by before Ida worked up her courage to visit Kitty. She realized she was afraid of Arthur. Which she knew was silly. After all, what could he do to her? He was only president of the Tenants Association, not the landlord, and in any case she hadn't done anything wrong. And she could always sic Dr. Barbara on him. Ida smiled at that thought. Her courage up, she patted her hair into place, took her keys and headed for the door. Her doorbell rang. She froze in the middle of her foyer. She crept up to her door and looked through the peephole. It was Kitty. Ida opened the door. Kitty held a four-cup measuring container in her hands.

"*Ni hau*," said Kitty. "Please may borrow sugar?" She held up her container.

"Of course," said Ida, and she motioned Kitty inside.

During most of her adult life, Ida had heard the phrase "borrow a cup of sugar," which alluded to a neighbor's ringing your bell to ask for some favor or other. She always assumed the cup of sugar was merely a figure of speech and no one really did such a thing. Although now that she thought of it, in her grandmother's day, when women did all their own baking, someone might have found themselves short of sugar, or flour, or milk, and had to borrow. Those were also the days when neighbors relied on each other for help. Nowadays, you hardly knew who your neighbors were, and if you needed help you summoned it on your cell phone. Ida went to her cabinet and brought her sugar canister to the table.

"Take whatever you need," she told Kitty.

"We go store, but not buy enough," Kitty explained as she scooped sugar into her container. "Lily not feel good. We go home fast, not buy many thing. Many cookie need make." She shook her head.

"Is Lily all right?" Ida asked.

Kitty put down the scoop and hesitated before she spoke.

"Lily think…" Kitty made an outward arc with her hand over her belly.

Ida knew it could mean only one thing: pregnant.

"Oh dear," said Ida.

Kitty nodded solemnly.

"Not want," said Kitty.

"But what will she do?" asked Ida.

"Tomorrow we go Chinese herb doctor," said Kitty. "Lily take herbs, baby go away."

Ida knew nothing about Chinese herbal medicine other than what was shown on an occasional segment of morning television. She remembered seeing a practitioner explain the use of acupuncture needles and how they regulated the body's functions. She herself was afraid of needles, not to mention the drawing of blood, and the dentist's drill. Now that she thought about it, her granddaughter Monica's aversion to such things might be an inherited trait that had skipped Barbara. But an herb to cause a miscarriage?

"Is it safe?" Ida asked, concerned.

"Chinese medicine very old, maybe one thousand year more," Kitty told her. "Very safe. No problem. Not tell Sen," she quickly added, "he very angry. Want have baby. Then Lily stay home all time."

Ida had never taken a position on abortion one way or another. She had heard stories of back alley abortions and women who died as a result. Years ago, a neighbor's daughter had been whisked off to Puerto Rico for the procedure. Ida didn't think women should be forced to have babies they didn't want and yet.... Then there had been the pro-choice movement in the 1970's, frequently on television news. By that time she herself was well into menopause, Barbara was married, and she felt she didn't need to take a position. Dr. Barbara had been quite active in the pro-choice movement, and had urged Ida to sign petitions and to write letters to her elected officials, pointing out that a woman never knew when she might need an abortion. By that time Barbara was living on the West coast, so Ida had said she would do as her daughter suggested, and then, somewhat guiltily, forgot about it. But now...well, Kitty wasn't asking her opinion. Ida pictured Lily's and Sven's child, dark-eyed and blond.

Kitty finished scooping sugar and put the lid back on Ida's canister. The news about the pregnancy had nearly caused Ida to forget to warn Kitty about Arthur.

"Don't leave yet," she told Kitty. "I have something to tell you about Arthur."

Kitty looked puzzled.

"The president," Ida said, realizing that the twins always referred to him by that moniker, rather than his name. "I saw him in the supermarket. He's determined to have another date with you."

"Not want," Kitty said emphatically. "What can do?"

"I don't know," said Ida.

The women stared at each other.

"The president can be very angry when he doesn't get what he wants," Ida told Kitty, "and that's what worries me."

"What he can do?" Kitty shrugged. "He not police. I not do wrong. Just not want date."

Ida sighed. She couldn't think how to explain that Arthur would try to find a way to make the China doll's life miserable. The situation was too complicated, with too many potential sparks to light a fire: the twins' illegal cookie business, Arthur being a lawyer and president of the Tenants Association, Kitty overstaying her visa.

"Is the Chinese herbal doctor close by?" Ida asked, returning to the more immediate subject.

"Very close," Kitty told her. "We go early in morning. Lily take herb, come home, wait. Maybe take one day. She stay my apartment. We tell Sen Lily sick, I take care. Then go back herbal doctor, check everything okay. Then Lily drink herb soup, rest few days."

As Ida listened, she reflected that the procedure sounded much gentler than Western style abortions, with their demeaning examinations and sharp instruments. Of course, any miscarriage could result in complications. She had a vision of Kitty knocking frantically on her door, asking for help. Ida would call 911 for an ambulance. She imagined the siren wailing on Bayside Avenue, and then Sven would find out about the pregnancy. And what if Lily died? Then Kitty would return to Hong Kong with Lily in a coffin. Ida shuddered.

"Not worry," Kitty told Ida, seeing her look of dismay. "Lily okay."

"I hope so," said Ida. Then she remembered the nighttime smell of peanut butter. "Kitty, do you ever bake at night?" she asked.

For a moment Kitty had the same inscrutable face she put on whenever Ida mentioned the Martha Stewart Cookies book. Finally, she nodded.

"In warm weather bake at night better," Kitty said. "Kitchen keep cool. Is good for Lily. Sen sleep, Lily come my apartment, we make cookie. Now many order," Kitty added proudly.

"About a week or so ago, I woke up in the middle of the night and smelled peanut butter cookies. Were they yours?" Ida asked.

Kitty nodded.

"Make many dozen. Mah Jongg lady like best," the China doll said. "Is okay? Not problem?"

Ida hesitated.

"Be careful," she finally said. "Some people might not like it."

Chapter 34

The next morning, Ida looked out her kitchen window and saw the Cheong sisters leave the building and make their way down Bayside Avenue. They seemed, from her fourth floor vantage point, to be very tiny, like actual China dolls. When they disappeared from view, she left the window. She ought to prepare something nice for Lily, she decided. The obvious choice was chicken soup. But this would necessitate a trip to the supermarket. She would need to buy a whole chicken, wait at the meat counter for it to be cut in pieces. Then there were the carrots, celery, onions, parsley and dill. She had not made her own chicken soup in over a decade. Now when she needed some, she bought it in a can. Dr. Barbara did not approve of this.

"It's been proven that preservatives in canned food leach out metal toxins from those cans," Barbara had informed her. "If you have to buy canned products, get organic. And instead of cans, get them in those waxy box containers."

Ida had pictured a small insect swimming in the can of soup, sucking toxins from the metal can and spitting them into the broth.

"But I like canned chicken soup," Ida had told Dr. Barbara. "It has very nice noodles."

"Don't eat that stuff," Barbara had advised.

Ida now concluded that chicken soup was out of the question. But she could bake. Lily would need something plain, sweet, and light: vanilla cupcakes. Ida hadn't made these in ages. Her best recipe had been cut out of a Women's magazine. It was fast and easy, the end product fluffy with a good crumb texture. And she would need frosting. She checked her refrigerator, found plenty of butter, and got to work.

By the afternoon, two dozen cupcakes, frosted and decorated with sprinkles, were ready. Ida supposed the twins had come back and that Lily had taken a rest. She hoped all had gone well, as Kitty had not come knocking at her door. She took the cupcakes down to the third floor and rang Kitty's bell. The apartment was silent.

"It's Ida," Ida called out, surmising Kitty might be reluctant to come to the door.

Soon the door opened a crack and Kitty peered out. Her face lit up when she saw the cupcakes.

"*Ni hau*," said Kitty as she opened the door wide. "Sorry you wait. I think maybe is president. Please come."

Inside the apartment, Ida was greeted with a strong, pungent smell. She couldn't help wrinkling her nose. In the kitchen, Lily sat at the table sipping a brownish liquid from a small bowl. Kitty took the cupcakes and nodded at an empty chair.

"So everything is all right?" Ida asked anxiously as she sat down.

"Is okay," said Kitty. "Doctor say Lily not have baby, just flu. I make herb soup, Lily drink." She pointed to a large pot on the stove. "Now feel better."

Lily smiled and nodded.

"Well, that's a great relief," said Ida.

Kitty lowered her voice.

"Doctor give Lily herb pill. Eat after sex. Not have baby," said Kitty.

A Chinese birth control morning after pill, Ida thought. She had read about the Western "morning after" pill in a magazine, touted as a great breakthrough in modern medicine. But apparently the Chinese had already thought this up a thousand years ago.

"But must not let Sen see," Lily said emphatically. "Sen want I have baby. Every night have sex many time."

"We keep herb my apartment," said Kitty.

Now that Lily mentioned it, Ida had been aware of a dim thumping sound from above her bedroom late at night. It was difficult to imagine Sven and Lily having sex. Lily seemed to be only about half Sven's height. Maybe they used one of those Oriental sex manuals that described contorted positions. When Dr. Barbara had moved to California, Ida and Irwin had cleared out a few boxes of things she had left behind, including books. They had found a book called Kama Sutra. Irwin had leafed through it, said it was a sex manual, but that there were no illustrations. They had put the book out in the trash with everything else.

"My lips are sealed," Ida assured Lily. "Sven won't hear anything from me."

Kitty poured tea and the women turned their attention to the cupcakes. Each China doll reached out and snatched a small cake, turned it this way and that as if inspecting it, and then in perfect synchronization took a bite. They chewed slowly, as if trying to save the taste as long as possible, even though there were plenty more cupcakes right in front of them.

"Very delicious," Kitty finally pronounced.

"Is difficult to make?" Lily asked.

"Very easy," Ida said. "You just need to buy cupcake pans and these papers," she added, pointing to a discarded yellow cupcake liner.

"Soon Mah Jongg lady have big party. Mother Day," said Kitty.

"In China we not have this day," said Lily. "But Mah Jongg lady say live in U.S. so must have this day."

"Anyway, Mother Day good for lady," Kitty pointed out. "Can receive many gift, have big party."

Ida had completely forgotten about Mothers Day. Although Dr. Barbara claimed not to buy into commercial holidays, last year she had sent Ida roses and a gift basket stocked with fruit, nuts, and chocolates. She wondered what this year's Mother's Day would bring.

"Please you can teach?" inquired Lily, pointing to the cupcakes.

"Of course," Ida replied, delighted at the prospect of another baking lesson. "I'll put a shopping list under the door tomorrow."

Ida was elated, visualizing a new era of baking lessons. After cupcakes, the China dolls would move on to simple loaf and layer cakes, then on to Angel Food and sponge. When she reached Lady Baltimore Cake, her train of thought was interrupted by the ringing of Kitty's doorbell. The three women froze and looked at each other, tea cups and cupcakes held in the air.

"Maybe it's Sven," Ida whispered.

Lily shook her head.

"Sven ring three time," whispered Lily. She poked the air with her index finger three times to demonstrate.

Ida was about to suggest one of the twins use the door's peep-hole, but realized the China dolls were too short to see through it.

"I'll take a look," Ida whispered.

She crept quietly to the door and peered through the spyglass. Arthur Sandowsky stood in front of Kitty's door. Ida crept back to the kitchen.

"It's the president," she whispered.

Lily and Kitty looked at Ida with dismay.

They sat for several minutes quietly drinking their tea. Ida got up and checked the spyglass again. Arthur was gone. But later, when she opened Kitty's door to leave, she found a note and a small bouquet of white flowers on Kitty's doormat. Kitty reluctantly picked them up. She and Ida returned to the kitchen.

"White flower for funeral!" Lily exclaimed.

Evidentally this was a Chinese cultural phenomenon of which Ida was sure Arthur was unaware. Kitty immediately put the flowers in the trash can. She opened the note and handed it to Ida.

"Please read," said Kitty.

Ida scanned the note and read aloud.

"'Kitty, I am so sorry about our previous misunderstanding. Please forgive me. I will ring your bell later in the week to personally invite you to dinner. From your admirer, Arthur Sandowsky, President, Tenants Association.'"

Arthur just didn't get it, Ida thought, and he never would. The time for subtlety and tact was over.

Chapter 35

"Did you see that notice in your lobby?" Sandy asked as she put her purse into the foyer closet.

"What notice?" Ida asked. "I haven't been downstairs yet this morning."

Ida was never out early in the morning, unless she went to the store or a doctor's appointment, and whatever happened in the lobby after she picked up the day's mail at three o'clock in the afternoon was a mystery.

"It's an eight by eleven piece of paper written in purple magic marker and scotch taped to the wall," Sandy explained. "It says something about a peanut butter odor in the middle of the night keeping them awake, and would the person producing that smell please stop."

Ida had been aware of more baking smells for the last few weeks. She had drifted half awake to the scents of not only peanut butter but ginger, lemon, and vanilla. Since she knew they were coming from Kitty's kitchen, she quickly went back to sleep. But she didn't want to let on that she already knew the origin of the lobby poster's complaint.

"That's odd," Ida said.

"It's not odd," Sandy countered. "I bet it's the twins. We know they've got a baking business. They're probably baking at night so nobody will notice."

"You're a good detective," Ida admitted. "But it's not illegal to bake in the middle of the night," she added. "And they're not making noise. I live in between them and I don't hear a thing."

"A strong smell might fit the phrase 'disturbing the peace,'" Sandy said. "Not that I want the twins to get into trouble," she quickly added.

"But they're pleasant smells," Ida pointed out.

"But they're waking someone up," said Sandy.

Ida wondered who the complainer was. They would have to live on her side of the building. Years ago, she knew most of the tenants, but many of those had died or moved away. Now there were younger people, with whom Ida had a nodding acquaintance. At least Arthur lived on the other side of the building, Ida thought, although she knew that as president of the Tenants Association he would have to get involved if there was a serious problem.

"Maybe the twins will see the note and take the hint," said Sandy.

"The twins don't read English," Ida reminded her.

"You might suggest they keep their windows closed," said Sandy, and she headed to the living room with a dust rag.

Ida looked at the kitchen clock. It was just about time for Dr. Barbara's weekly phone call. Ida wondered what her daughter would say if she knew about the goings-on at 388 Bayside Avenue. She would say it was time for Ida to move to Assisted Living, that's what. The subject of Assisted Living had come up many times in the past several years, but Ida had been adamant about staying in her apartment.

"I don't want to live with a bunch of old people," Ida had said. "It's too boring."

She knew this was not necessarily true. Some of her friends had moved into such places when they were in their early eighties. They had told stories of plenty of goings-on there: men dying of heart attacks while having illicit sex with another resident, men using the Assisted Living computer room to visit pornography sites, and the smuggling in of liquor which was then served at midnight card parties.

"Anyway, I'm getting along fine in my apartment," Ida had concluded.

Now the telephone rang right on schedule.

"I've selected the menu for my wedding reception," Dr. Barbara announced. "I'm mailing you a copy."

Ida noted, as she often did, that Barbara plunged right into the conversation and never asked her mother how she was. Maybe Barbara assumed that if Ida was able to answer the phone then all was well.

"You could just read me the menu," Ida suggested.

"It's too long and complicated," Barbara said. "First there are the cocktail tidbits. Then there's the sit-down dinner. And finally there's the dessert buffet.

"Dessert buffet?" Ida asked. The term made her think of PTA bake sales: a long table laden with the mothers' contributions of cakes, cookies, and brownies. "Won't you have a wedding cake?"

"Of course," Barbara said, "but it will be small. Anyway, what with people being on diets, we felt there should be some healthy choices. You'll see."

To Ida's mind, the words "dessert" and "healthy" were diametrically opposed.

"It all sounds very nice," Ida said. "What is the date?"

"September first," Barbara replied. "I'll arrange for your flights and hotel room. Have you gone to see Dr. Schwartz?"

"Not yet," Ida told her.

"Well, when you do, be sure to tell him about the trip and get his okay," Barbara instructed.

Barbara must have forgotten the memory thing, Ida thought. Maybe her daughter needed a check-up.

"And how about you?" Ida asked. "Do you have regular check-ups?"

"I'm a doctor, of course I have regular check-ups," Barbara snapped.

"Many doctors are remiss about taking care of their own health," Ida retorted. "I saw a program on t.v. that said doctors were no better than other people at getting check-ups."

"Those television medical presentations are a load of crap," said Dr. Barbara. "A lot of them give inaccurate information. You shouldn't waste your time watching them."

"What about Dr. Oz?" Ida asked. She occasionally watched his program, and she thought Dr. Oz very attractive. She supposed the modern term was "hot." But Barbara didn't need to know that this was the real reason Ida watched his show.

"Some of his information is good," Barbara admitted, "but most people aren't going to do what he suggests. He should leave television, or at least cut back and attend to his patients. I've got to go," Barbara said. "Be on the lookout for my menu."

Later in the afternoon, Ida went down to the lobby for the mail. Just as Sandy had described, there was the sheet of paper taped to the wall, purple pen describing the late-night odor of peanut butter. To this had been added a remark in red pen: "Cool it with the peanut butter! It stinks!" The sign seemed very childish, with its colored inks and silly remarks. It reminded her of the way teenagers would write things on the white plaster casts of a friend who had broken an arm or a leg. Did the person putting up the sign think anyone would take it seriously? She was tempted to pull the paper off the wall, crumple it up and throw it away. But she reminded herself of her resolve to stay out of further involvement with the China dolls' cookie business or Arthur's pursuit of Kitty. Surely Arthur had seen the paper on his way in or out of the building. And surely he would put two and two together, knowing the Cheong sisters baked. Or maybe he would delude himself into thinking that Ida was the midnight baker. She pictured him stalking in the hallway, listening at her door for the rattle of baking pans, the whir of an electric mixer. Well, he would hear nothing, because there would be nothing to hear. She definitely didn't want to run into him here in the lobby and be forced into a discussion of the problem. She hurried to the elevator and returned to her apartment.

Chapter 36

The China dolls arrived for their cupcake-baking lesson pushing a shopping cart filled with supplies and equipment. They unloaded cupcake pans, paper liners, and jars of colored sugars and sprinkles, in addition to the necessary ingredients for the cakes and frosting. Ida realized the twins had risen to a professional level, and she felt as if the Good Fortune Cookie Company had moved into her kitchen.

The China dolls were beaming ear to ear.

"Before start, we tell you something," announced Kitty.

Lily giggled.

Ida tried to think what the news could be. Were the China dolls returning to Hong Kong?

"We see president," said Kitty.

Ida noted the use of "we" instead of "I."

"We see president on street," Lily explained. "On way home from supermarket."

Ida frowned. Despite the twins' apparent joy, she had an uneasy feeling.

"He invite me eat dinner," said Kitty, "at his home."

Lily nodded, as if corroborating the accuracy of Kitty's statement.

"What did you tell him?" Ida asked.

"I say I am Chinese. Only date Chinese man. Not date American," reported Kitty.

Ida thought this was a perfectly reasonable tactic. Why hadn't she and Sandy thought of it?

"President not happy Kitty say this," said Lily. "President look at me. Say to Kitty your sister marry man not Chinese."

"I tell president I am not Lily," Kitty continued. "We not same person. Maybe look like same person, but not. Lily do she want, I do I want."

Ida could imagine Arthur taking this in. Kitty's saying she would only date a Chinese man was one thing. Telling him that just because she and Lily looked alike didn't mean they thought alike—Arthur would doubtless take this as an insult to his intelligence. Of course, if he were truly intelligent he would never have made his statement about Lily and her husband.

"What did the president say?" Ida asked.

"First not say, just look angry," said Kitty.

Lily made an angry face as if to illustrate.

"Then he say some word I not understand," continued Kitty. "Sound like dis..."

"Is law sounding word," said Lily. "He explain say this word when you not like people of other culture. Like Kitty say not want date American, only Chinese."

"You mean 'discriminate'?" Ida asked.

The China dolls' faces lit up and they nodded vigorously. Ida had to control herself to keep from laughing.

"In the U.S. we have laws against discrimination, but only in public life," Ida explained. "You can't be fired from your job because of what culture you come from, you can sit wherever you want on the bus, and you can buy or rent a house in any neighborhood as long as you have enough money. But when it comes to your own private life—like dating and marrying—you can decide to go with whomever you prefer."

Ida knew this was correct in theory and mostly in practice, but Arthur Sandowsky was raising it to a level to suit himself.

"What did you say to him then?" asked Ida.

"Say I not understand he say what," replied Kitty. "Tell him I only date Chinese man."

"He still angry, yell something in street," said Lily. "Many people look us. Then president go away."

Ida could imagine Arthur stalking off.

"We afraid come back, maybe president wait in building for us. But we go back, is okay," said Kitty, concluding the story.

Ida knew that though this might be the end of one story, it was probably the beginning of another one, equally unpleasant. But she would have to let the China dolls discover this for themselves. She turned her attention to cupcakes.

Ida recalled her cupcake-baking days during Dr. Barbara's childhood, for the school bake sales, Girl Scout events, and for parties at the Ladies Auxiliary at the Jewish Center. (She had always wondered why ladies were termed "auxiliary;" they did all the social work including food preparation, party organization, hostessing, sending out invitations, and secretarial work without which the Center would no doubt fall apart.) The advantage of cupcakes was that they were cake in single-serving portions with no need for slicing, no need for forks or plates. They could be held in the hand and demolished in a few bites. The cakes themselves could be made in a variety of flavors: vanilla, chocolate, lemon, coconut, banana. Ida's greatest cupcake achievement had been banana cupcakes decorated with a fluffy marshmallow frosting and topped with toasted banana chips. For a long time, cupcakes seemed to disappear except for Hostess Cupcakes with their crème filling and squiggled icing on top, or bakery cupcakes that were usually vanilla cake with vanilla or chocolate icing. Then, a few years ago, cupcakes had made a comeback. Specialty shops selling only cupcakes proliferated. And the Food Network had produced the Cupcake Wars, in which teams of would-be chefs competed to produce vast amounts of professional-quality cupcakes in a time squeeze. Ida couldn't see the sense in this. Cupcakes were fun. Why make them into a high-stress competition?

"Now we'll have some fun and make cupcakes," Ida announced to the twins.

The China dolls whipped out their aprons and put them on. Then they took shower caps from their shopping cart and donned them.

"We professional now," explained Kitty. "Must take care for clean."

"When we go bake shop, we see in back, baker all wear this hat," added Lily.

Ida explained the batter-making process: sifting the dry ingredients, creaming butter and sugar, then adding eggs, and then adding milk and dry ingredients alternately to the butter- sugar-egg mixture. Soon the batter was done. Lily filled the cupcake pans with paper liners and Kitty poured the batter. While the cakes baked, the twins, to Ida's surprise, efficiently washed the mixing bowls and utensils and set them on the drain board.

"We can't frost the cupcakes until they've cooled," said Ida. "Let's have tea."

"Cookie business very success," Kitty revealed as she waited for her tea to cool. "Sell many cookie."

"So you'll go back to Hong Kong soon?" Ida asked.

"Not soon," Lily said sadly. "Cookie business very success but not yet have money for air ticket."

"Will take some time," agreed Lily.

Ida imagined the profit on cookies, after the expenses were deducted, were not huge. The Cheong sisters had to be competitive, otherwise the Mah Jongg ladies would get their refreshments elsewhere.

"How many cupcakes will you need for Mothers Day?" asked Ida.

The twins thought for a moment.

"Maybe twenty dozen," Kitty said.

Ida's mouth dropped open. Math had not been her best subject but she knew this meant at least two hundred cupcakes. She pictured Kitty's kitchen, the counter and table covered with cupcakes.

"Not worry, we can do," Kitty assured Ida.

"We buy special tray," said Lily. "Many tray stack up. Have wheel."

Ida realized they had gotten a rolling cart with metal trays used in commercial bakeries.

The women quietly sipped their tea.

"I think we can get to work on the frosting," Ida finally said. "By the time it's ready, the cupcakes should be cool enough.

One hour later, the kitchen table was covered with a rainbow assortment of flower cupcakes. The China dolls had bought a pastry bag fitted with fancy tips. They divided the frosting into several bowls and made batches of different colors. After piping the frosting flowers, they dusted the cakes with matching colored sugar.

Kitty took her cell phone from her pocket.

"I take picture, send mother in Hong Kong," said Kitty, snapping a photo.

Ida was impressed, and was sure Mrs. Cheong would be, too.

The twins had brought cupcake carriers, and they began to load the cakes. Lily selected the two prettiest cupcakes and put them on Ida's kitchen table.

"For teacher," said Lily.

After the twins had gone, Ida reflected that the scent of vanilla cake would waft through her open window that night. At least the scent of vanilla was not as distracting as peanut butter.

Chapter 37

Ida walked through her lobby to check the mail and saw that the sheet of paper with baking smell complaints was still taped to the wall. A third remark had been added, scrawled in black ball-point pen.

"The smell is leaking under our apartment door," the addition read. "It's gross."

Again Ida was tempted to rip the paper from the wall and throw it away. Or add her own remark: "Grow Up." She did neither of these things and opened her mailbox. She removed two envelopes, one from Dr. Barbara and one from Charlene.

Back in her apartment, she decided to open Dr. Barbara's letter in the comfort of her sofa. Although the envelope probably contained the wedding menu and the kitchen might be a more appropriate location in which to read it, Ida already knew that the contents might be unusual, and in case of shock it would be better to be reclining against cushions. The envelope contained two type-written sheets of paper. There was no note or even a post-it with a scrawled "Here it is!" Well, Barbara had never been one for the little niceties. Ida unfolded the sheets and read the contents.

Menu

Rolling Hors d'Oeuvres

She assumed this meant a waiter would come around the reception area pushing a cart laden with goodies. She soon realized the word "goodies" might not be the best description.

Pickled Quail Eggs
Prawns in Lettuce Cups
Eggplant Caviar on Rice Crisps
Julienne of Radish and Celery in Bean Curd Wrappers
Mushrooms Stuffed with Minced Lobster

This selection was a far cry from the tiny hot dogs wrapped in pastry that were so popular decades ago. Ida read on, and was surprised to learn the wedding was to be followed by a lunch rather than a dinner.

Luncheon Table Service
Tomato Gazpacho with Buckwheat Crackers
Salad of Arugula, Heirloom Tomatoes and Fennel
Choice of Entrée:
Crustless Asparagus Quiche, New Potatoes
Poached Filet of Sole, Rice Pilaf
Angus Beef Roulade, Carrot Puree
Palate Refresher: Lemon Sorbet

Ida took a deep breath and sighed. She supposed this was the California way of eating. But the best was yet to come.

Dessert Buffet
Citrus Fruit Compote
Crème Caramel
Mixed Berries and Cream
Three-tiered Nut Cake with Crème Anglaise

This was definitely not Ida's idea of a dessert buffet. There should be at least two different cakes, and something chocolate. And pudding or parfait. Mini-cakes or doughnut holes. Something suitable for dunking in tea or coffee. Then she realized the entire menu was gluten free. As was Dr. Barbara. But why inflict your food limitations on all of your guests? Ida tried to imagine what sort of person would attend her daughter's wedding. Obviously they would be thin, or if not, then aspiring to it. She wondered if Barbara would expect her mother to comment on the menu, and decided she had better prepare some non-judgmental things to say. The word "interesting" came to mind. There were also "original" and the obvious "healthful." After a few more minutes of thought, she came up with "daring." But this was not a good word to be associated with a wedding. She was still miffed at the prospect of no real wedding cake. Maybe she could make one and bring it on the plane. But there were all these new security rules now. It would be better to find a bakery in Barbara's area, order the cake, and have it delivered to the reception hall. Surprise! She could have Monica look into it. She replaced Dr. Barbara's menu in its envelope and picked up the envelope from Charlene.

Her sort-of-former cleaning girl's envelope contained a thank-you note. It was not one of those fancily printed things that said "the family of— thanks you," or "Mr. and Mrs." thank you. It was simply an attractive Hallmark card. In addition to the pre-printed greeting, Charlene had hand-written a note: "Dear Ida, thank you so much for coming to our wedding, and for the lovely gift." What gift had Ida given the couple? She couldn't remember. That memory thing! "I am doing well now," Charlene continued, "and starting to think of the future." Ida paused in her reading. Did this mean Charlene was thinking about coming back to work? And if so, would she displace Sandy? Though displace was not the right word, as the job had been Charlene's to begin with. Ida finished reading the note: "And thank you so much for those cookie bars—we loved them!" Light Rocky Road! Ida smiled. She would postpone thinking about who would clean her apartment. Maybe Sandy would have some information.

She returned the thank-you note to its envelope and placed it on the sofa cushion next to Dr. Barbara's menu. It was an interesting contrast, Ida thought: no-nonsense Barbara and the more thoughtful Charlene. Ida wondered what Dr. Barbara would make of this comparison. She would probably think there was no comparison, and maybe she was right. People were themselves. As she concluded her reverie, the telephone rang.

Ida reached the kitchen on the fifth ring and managed a somewhat breathless "hello."

"Arthur Sandowsky here," said the president.

Ida's heart sank as quickly as a botched soufflé.

"Hello, Arthur," she said.

"I wonder if I might have a word with you," Arthur asked.

"You're having a word with me right now," Ida pointed out, pulling herself together.

"I meant in person," said Arthur.

Ida sighed. She could not face another session in the Man Cave, nor did she want Arthur in her apartment.

"I was just about to go downstairs for the mail," Ida said. She thought of the two envelopes on her sofa. Arthur would never know. "Why don't you meet me in the lobby?"

"Well, all right," the president agreed, clearly not happy with this arrangement.

"See you in a few minutes," Ida chirped, and hung up.

There were several advantages to meeting Arthur in the lobby. The first was that the time involved would be relatively short, because if Arthur went on and on, Ida would indicate that due to her age she could not remain upright for a protracted amount of time. The second was that the lobby was a public place, which would inhibit Arthur from discussing his eternal love of Kitty Cheong. She decided to wait a few minutes before going downstairs, mainly to avoid being cornered by Arthur in the elevator. Finally, she left her apartment and looked at the elevator floor indicator. It was resting on six: Arthur's floor. In a moment it began its descent. Ida waited until it landed on the first floor. Then she pressed the call button.

When she emerged in the lobby, Arthur was standing in front of the paper taped to the wall.

"Have you seen this?" he immediately asked, indicating the mounted paper with a nod.

"I noticed it, but I didn't actually read it," said Ida. "It looked like a personal note of some sort." She didn't like to lie, but as she had already lied about needing to get the mail, she felt another lie would make no difference.

"It's actually a complaint," Arthur enlightened her. "Some tenants are saying there's a strong smell of peanut butter and other things entering their apartments in the middle of the night. Have you smelled anything lately?"

"No," said Ida, going for lie number three. "I haven't smelled anything."

"I'm going to have to track down the culprit," Arthur declared. "It's my duty as president."

"How do you know the smell is coming from our building?" Ida asked. "It could be blowing over from across the street."

Arthur frowned.

"I hadn't thought of that," admitted the president.

"Well, good luck," said Ida, turning back to the elevator.

"You forgot to check your mail," said Arthur. He gave her a piercing look.

"Oh, goodness!" Ida exclaimed, bordering on lie number four. "At my age you forget everything!"

She went to her mailbox, made a show of opening it and peering intently inside.

"Nothing today!" she announced, and she returned to her apartment.

Chapter 38

During the week before Mothers Day, Ida did not see the China dolls anywhere. She frequently glanced out her kitchen window, from which she sometimes saw them with their shopping carts leaving for or returning from the supermarket. Occasionally on a Saturday morning she would see them pushing a loaded shopping cart out of the building and along Bayside Avenue, bringing cookies to the Mah Jongg ladies. Ida knew the twins had been busy baking cupcakes the last few days, because at night, before she went to bed, she had smelled the scent of vanilla cake in the air. She wondered how they kept the cupcakes fresh. Had they installed an industrial-size freezer in Kitty's apartment? Was such a thing legal in an apartment? But the frosting and decorating could not be done in advance. Now, on Mothers Day morning, Ida reflected that the twins must have been up all night finishing the cakes.

She could imagine the China dolls competing on the Food Network's Cupcake Wars. Of course, they would need more experience at cake-baking than they now had, but given their rapid progress with cookies, she was sure that experience could be gained quickly. And they would need an interpreter. Their English was serviceable but might not be up to the technical jargon and speed of television. Or perhaps Hong Kong television had its own version of Cupcake Wars. They could compete in Hong Kong and triumph. Ida smiled. It was a fantasy, but it could become a reality.

Ida did not expect Dr. Barbara to call her on Mothers Day, as they had had their usual weekly conversation on Friday morning.

"Did you get my menu?" Barbara had asked.

"Yes, I did, and I looked it over," Ida had replied.

But instead of asking Ida what she thought of it, Barbara had given her own opinion.

"I think it hits just the right note," Barbara had said thoughtfully. "Healthy, elegant, with plenty of choices."

"Yes," Ida had agreed, although she thought the menu was weird.

"So I've got everything but a dress," Barbara went on. "I'll have to start shopping."

Ida thought of her own outfit, ready and waiting in her closet.

" I'll wish you a happy Mothers Day now," Barbara had continued. "We're going to a winery on Sunday, so I'll be busy."

Ida assumed the "we" meant Dr. Barbara and her fiancé.

"Well, thank you, dear," Ida had said. "We'll talk next week."

Now, when the telephone rang, Ida was startled. She had a moment of trepidation, thinking it might be Arthur calling to cross-examine her about nighttime baking smells or the whereabouts of Kitty Cheong.

"Hello?" she said cautiously.

"Hi Grandma! Happy Mothers Day!" said Monica.

A call from Monica was rare. Ida remembered the last time she had called, in tears, expelled from the nunnery. The young woman now on the line sounded cheerful and upbeat.

"Oh, Monica, thank you!" Ida exclaimed. "How are you? Do you like your new career?"

"I'm very happy," Monica gushed. "It's so interesting. And I love working with the patients."

"Really?" Ida asked. She could not imagine Monica happy in a hospital environment. No doubt she had not yet dealt with body fluids.

"Grandma, I have a favor to ask you," Monica continued. "I want to bake something and I need a recipe."

"Of course!" Ida exclaimed, delighted that the family baking gene might be asserting itself in Monica. "What would you like? Oatmeal chocolate chip cookies?"

"Actually, I was thinking of something a bit faster and easier," Monica said. "Maybe something I could make in a brownie pan and cut into bars."

"Brownies?" Ida asked, immediately thinking with annoyance of her Martha Stewart Cookies book sitting on Kitty Cheong's kitchen counter.

"Sort of," said Monica. "Maybe something a bit more…special. Something a man would like."

Ida couldn't imagine a man not liking brownies, but she wanted to please her granddaughter.

"Let me think for a moment," Ida told Monica. Her thoughts were actually racing not to recipes but to Monica's mention of a man. Was she seeing someone? Ida pictured a handsome young doctor, like one who appeared on the afternoon soap opera "General Hospital" many decades ago. She could already picture Monica walking down the aisle in a white dress festooned with layers of lace and ruffles. Actually, Ida could not see her granddaughter wearing such a dress. And who would give the bride away? Was Monica in touch with her father? Ida had no idea. She reined in these thoughts and turned her attention to the recipe request.

"I've got just the thing!" Ida told Monica. "It's called Dark Rocky Road." She described the cookie bars with their nuts, chocolate and marshmallows.

"That sounds perfect," Monica said.

"I'll copy out the recipe and put it in the mail tomorrow," Ida promised.

"Thanks a million, Grandma," Monica told her, "and happy Mothers Day."

Ida stood at the telephone for several seconds. Then she sat at her kitchen table to ponder this possible major development. It was the first time Monica had mentioned a man. Not that she hadn't dated. According to Dr. Barbara, there had been too many men, none of them "suitable." Ida had never asked Barbara what she meant by "suitable" but assumed it meant a professional man: doctor, lawyer, dentist. Ida thought this was unrealistic on Barbara's part, as Monica was clearly not cut out for this type of life. But maybe now she was. Monica's reaching age twenty-five might have been a turning point. And now, thrown into a professional environment, she might have seen a possible future.

Ida supposed Monica must be in the early stages of involvement, too soon to contemplate a possible double wedding. In any case, Dr. Barbara would not want to share the spotlight. On the other hand, a double wedding would save a lot of money. Ida thought of her wedding outfit. Could she wear it to both weddings? Many of the same people would be in attendance. Maybe she could get away with the same dress but different accessories. She would have to ask Sandy for advice.

She took out her copy of Maida Heatter's book and opened it to the Dark Rocky Road recipe. She read it over; it was not quite as simple as putting together brownies, but she was sure Monica would manage. Her granddaughter was motivated by love. Or maybe by sex. Ida now recalled that one of the reasons for Monica's expulsion from the nunnery was for telling the other nuns that she missed sex. Ida was sure Dark Rocky Road would please any man. Unless he was allergic to nuts. She should have asked about that. Well, she would write a note advising Monica to check on this and enclose it in the envelope.

After addressing and sealing the envelope, she affixed a stamp and a return address label and left it prominently on the table, to be mailed the next morning. She was contemplating what to do about dinner when the doorbell rang. Again she had a feeling of trepidation. Could it be Arthur, seeking information? She went to the door as quietly as she could and raised the peephole cover, but there seemed to be no one there.

"Who is it?" she asked warily.

"Is Kitty," said the China doll.

Ida immediately opened the door.

"*Ni hau*," said Kitty. "Lily and I please invite you my apartment eat special Mother Day dinner. Please come six o'clock."

"I'd love to," said Ida, astonished. "I'll be at your apartment at six."

After closing the door, she looked at the clock: four-thirty. There would be just enough time to bake a simple loaf cake. But the China dolls would doubtless have Mothers Day cupcakes to serve. She decided to forgo the baking. It would be the first time in her life that she accepted an at-home dinner invitation without bringing a cake or cookies. And she wondered what strange foods she might encounter.

Chapter 39

Promptly at six, Ida arrived at Kitty Cheong's apartment. Once inside, the first thing she noticed was a large white metal box near the window: a freezer. It was the sort people who lived in houses kept in their basement to stockpile food. Dr. Barbara had one in her first house during her first marriage. The table was set with small bowls and plates, and tiny teacups. Two of the settings were accompanied by chopsticks and one by a fork. It was obvious which place was Ida's.

"Not worry, we this night not eat cow stomach," said Lily, and she giggled.

Ida smiled, but she knew there were plenty of foods besides cow stomachs to worry about. She recalled Sandy's tales of large fried insects, strange gnarled roots, even dog and cat dishes. But the air had a pleasant aroma and Ida hoped the food would be pleasant, too.

Lily poured tea while Kitty placed a soup tureen in the center of the table.

"Winter melon soup," Kitty announced. She ladled soup into each bowl and sat down.

"You forget spoon," said Lily. She got up and returned with three ceramic spoons.

A slurping sound filled the kitchen.

"This soup is delicious!" Ida exclaimed. "What is in it?"

As soon as the words were out of her mouth, Ida knew she had made a mistake. It was not because it was thought to be impolite to ask such a question.

"Never ask what's in a Chinese dish," Sandy had warned her, "because you don't want to know."

Well, too late now, Ida thought, and she braced herself.

"Is winter melon and soup," said Lily.

Ida peered into her bowl. There were little bits of what looked like vegetables. She hoped they were vegetables and continued eating.

When the soup was finished Lily cleared away the bowls. Kitty brought out a platter of scrambled eggs with tomatoes. Lily took Ida's plate and heaped it with eggs.

"Delicious," Ida said approvingly. "I've heard of Egg Foo Young but I never knew the Chinese ate scrambled eggs."

"Chinese eat many egg dish," said Kitty. "Egg drop soup, egg pudding, tea egg, preserve egg," Kitty rattled them off. "Many more."

Lily removed the plates and put out clean ones. Kitty fussed at the stove, then brought a large platter containing a fish with its head still attached, swimming in a brown sauce.

"Steam fish garlic ginger," Kitty announced. She turned and came back with another dish. "*Bai tsai*," said Kitty. "Green vegetable."

Lily took Ida's plate and served her generous portions of each dish.

There was silence at the table while the women ate. The food was tasty, Ida thought, not what she had expected. Her experience of Chinese food had been at Chinese-American restaurants, dishes like beef with broccoli and sweet and sour chicken, each with a thick sauce. There had also been deep fried greasy eggrolls and wonton soup with its cornstarch thickener and chewy dumplings. But nothing like what she was now eating.

The fish and vegetables demolished, Lily again cleared the table and brought fresh plates. Ida was glad the apartment had a dishwasher.

"Drink tea and rest," said Lily.

But Ida was watching Kitty at the stove. A large pot with steam rising above it sat beside a wok, from which a sizzling sound pierced the air. With one hand Kitty tossed the contents of the wok and with her other hand she stirred the pot. Ida now understood how the China dolls were able to produce such large quantities of baked goods. They were already adept in the kitchen, and they utilized teamwork. Kitty emptied the steaming pot into the sink, then lifted out a colander filled with noodles. The noodles were then added to the wok and vigorously tossed with tongs. Lily jumped up and brought clean bowls. The wok was then ceremoniously placed on a trivet in the center of the table.

"Long life noodle," said Kitty.

"We eat this dish for Chinese New Year or for birthday," Lily explained, "but we want serve you this dish, hope you live many more year."

Ida didn't know about living many more years, but she loved noodles. Lily stood up, plunged a pair of clean chopsticks into the wok and wound some noodles around them. Then she lifted them high in the air. Ida now understood why the dish was called "long life." She had never before seen such lengthy pasta. Lily lowered the mass of noodles into Ida's bowl with a flourish. She repeated the procedure with the other two bowls. After Ida's first attempt at eating the noodles, in which she had to bite some off her fork and let the loose ends fall back into her bowl, Lily spoke up.

"Eat like this," Lily demonstrated, sucking just a few noodles into her mouth.

This method was more successful, and Ida managed to finish two bowls.

"I'm quite stuffed," Ida said contentedly. "I hope this is the last course."

"Not finish!" said Lily, bursting into a round of giggles. "Must eat more."

Lily cleared the noodle bowls and brought clean ones. Ida wondered how many bowls the twins owned. Meanwhile, Kitty attended to yet another pot on the stove. Soon another serving bowl was brought to the table.

"Fry rice," announced Kitty.

Lily served Ida a bowl of the rice. It bore no resemblance to the brownish oily rice chock full of hard salty lumps of roast pork that was the fried rice Ida knew. This rice was lightly browned and clean-looking, with bits of egg and bright green and orange vegetables. Ida protested when Lily tried to give her a second bowl.

"Okay okay, now dessert," said Kitty.

Ida sighed with relief. She had survived a real Chinese meal. She tried to imagine dessert. Probably fruit. Maybe the China dolls had baked almond cookies. But to her surprise, Kitty brought yet another soup tureen to the table.

"Red bean soup," Kitty announced.

Ida looked doubtfully at the thick dark red liquid in front of her.

"Is good, you try," said Lily.

Ida brought a spoonful of soup to her lips, hesitated, then sucked the liquid into her mouth. It was sweet! She swallowed and smiled.

"Only one bowl," Ida said firmly as Lily moved to give her a refill.

Finally the table was cleared and the women sat contentedly drinking tea.

"Mother Day very success," Kitty said.

"Lady eat many cupcake," Lily added.

"Mah Jongg lady ask we make big cake," said Kitty. She held her hands a foot apart to clarify what she meant. "Maybe for wedding."

"We can make much money if do this," said Lily.

There was a moment of silence, and suddenly Ida knew why she had been given this lavish dinner. The China dolls wanted her help. She wondered why they didn't just ask. Then she realized they didn't mean an ordinary layer cake. They meant a Big Cake. One with a huge bottom layer and progressively smaller layers on top. Ida had never made such a cake. But her mind was already racing, thinking of special baking pans and Seven Minute frosting.

"I'll help you, of course," she told the twins.

Kitty and Lily beamed.

"Thank you thank you," said the China dolls in unison.

"We have special dessert for you," said Lily, jumping up from the table.

She went to the refrigerator and brought back a plate. On it were three cupcakes. Each was decorated with a letter of the alphabet. Put together, they spelled I D A.

"That's wonderful!" Ida exclaimed. "If you don't mind, I'm going to bring them home. I can't eat another bite!"

Chapter 40

"Did you see that paper in the lobby?" Sandy asked as soon as she came in the door.

"I saw it yesterday," Ida told her.

"I think it means trouble," Sandy said.

They referred to a new piece of paper mounted on the wall. It had replaced the paper with scribblings about the baking aromas. This one appeared to have been printed from a computer. ATTENTION ALL TENANTS was centered in bold face at the top. Beneath this heading was a short paragraph: "If you have been bothered by unusual odors late at night, please sign the list below. Arthur Sandowsky, President, Tenants Association." The remainder of the page was filled with horizontal lines and two column headings: Name and Apartment Number. When Ida had seen the list the previous day, three names had been listed, the same, she assumed, as those on the original sheet of paper.

"There are five names on it," Sandy continued.

"Five!" Ida exclaimed. "There were only three yesterday."

"Now don't you go and get involved in that business," Sandy said firmly. "You'd best stay completely out of it. With that Arthur in charge, things could get nasty."

Ida reflected that Arthur had already gotten nasty. He knew she was friendly with the China dolls. But she'd already told him she hadn't smelled anything.

"I had the most wonderful Chinese dinner at Kitty Cheong's apartment," Ida told Sandy, trying to move the conversation off the baking smell problem. She described the dishes.

"You got off easy," Sandy said with a chuckle. "What you ate was simple home cooking. Was it for Mothers Day?"

"That's what I thought," Ida said. "Then at the end of the meal, they asked me to help them bake a special cake. They didn't mean just any cake—it's either for a wedding or a birthday, but it sounded like they were thinking of one of those multilayered cakes with extravagant decorations."

"Sounds right up your alley," Sandy said as she pulled on her work gloves. Then she frowned. "You know, Ida, if I were you, I'd stop the baking lessons for a while. Arthur knows you bake with the twins. He might think you're helping them create a nuisance."

"I already promised to help them with this cake," Ida said. "But after we do it, that's probably the end anyway. We've done cookies, cupcakes, and now cake. That's the end of my repertoire."

Over the years, many people had asked Ida why she didn't bake pies, muffins, scones, even bread. She couldn't really say. She supposed these items had never called her, and if they hadn't by now, they were never going to. They lacked a certain something—sugar, for one, a quality that made people light up. A muffin just didn't elicit the same response, no matter how many little goody bits you threw in—nuts, chocolate chips, banana chips, swirls of peanut butter. A muffin would never have the cachet of a devil's food cupcake with marshmallow frosting. She lit up just at the thought of such a confection. Pies she found boring; rolling out the dough for the crust was a chore. And bread, well, it took too long, what with letting the dough rise and punching it down. Maybe some people liked to take out their frustrations on bread dough, but Ida didn't have frustrations to take out. Now she felt sad at the thought of no more baking lessons.

"Anyway," she said to Sandy, "if they're busy with this cake, they won't be doing all those cookies and won't be baking in the middle of the night."

"Of course they'll be baking cookies," Sandy retorted. "Just because one person ordered a cake doesn't mean everyone else stopped wanting cookies. The twins will just work harder and bake more. They need the money."

Ida knew Sandy was right. In fact, the Big Cake project would just increase the baking smells. A cake with multiple layers would require several rounds of oven time, as the oven would hold just so many baking pans. Unless the twins were going to buy a commercial stove. The landlord would never allow it. Not that that would stop the China dolls.

"I have created a monster," Ida said to herself out loud. "Two monsters," she corrected herself.

The telephone rang. She remembered it was Dr. Barbara's morning to call.

"Monica is baking," Dr. Barbara announced. She sounded puzzled, which was rare. "She made a pan of something called Dark Rocky Road," Barbara continued, "and a big mess in the kitchen. Did you give her the recipe?" she asked suspiciously.

"She asked me for it," Ida said defensively, "so of course I gave it to her."

There was silence on Barbara's end, another rare occurrence.

"But why would she want to bake?" Barbara finally said.

Obviously Monica had not told her mother there was a man in the picture. Ida wondered why not. Surely Barbara would be thrilled to see Monica involved with any kind of medical man. Most people would put two and two together and surmise there was a budding romance in the wings. But Dr. Barbara had never baked anything for anybody, except the Girl Scouts, so such a thought would never cross her mind. And if Monica hadn't told her mother, Ida certainly wasn't going to either.

"Maybe she's got the family baking gene," Ida suggested. "Remember when she lived on the commune, she baked pies."

Ida could picture Barbara wrinkling her nose at the mention of the commune.

"And what kind of name is Dark Rocky Road for a cake?" Barbara demanded.

"They're cookie bars. The recipe is from a book by Maida Heatter. She's quite well known in the baking world," Ida explained. Of course, Barbara would never have heard of Maida Heatter.

"Well, I hope this isn't going to be a regular thing," Dr. Barbara said with an accusing tone, as if Ida was the cause of this unpleasant development.

"Maybe Monica will get her own apartment soon, and move out," Ida said.

She suspected the real issue was not the baking but Monica's presence in Barbara's house. But surely Barbara had enough money to pay rent for a small studio apartment so mother and daughter could each have their own space. Ida decided not to broach this subject.

"She won't finish this course for at least two years," said Barbara. "It might take longer, depending on how many credits she can handle each semester. I don't like the smell of chocolate," Barbara added.

Ida was about to say she would send Monica some non-chocolate recipes when the roar of the vacuum cleaner fortunately stopped her.

"I can't talk, the vacuum is running," Ida said.

"Next week, then," said Barbara, and the women hung up,.

Ida was extremely pleased with her granddaughter's desire to bake. She decided to look through her baking books and select some good and simple recipes and then copy them out. Dr. Barbara would be annoyed, but she was always annoyed at something. Ida reflected that her baking endeavors were creating annoyance to someone or other. But this was not her concern. After she did the recipes for Monica, she would forge ahead with plans for the China dolls' cake. With a sense of great purpose, she stacked some books on the table and took out pencil and paper.

Chapter 41

On the day the Cheong sisters were to meet with Ida to plan the Big Cake, there were seven names on the list taped to the lobby wall. Ida stopped to look at the list when she went down for the mail. She spent some time studying the apartment numbers and names but she didn't recognize any of them. She knew most of the tenants only by sight. She calculated the number of apartments that could be affected. Each floor had eight apartments; half faced east and half faced west. The building was six stories high. Assuming the odor traveled only upward, that meant four floors times four apartments. Sixteen. Minus Kitty's own apartment and Lily's (unless Sven signed the list, which Ida doubted). Which made fourteen. But if what one of the earliest signees claimed was true, everyone on Kitty's floor could smell her baking. Which added four more apartments, a total of eighteen. Which was a sizable number of apartments. As Sandy said, it could be trouble. But so far only seven had signed. Ida went back upstairs.

Ida had explained to the China dolls that this meeting would be a planning session and they would not actually bake anything. The twins arrived with no supplies other than pads of paper and pens. Now that the weather was warmer, they were dressed in tank tops (Lily's yellow, Kitty's orange) and blue cotton mini-skirts.

"*Ni hau*," the China dolls said cheerfully as they entered Ida's apartment.

After they were all seated and drinking tea, they began to discuss the cake.

"Who is this cake for?" Ida asked.

"Is birthday of big Mah Jongg lady. Fifty year. Very important," said Kitty.

"Lady sister ask us bake this cake. Big surprise. Ask we decorate with Mah Jongg cookie. You remember we make," said Lily. "Many month before."

Ida remembered those cookies and how impressed she was. Now she tried to visualize a cake that would make the most of these cookies.

"We have idea," said Kitty. "Make very large cake like Mah Jongg set. Have row of cookie decorate like Mah Jongg tile." She drew a picture on her pad and showed it to Ida.

"But we need very big," said Lily. "Not fit in oven to bake. And how can bring to party?"

"Are you walking to the party?" Ida asked.

The twins nodded.

"I know how to do it," Ida said excitedly. "You can bake it in sections, and bring the sections on your rolling tray. Then you can assemble the cake at the Mah Jongg place before the party. On a big table."

The twins nodded rapidly in comprehension.

"So the first thing we have to figure out is how much cake you need. Then you'll have to buy pans," Ida explained. She went to her cabinet and removed a nine by thirteen inch pan. "Like this," she showed them. "You can borrow mine, but I've only got one. I think you should have three more."

Kitty scribbled on her pad.

"When you decide how many pans you need, we can figure out the icing," Ida told them. "And what about the cookies?"

"Need one hundred forty-four cookie," said Kitty. "No problem."

Considering the twins' cookie output, Ida was sure that it would be a piece of cake.

"We make and freeze," said Lily. "Then decorate same day. Get up very early."

"And what kind of cake will it be?" Ida asked. "Vanilla? Chocolate?"

"If use many pan, can make many flavor," Kitty said thoughtfully. "One vanilla, one chocolate."

"One ginger," said Lily. "One lemon." She looked at Ida. "What more?"

Ida tried to think of other cakes she had made over the years. There was a sweet potato cake with rum-soaked raisins that was truly delicious. But the extra work—cooking and mashing the potatoes, soaking the raisins—would be prohibitive, given all the work of the entire project. There was applesauce cake, easily done by dumping the contents of a jar of applesauce into the batter. Then she recalled a recipe for Madeleines, those French tea cakes, flavored with Earl Gray tea.

"What about a tea-flavored cake?" Ida mused aloud.

The China dolls' mouths dropped open and they looked at each other as if a lightening bolt had hit them simultaneously.

"Green tea cake!" they shouted.

"We have in Hong Kong many time," said Kitty, shaking her head. "Now forget. Live in U.S. too long."

"Make with green powder tea," said Lily. "Japanese. Very expensive."

"But only need one small can," Kitty pointed out. "Lady very impress."

Lily nodded.

"Maybe make one vanilla, one chocolate. One lemon, one ginger. Two green tea," said Kitty.

"We need make list for shopping," said Lily.

The twins finished their tea.

"Thank you, thank you," they said in unison, and they stood up to leave.

"Let me know if you need any help," Ida told them.

After the twins had gone, Ida sat down to write out recipes for Monica. She had initially thought this would be easy. But as she now realized, being limited to bar cookies baked in one square or rectangular pan and then cut into pieces narrowed the field considerably. Maida Heatter devoted an entire chapter to bar cookies in her Cookies book. But on closer examination there were many variations on the same theme. There were several recipes for Brownies. There were numerous recipes for cookies with oatmeal crusts on top and bottom, filled with fruit or chocolate or nuts. Some of these recipes were surprisingly complicated. She finally settled on Supremes, oatmeal walnut bars with a sweet chocolate filling. She also selected Butterscotch Brownies, usually called Blondies. And finally she added Toasted Coconut Bars, a recipe she had developed years ago for the Ladies Auxiliary's Hawaiian Night. What an extravaganza that had been! Flower leis, pineapples. Had they danced the hula? She couldn't remember. That memory thing again! But maybe it was better she didn't remember. She did recall drinking too many Pina Coladas. She wrote out the recipes, put them in an envelope and addressed it to Monica.

That should keep her granddaughter busy, Ida thought. And keep Barbara annoyed.

She decided to stroll out to the corner mailbox to mail the recipes—love would not wait, and Monica was already past age thirty. When she returned, she walked through the lobby and stopped in front of the Tenants Notice. Two more names had been added, making a total of nine. As she stood there, she heard the lobby door open. Arthur Sandowsky entered and strolled over to her.

"Hi, Ida," the president said. "Looking at the Tenants Notice, I see."

"Just looking," Ida replied, thinking that Arthur frequently remarked on the obvious.

"I notice your name isn't on the list," Arthur continued. "Don't you live on the same side of the building as most of these people?"

"I suppose I do," Ida replied, thinking what an idiot Arthur was.

"Then why isn't your name on the list?" he persisted.

"Because I haven't smelled anything," said Ida. She was tempted to put her hand in her housecoat pocket and cross her fingers, but she decided she didn't care if she was lying.

"Really?" There was a note of sarcasm in Arthur's voice.

Ida shrugged.

"When you get to be my age, your senses lose their edge—vision, hearing, taste, smell. You'll see for yourself in just a few years," Ida said ominously. "It will happen to you."

Arthur frowned. He rang for the elevator, which was already at the lobby.

"Have a nice day," he said as the elevator door closed.

Ida had shut him up, but she knew it was temporary.

Chapter 42

"That list has twelve names on it," Sandy announced when she arrived the following Friday.

Ida was not surprised. While passing through the lobby she had avoided looking at the list, but the last few nights she had smelled first the scent of vanilla cake, then chocolate. She had wondered what green tea cake smelled like, and she supposed she'd soon find out.

"What do you think will happen?" Ida asked Sandy.

"I don't really know," Sandy admitted. "Arthur could get those people on the list to sign a petition or a letter of complaint and send it to the building management. But they'd have to prove which apartment the smell was coming from."

Ida was sure Arthur had figured out which apartment the smell was coming from. She pictured him camped out at night across from Kitty Cheong's door. But he could not give evidence alone. Kitty could say he was harassing her because she wouldn't date him. But Arthur was too smart to let that happen. He would bring an impartial witness with him. Ida wondered who else in the building would do such a thing. Obviously he would ask one of the tenants who had signed the list.

"Suppose he has proof?" Ida asked. "Then what?"

"Well, first Kitty would get a letter from the management telling her there had been complaints, and that the cause of the complaints had to cease and desist, or whatever legal jargon they use. And if Kitty doesn't stop, they could start eviction proceedings."

"Eviction!" Ida exclaimed. "It's that serious?"

"Evictions take a long time," Sandy told her. "By the time they would get the final notice, the twins might have made enough money for their tickets to Hong Kong and have left."

Ida wondered how much money they had actually made. Then she remembered the Big Cake. If this was successful, they might get many more cake orders. Which would mean more baking. Which would mean more late-night baking smells. It was a vicious cycle.

"Do you think I should talk to the twins?" Ida asked.

"Don't you dare," Sandy chided her. "Don't get involved."

A few minutes of silence went by as Sandy began to scrub the stove.

"Oh, Charlene sends regards," Sandy suddenly turned around and told Ida, as if the talk of the baking smells had distracted her.

"How is Charlene?" Ida asked.

She had completely forgotten about Charlene, taken up as she was with the twins, Arthur, and her granddaughter's baking.

"Charlene's good," Sandy reported. "She's starting to get her life back together."

"Will they try for another baby?" Ida asked.

"They'd like to, but the doctor thinks it's too risky," Sandy said. "They're looking into adoption. And she's also thinking about going back to work."

"Oh?" Ida said, suddenly wary.

She had pushed the knowledge that Charlene might someday soon decide to return to cleaning for her former clients to the back of her mind. Ida wondered how many of those clients there were, and whether they had found permanent replacements. It had, after all, been several months since Charlene's appendix attack. But how could her sort-of-former cleaning girl go back to work if she and Charles adopted a baby? And if Charlene's doctor felt pregnancy and childbirth were too risky for her, maybe scrubbing tubs and floors was too risky also. Ida suddenly thought that maybe Charlene had some innate abdominal defect which had actually caused her appendix to rupture and had also caused her to miscarry. Ida had of course never been to medical school. But her television-viewing experience encompassed The Doctors, Dr. Oz, and the medical mystery solver Dr. House. Her hunch just might be correct. She could call Dr. Barbara and ask for her professional opinion. But she could not call Dr. Barbara because Dr. Barbara would launch into an inquisition as to why her mother needed to know such a thing, and they would never get around to an answer. Then Ida had a brilliant idea: she would call Monica.

Monica had only been in her medical studies for a couple of months, and might not yet know enough to answer Ida's question. But she did have access to medical professionals and could make discreet inquiries that would not get back to Dr. Barbara. The point of all this was that if Charlene did have some abdominal issue, her doctor would probably advise against her going back to cleaning. Which would set Ida's mind at rest that she would not have to give up Sandy.

"She's just thinking about it," said Sandy, interrupting Ida's train of thought. "Don't worry."

Ida was about to falsely protest that she wasn't worried when the telephone rang. She sighed and braced herself for the weekly onslaught from Dr. Barbara, but to her surprise it was her granddaughter Monica.

"Hi, Grandma!" Monica chirped.

"Hello, Monica," Ida said. "How are you? I mailed more baking recipes to you a few days ago. Did they arrive?"

"Oh, yes, thanks a million. I'm going to try one this weekend." Monica paused. "But I need another kind of recipe."

Ida was momentarily confused. Did Monica mean cookies or a cake?

"I need a recipe for real food," Monica continued. "I'm cooking dinner tomorrow night. I was hoping you could give me an easy main dish."

"Let me think a minute," Ida said.

She was totally unprepared for such a request. Besides, it had been years since she'd done any real cooking. She wracked her brain.

"Well, there's always meat loaf," she finally said. "It's good with mashed potatoes and carrots and peas."

"I was really hoping for a casserole," Monica told her. "You know, all in one pot."

Ida wracked her brain again. Then she recalled a chicken and rice casserole, made with Campbell's Cream of Something soup. The recipe was probably in one of her old metal recipe boxes.

"I think I've got something," Ida told Monica, "but I'll have to look for it."

"Could you call me when you find it and read it to me?" Monica asked. "That way I can write it down and have it right away. I'll need to go shopping for the ingredients."

"Of course," Ida said. "Give me your phone number."

She jotted down the number, said goodbye, and hung up.

There were three metal recipe boxes on her shelf. She probably hadn't opened them in years, probably decades. It took some time to go through them, as there appeared to be no particular organization of the recipes: chicken followed meat followed vegetable. There was something interesting, a three-layered vegetable loaf recipe and photo of the finished dish torn from a magazine. Ida couldn't remember ever making it. Finally, in the third box, she found it: Magic Celery Chicken. And now she remembered it had been one of Barbara's favorite dishes when she was a child. Ida wondered if Barbara would remember it when Monica served it to her. But now Ida recalled seeing a television segment on manufacturers' trend to cut fat from their products to go along with the public's desire to reduce fat and calories. Of course, the public didn't really want to reduce fat and calories, but some people were intimidated by the media's threat of death by obesity. This recipe called for one can of Cream of Chicken soup and one can of Cream of Celery soup. Were these soups still available? Surely they must be. But were they the same fat-logged things that she had used years ago, which had made the dish so delicious, or were they now low-fat? It would make a big difference in the result. Well, Monica would figure it out. She called her granddaughter's number and read her the recipe. After she hung up, she wondered if Barbara owned a casserole dish.

Chapter 43

The only indication of the China dolls' existence over the next several days was the scent of baking wafting through Ida's apartment at night. Then Ida met them in the lobby. She was on her way out to the supermarket, shopping cart empty. The twins were obviously on their way back from the supermarket, shopping carts overflowing.

"*Ni hau,*" said the China dolls in unison.

"I see you're very busy," Ida remarked with a nod at their carts.

She was standing near the Attention All Tenants list, and couldn't help noticing there were now fifteen names on it, close to the possible maximum.

"Cake finish," Lily reported. "Now make cookie."

Ida actually remembered they needed one hundred forty-four cookies, plus some extra in case of mishaps. Could her short-term memory be improving? More likely, she recalled the number of cookies because she had played Mah Jongg years ago, and one hundred forty-four was the number of tiles used.

"Sugar cookies?" she asked.

The twins nodded. At least the baking smells would be plain vanilla, what she considered the least offensive.

"We try new idea," said Lily. She rummaged in one of her grocery bags and took out several small bottles of flavored extracts:

lemon, orange, coconut, banana, almond, peppermint, coffee. "Make each dozen cookie different flavor," Lily explained. "Mah Jongg lady have surprise."

"Maybe order more cookie," said Kitty. "Make more money."

So much for innocuous baking smells, Ida thought. The surprise would not be only for the Mah Jongg ladies. The Bayside Avenue tenants would be treated to new wake-up odors.

"Let me know when you're ready to frost the cakes and I'll come and help," Ida told the twins.

"Thank you, thank you," chirped the China dolls, and they hurried into the elevator, completely oblivious to the piece of paper taped to the wall that might prophecy their doom.

On her way to the supermarket, not wanting to dwell on the tenants against baking smells, Ida focused on Seven Minute frosting. Although several of her baking books contained the recipe, she knew it was also featured in the Martha Stewart Cookies book. If she went to Kitty's apartment, she might drop a hint that the best Seven Minute frosting recipe was in the Martha Stewart Cookies book, which she had misplaced and couldn't find. (That this was "the best" Seven Minute Frosting recipe was a lie, as the recipe was standard. Ida reflected that she had been doing a good bit of lying lately, with and without her fingers crossed, but she excused herself on the grounds that her lies were all for good causes.) But if she made such a remark about the book, the China dolls would most likely be their inscrutable selves and ignore it, even if the book was in full view on the kitchen counter.

An hour later, returning from the supermarket, she passed by the Tenants Notice on the lobby wall, glanced at it and came to a dead halt. The list of tenants signatures had been replaced with a new notice. Attention All Tenants was still at the top. But now this was followed by Tenants Meeting Saturday May 23, 11:00 a.m. in the lobby. Ida began to read the paragraph underneath.

"There will be a meeting of all tenants on Saturday May 23 at 11:00 a.m. in the building lobby to discuss the problem of the late-night baking smells. Please plan to attend. Refreshments will be served. Arthur Sandowsky, President, Tenants Association."

Ida was momentarily distracted by the word "refreshments." If the meeting was about complaints related to baking smells, how could Arthur serve cookies? Of course, he would buy something in a package. She had once seen him in the supermarket with a package of Entenmann's Chocolate Chip Cookies in his cart. Or maybe he would serve pretzels or chips. She knew the real motive behind refreshments was an extra enticement to come to the meeting. People who were willing to put their names on a list were not always as willing to show up in person.

Which brought her back to the real issue: Arthur was taking action against the China dolls. Ordinarily, this kind of situation would be handled very differently. Arthur, suspecting Kitty Cheong was the culprit, would ring her bell and ask to speak with her. If she was not at home, he would leave a note requesting a meeting. But Ida already knew what would have happened if he had left a note, the same as the recent communication disaster regarding a date. And just as the China dolls were inscrutable regarding the Martha Stewart Cookies book, so would Kitty Cheong be regarding her late-night baking. Ida wondered what would have happened if Kitty had agreed to date Arthur. How would he handle the baking smell problem? She would never know.

And what would Ida herself do about this Tenants Meeting? She supposed she would have to put in an appearance. She couldn't remember when the last Tenants Meeting had taken place—the memory thing again—but it must have been at least several years ago, and for some equally trivial situation. As these thoughts went through her mind, she heard footsteps approaching from the secluded mailbox area, and none other than the president of the Tenants Association himself appeared.

"Hi, Ida," Arthur greeted her. "I see you're reading my notice."

"Yes," said Ida, thinking for the umpteenth time of Arthur's habit of belaboring the obvious.

"It's hot off the press," Arthur continued. "You might be the first tenant in the building to see it."

"Really," said Ida, unimpressed.

"So will you come to the meeting?" Arthur persisted.

Once again, Ida was seized with the urge to rip the paper off the wall.

"Well, I'll have to see," she told him. "I'll need to check my appointment book."

Ida did not actually have an appointment book. She had a calendar on the wall on which she scribbled her few appointments with Dr. Schwartz, and other important events such as Charlene's wedding. But she had heard Dr. Barbara and several television series characters refer to their appointment books and felt the possession (yet another lie!) of one would give her some stature with Arthur.

"It's really essential that all tenants attend," Arthur pontificated. "It's only with complete cooperation that we can get some action from the management."

"What action are you looking for?" Ida asked.

Arthur looked at her as if she was a total nincompoop.

"We want the night-time baking to stop," he answered. "People need their sleep. They have to go to work in the morning."

"I've always found baking smells rather pleasant," said Ida. "I can't imagine who complained."

"There were fifteen signatures on that list," Arthur reminded her.

"Whatever," said Ida, borrowing the phrase used by young people. She had heard it on television.

Arthur seemed a bit startled by this rejoinder, but Ida pretended not to notice.

"Excuse me," Ida said, nearly running him over with her shopping cart as she headed for the elevator. "I've got to get my perishables into the fridge."

After she returned to her apartment and put away her shopping, the real scenario behind the baking smell uprising suddenly spread out before her. "Someone" in the building had mentioned to Arthur in passing that they had smelled baking late at night, but without any negative commentary. Arthur had immediately suspected the source: Kitty Cheong. He might, as Ida had previously imagined, have camped out in front of Kitty's door to assure himself he was right. Then, to get back at Kitty for refusing to date him, Arthur had anonymously posted the original piece of paper with the complaint in the lobby. And that had started the ball rolling. Like rats following the Pied Piper, other tenants who might have otherwise ignored the odors jumped on the bandwagon. And the rest, unfortunately, was history.

Chapter 44

"It's an interesting theory," said Sandy after Ida had excitedly explained her insight the following Friday. "But I don't think it would hold up in court."

"True," Ida admitted. "But in the court of public opinion, I think it might hold water."

"Problem is, there isn't any public here," Sandy pointed out. "Fifteen people already signed Arthur's list. And I'm sure none of them know he was jilted by Kitty Cheong. In fact," Sandy continued, "they don't even know Kitty is the culprit. And if anyone tried to publicize that situation, it would just be a case of 'he said, she said.'"

"You should have become a lawyer," Ida told Sandy, impressed.

"No, I just watch too much Judge Judy," Sandy laughed.

Ida was not surprised at the holes in her theory. It had simply been a layperson's uninformed deduction, similar to her theory about Charlene's abdomen. And now that she thought of it, she had forgotten to ask Monica to look into it, distracted by the recipe for Magic Celery Chicken.

"The real issue here," Sandy went on, "is whether you're going to the Tenants meeting." She stood with hands on hips, looking at Ida expectantly.

"Of course I'm going," Ida told her. "I have to."

"But you're not going to make any trouble," Sandy said emphatically.

"I will be meek as a lamb," Ida assured her. "I'll wear my best housedress and slippers."

"But you can't be dismissive either," Sandy advised her. "You have to show interest."

"I hate the idea of kowtowing to Arthur," Ida admitted. "But I'll hold my tongue. Anyway, I'm of the philosophy that if you give someone enough rope, they'll hang themselves."

Ida pictured Arthur Sandowsky dangling from the ceiling with a rope around his neck. It was a highly satisfactory picture. Then she remembered Arthur's mother had been her friend. But if Mrs. Sandowsky had known about all of Arthur's shenanigans, she might have thought it a pretty picture, too. Continuing with the rope image, the telephone rang: time for Dr. Barbara's weekly call.

"I hear some hot weather is coming your way," said Dr. Barbara. "I hope you've had your air conditioners serviced."

Ida had not had her air conditioners serviced since she had bought them ten years ago. She'd decided that if either of them stopped working, she would just buy a new one.

"Of course," she told Barbara, adding another lie to her ever-increasing total.

"And you replaced the filters?" Barbara persisted.

"The serviceman did that," Ida lied again. "By the way, how did you like Monica's chicken dinner?" she asked, trying to hustle onto a safer topic.

"What chicken dinner?" Barbara asked.

"The one Monica made. With soup and celery," Ida prompted. "I gave her the recipe. It used to be one of your favorites."

There was silence on Barbara's end.

"Monica doesn't live here anymore," Barbara finally said.

Ida was silent, taking this in.

"So she's found her own apartment?" Ida asked, not surprised. She had doubted mother and daughter would last long under one roof.

"No, she moved in with a friend," Barbara said.

As far as Ida could recall with her compromised memory, Monica had not lived in the Los Angeles area for several years, and even when she had, she hadn't been the social butterfly. So Ida deduced her granddaughter had made new friends at the medical center.

"A student at her medical program?" Ida asked expectantly.

"Sort of,' Barbara hedged.

"Well," said Ida, trying to glide past what she realized might be a sticky situation, "you must be relieved to have your house to yourself again." She was thinking of Barbara's fiancé and their sex life.

"Right," Barbara said.

Ida didn't know what to make of all this. Dr. Barbara hadn't looked forward to her daughter's return because she needed "her space," which Ida interpreted as privacy for sex with her fiancé. Having one's children aware of one's sexual activity was uncomfortable for most people, though she supposed those of the hippie sixties might not be so squeamish about it. Barbara came of age during those times but had not gone the psychedelic route. She hadn't let her hair grow down to her behind and she hadn't worn Granny dresses. She had actually been more the Jewish Princess type, Ida now reflected, and she wondered if this outcome had been her own and her husband's fault. Not exactly fault, as being a Jewish Princess was not a crime, only a state of being. And given a choice between Psychedelic Earth Mother and Jewish Princess, Ida would definitely prefer the princess.

"So are your wedding plans all in place?" Ida asked Barbara, thinking a shift to a safer subject was in order.

"Everything is status quo," Barbara said.

Ida assumed that meant the wedding was still on. But at the same time she sensed the topic should not be pursued.

"Well, I'll have to call Monica and congratulate her on her move," Ida told Barbara, and immediately realized she had again put her foot in it. She wanted to add that Barbara should ask Monica to make the Magic Celery Chicken for her, but decided the best course of action was to end the conversation. "Sandy's about to vacuum, so I'll have to go," she said, and hung up.

Over a cup of tea, Ida thought about Barbara's news. Then the truth dawned on her: Monica had moved in with a man. Surely Barbara would not object to such an arrangement on moral grounds. Therefore, it had to be the specific man she objected to. Ida assumed the man in question was in the medical field. She couldn't imagine any medical field being objectionable, except possibly infectious diseases. But then, Barbara had not approved of any of her daughter's boyfriends, so maybe she was just in the habit of disapproving. Perhaps Monica could invite Dr. Barbara and her fiancé to dinner and serve the Magic Celery Chicken. It was gluten free.

The noise of the vacuum cleaner abruptly stopped, jolting Ida from her reverie.

"We've got a problem," said Sandy as she entered the kitchen. "How old is your vacuum cleaner?"

"Let me think," Ida said.

Her memory being what it was, this was not easy. She vaguely recalled Dr. Barbara going with her to Sears to buy it.

"I'm not sure," Ida said. "I think I had it before Charlene came to work for me. Ten years?"

"I think the motor burned out," Sandy explained. "I can go to Sears over the weekend and order one for you. I'll put it on my credit card and you can write me a check. If this one is ten years old, it doesn't pay to fix it. They make more powerful, lighter weight ones now."

"That's fine," Ida said. "Thanks a million."

She could not picture herself going to Sears. But after Sandy left the kitchen, Ida began to think. A lighter weight vacuum would require less strength. Charlene might be able to use it. Was Sandy buying this vacuum with a view toward Charlene using it and coming back to work? Ida didn't want to ask Sandy or bring up the subject of Charlene. She didn't want to ruffle any feathers. Suppose Sandy had to leave? If Ida implied she preferred Sandy to Charlene, Charlene might be insulted and not want to come back. If she could come back. And where would Ida be then, with no one to clean her apartment?

She decided not to worry about who would clean her apartment. If the new vacuum was light enough, she could use it herself.

Chapter 45

"Are you sure I shouldn't mention the Tenants meeting?" Ida asked Sandy.

She was on her way to the China dolls to assist with the Seven Minute Frosting.

"Absolutely not," said Sandy, looking up from the new vacuum's instruction booklet.

The vacuum, looking distinctly more streamlined than the old one, sat in the middle of the living room surrounded by its box and various packing materials. Ida had wanted to give it a push to see how lightweight it actually was, but Sandy advised against this until she had everything figured out.

"What would be the point?" Sandy continued, referring to the China dolls. "They might not understand half of what was said, and I'm sure Kitty doesn't want to see Arthur."

Ida had to admit Sandy was right, and yet she felt the Cheong sisters ought to know there was a plot against them. But even if they knew, what could they do about it? Stop baking was what, and that wasn't going to happen.

In Kitty Cheong's kitchen, cakes were lined up on the counter and on top of the freezer. Two of the sheet cakes were a pale green color and Ida realized they must be the green tea ones.

"We'll make one batch of frosting and frost one cake," Ida explained. "Then we'll do a second one. Doubling or tripling the recipe might not work. And then if you think you've got the hang of it, I'll leave you to do the rest."

Kitty frowned.

"Why leave? You are Cake Master!" Kitty declared. "We need you stay."

"In case we have problem," said Lily. "I make tea. You sit and drink."

Ida now noticed a teapot and tiny teacups on the table. She remembered the success of this cake could make or break the sisters' plan to escape to Hong Kong. And she wondered how Lily would manage to spend the coming night frosting cookies instead of ministering to her husband. Maybe Ida would be called into service, frosting and decorating cookies. Just like a bakery worker. She rather liked the idea. When she was very young and assisting her grandmother in the kitchen, she had fantasized being a professional baker. Of course, she had no idea of the hard work and early hours involved. In her mind she had seen herself as a pastry chef at the Waldorf Astoria, creating multi-layered, feather-light cakes filled with fluffy frosting and topped with a shiny chocolate glaze.

"Tonight I make Sven special dinner," said Lily, and she giggled. "Use special Chinese herb. After eat, will be very sleepy. Sleep very many hour. I can come Kitty, decorate cookie."

Ida was both relieved and disappointed. But she didn't have time to dwell on her lost baking career. Kitty was ready at the stove.

"Please now do what?" asked Kitty.

Ida went to the stove. A small saucepan was waiting, filled with what Ida hoped were the correct amounts of sugar, corn syrup, and water. Lily stood by, with a candy thermometer and a bowl of fluffy beaten egg whites ready, as if assisting at a surgery. Following Ida's instructions, Kitty made the sugar syrup and Lily handed her the thermometer to check the temperature. When the syrup was done,

Kitty slowly poured it into the bowl of egg whites as Lily wielded the electric mixer. When the pot of syrup was empty, Kitty quickly set the timer for seven minutes, and at the halfway point took over at the mixer. When the timer rang, Lily was ready with the vanilla extract. And then, without missing a beat, the frosting was spread over one of the sheet cakes. Seeing the China dolls at work as a team was like watching a perfectly orchestrated ballet, Ida thought.

"Brava!" Ida exclaimed when Lily finally put down the offset spatula, and she clapped her hands.

The twins bowed slightly and Lily giggled.

"We now wash, do again," said Kitty.

While one twin washed pot, bowl, and utensils, the other dried the measuring cups and measured ingredients for the next round. Ida sat and sipped her tea, watching the show. Finally, one and a half hours later, the cakes were done.

Lily made a fresh pot of tea and the twins joined Ida at the table.

"Soon we buy new stove, have two oven," said Kitty.

"Bake more fast," said Lily.

For a few seconds, Ida said nothing. She looked at the large freezer that was humming away against the window.

"Are you sure you're allowed to do that, buy a new stove? Don't you need the building manager's permission?" she asked, knowing as the words came out of her mouth that it was a useless question.

"We ask Super," said Lily.

"He say no problem," said Kitty. "He take away old stove, keep in basement. When we go back Hong Kong he put back old stove, keep new one himself."

And then he'll sell the new one and make some cash for himself, Ida thought.

"But what about the electrical wiring?" Ida persisted. "This is an old building. The new stove might use more power than the old one. If you overload the circuits, you could blow a fuse and you won't have any power." Or you could start an electrical fire and be in a lot of trouble, she thought but did not say.

"What is fuse?" asked Lily.

Years ago, when she lived in the Bronx, someone in her apartment building had loaded their outlets with all the latest appliances, not checking with the Super or anyone else as to whether the building's ancient wiring could support everything. They were soon in darkness. The wife became hysterical and ran screaming into the hallway, which set all the dogs barking, which caused those tenants who were at home to open their doors. Somehow the fire department was called and during their stampede through the dark apartment they saw the load of electrical appliances and the tangle of extension cords and issued a violation to the building's owner. Eviction proceedings commenced against those tenants and after several months, city marshals arrived, carried out the furniture and placed it on the sidewalk. The China dolls already had enough of a problem, Ida thought, and they didn't even know it. What if Arthur Sandowsky saw the stove being delivered? Their goose would be cooked for sure.

"A fuse is something in the wall," Ida told Lily. She couldn't really explain it.

"In my apartment, not use many electricity," Kitty said. "Just one person, not need." She waved her hand expansively as if to indicate the lack of electrical usage on her premises.

"Don't you have an air conditioner?" Ida asked.

"Only in bedroom," Kitty answered. "Not bake and sleep same time. No problem." She beamed as if she had everything under control and figured out.

"Well, I hope you're right," Ida said.

She knew there was no point in discussing the subject any further. Instead, as she sipped her tea, she tried to remember the location of her flashlights and resolved to keep one on her night table just in case. She frequently got up during the night to use the bathroom. Since the twins did much of their baking at night, that would be when a potential power outage would occur.

Lily suddenly jumped up, went to a cabinet and returned with a tin. Inside were Chinese almond cookies, the kind Ida had eaten years ago. Lily removed several cookies and put them on a plate.

"From Chinese bake shop," Lily explained. "Please eat."

Ida reached out and took a cookie. It went very well with the green tea. She finished it and took another. Live for today, she thought.

Chapter 46

The Tenants meeting was scheduled for eleven o'clock but Ida decided to be fashionably late. She dressed in a blouse and skirt but wore her best slippers. She emerged from the elevator with her cane and her folding seat, both of which she hardly ever used, the folding seat having been sent by Dr. Barbara years ago. She had decided it best to capitalize on her advanced age, the better to be ignored. Arthur had set up a card table in the lobby and he stood beside it. The lobby seemed filled with tenants. Then Ida realized the lobby was not very large, so that even a dozen or so people made it look full.

Ida recalled a Tenants Holiday Party many years ago, when the Tenants Association had just been organized. Arthur had set up a card table then, too, with punch, paper cups, and cookies baked by Ida herself. That party had not been terribly successful. For one thing, the lobby was too small and quickly became too crowded. And most of the tenants came just for the refreshments, which despite Ida's cookies, were not what they expected. Arthur's card table of the moment held a few cartons of orange juice, small paper cups, and two boxes of Entenmann's muffins. Arthur looked around the lobby as Ida opened her seat and positioned herself.

"I think we can start," he announced. He looked at his watch and cleared his throat. "The reason you're all here," he said, "is an unpleasant cooking odor that's been waking you up in the middle of the night."

Nods and murmurs of assent went through the assembled group.

"I think I've discovered the source of these odors," he continued. "It's obviously one of our own tenants. I believe the culprit is Miss Kitty Cheong of apartment 3C." Arthur paused, as if waiting for a reaction. But there were no gasps, only puzzled looks.

"Who is Kitty Cheong?" someone finally asked.

"The Chinese woman who lives in apartment 3C," Arthur replied. He reached into his pants pocket, removed a business card and held it up.

Ida knew that this was the China dolls' business card, same as the one they'd shown her: Good Fortune Cookie Company.

"I found this on the floor by the mailboxes," Arthur continued. "It's written in Chinese. Since only two Chinese people live in our building, I couldn't imagine what it was. So I called our local high school, which teaches Chinese, and arranged for their Chinese language teacher to translate it. What it says is "Good Fortune Cookie Company, 388 Bayside Avenue, Apartment 3C." He paused.

For a few seconds no one spoke.

"That means it's a business," a tenant finally said. "A bakery business. Here in our building."

Surprised murmurs and shaking of heads now took place. Ida sat on her portable seat, poker-faced. She could always pretend to be hard of hearing.

"Right," Arthur responded, "and it's illegal."

Murmurs of surprise and shaking of heads now took place. Finally the noise subsided.

"So what are we going to do?" someone asked.

Now Arthur smiled.

"What we're going to do is inform the building's management and demand an investigation," Arthur explained. "I've prepared a letter summarizing the situation, and I need everyone here to sign it. We can do it right now." He removed a folder from the card table, took out a typed letter and held it up.

"This letter is very brief," said Arthur. "You can come up here, give it a quick read, and if you agree, sign your name and apartment number. After everyone signs, I'll send it certified mail to the building manager. And have some breakfast," he added, pointing to the meager offerings on the table.

There was a sense of hesitation in the lobby. Coming to a meeting was one thing. Signing one's name to a certified letter of complaint was something else.

"What exactly will happen after we send this letter?" someone finally asked. "What will happen to this Chinese woman? I mean, I don't want to send anyone to jail or anything just over the smell of a peanut butter cookie."

Arthur frowned.

"This is not just about the smell of cookies," Arthur said sternly. "If this woman is operating an illegal business she could be using dangerous equipment. Industrial stoves not meant for a residential building. Mixing machines. A conveyer belt operation in the living room. Who knows what's going on in that apartment," he said ominously.

"But what will happen to that woman?" another tenant asked.

"First the management will come in and inspect. If they find evidence of an illegal business, they'll send the tenant a cease and desist notice. And if the tenant doesn't cease and desist, the landlord will begin eviction proceedings." Arthur gave the assembled tenants a tight smile.

"Well, that seems fair," a tenant decided, and he walked to the table. He picked up Arthur's letter, read it, and picked up the pen.

Until this moment, no one had either entered the lobby from the outside or come down in the elevator to leave the building. But now the elevator door opened and the China dolls emerged, pushing and maneuvering their multi-layered tray on wheels contraption, which was laden with boxes of what Ida knew were cookies and cakes for the special birthday of the Mah Jongg lady. The twins gave the assembled group only a passing glance as they made their way and headed for the ramped service entrance. For a moment everyone, including Ida and Arthur, froze, watching the spectacle. The Cheong sisters couldn't have had worse timing, Ida thought.

"Was that the Chinese baker?" someone asked.

"I believe so," said Arthur.

The man holding the pen quickly signed the letter, poured himself a cup of juice and took a muffin. Then he stepped away from the table and looked out the lobby's front window while he ate and drank. The remaining tenants quickly formed a line leading to the table. The line moved quickly, each person taking barely a moment to scan the letter and sign it.

Ida remained on her portable seat. She certainly wasn't going to stand on a line. She wondered if there would be any muffins left—she'd always had a weakness for Entenmann's baked goods, even though she preferred home-made. She still remembered a certain cinnamon crumb coffee cake that she'd sometimes bought when she'd lived in the Bronx. When the last person began to pour their juice, she got up, collapsed the folding seat and made her way across the lobby, walking as slowly as she could. If Arthur wanted her signature, he would have to wait for it. She reached the table, picked up the letter and squinted at it. Arthur picked up the pen and handed it to her. She signed her name as illegibly as she could, then handed Arthur the pen.

"I'd just like to have a bit of juice, if you don't mind," Ida said.

She leaned over the letter, preventing Arthur from picking it up. She lifted first one juice container, and then another, but they were empty. The third had some liquid sloshing towards the bottom. Ida tipped this over a cup. But somehow, as she poured, the cup tipped over and a cascade of juice ran over the letter.

"Oh, Arthur, I'm so sorry!" Ida exclaimed.

Arthur, aghast, whipped a handkerchief from his pocket, mopped the juice, and held the letter up between two fingers, waving it dry.

"I'm so sorry!" Ida repeated. "I hope the letter is still usable." Then she turned, got into the elevator, and went upstairs.

Chapter 47

"They bought what?!" Sandy exclaimed after Ida told her about the China dolls' newest purchase. "What will they get next, a French door refrigerator?"

Ida had never heard of a French door refrigerator but she supposed it was just what it sounded like, a refrigerator that opened like French doors. She failed to see the advantage of such a refrigerator. If you opened one side and didn't find what you wanted, you just had to open the other side and look again. Of course, this spoke more of the state of Ida's own refrigerator than the design of refrigerators in general. Sandy put it in order every Friday, but by the next week it had returned to a state of chaos.

"It can't be legal to put in all these fancy appliances," Sandy continued. "I bet they never checked with the building management, and if management finds out, those women will be in a heap of trouble." She paused. "And speaking of trouble, how did the tenants' meeting go?"

"Pretty much the way Arthur wanted," Ida told her, trying and failing to keep a straight face. She described the signing of the letter and her spilling the orange juice on it.

"You didn't!" said Sandy, and she grinned. "And here I thought I was working for a docile old lady."

"He mopped up the juice right away," Ida explained, "so it's probably still usable. Anyway, it was not a premeditated act. But when the twins came out of the elevator pushing that load of cake, I felt so sorry for them..."

"That you had to make a political statement," Sandy nodded.

"So now they'll send someone to inspect," Ida lamented.

"Eviction takes a few months," said Sandy. "Maybe by then they'll have enough money to leave."

Ida had often thought of giving the China dolls the money for their air tickets. She had some savings in a bank account. The twins could return to Hong Kong and then, after they began to earn money, they could pay her back. Of course, she might be dead by then, and if she was dead, the money wouldn't matter. The problem was that her account was held jointly with Dr. Barbara, and Dr. Barbara would totally disapprove of such an expenditure. If Ida died, it wouldn't make any difference. But suppose a situation evolved where Ida was still alive and Barbara had to take money from the account? Ida didn't want to imagine the scene that would take place.

Thinking of Dr. Barbara, Ida looked at her clock and realized her daughter's weekly phone call was half an hour overdue. This was worrisome, as Barbara was always very punctual. She never scheduled surgeries on Friday, so she would not now be in the operating room. Ida wondered if her daughter had had an emergency herself. But if that were the case, Monica would have called. Or would she? Though she was technically an adult, she still lacked whatever it was that made a person an adult. Just then, the phone rang.

"I was in a meeting," said Dr. Barbara. "I hope you weren't worried."

"A little bit," Ida said, not admitting half an hour had gone by before she'd noticed.

"My department is being reorganized," said Dr. Barbara.

Ida wasn't sure how a surgery department could be reorganized. Surely it couldn't mean that surgeons would operate on different organs than they had previously.

"Will you still have your job?" Ida asked.

"I think so," said Barbara. "But if not, I have options. I can retire from here. And when I was at the thyroid conference in Honolulu, I was offered a part-time teaching post at the University Hospital. I was planning to retire to Hawaii anyway," Barbara continued, "so it could all work out perfectly."

Things working out perfectly was just what Barbara liked and expected. Ida thought to ask how this would impact on Monica. Then she remembered Monica was no longer living with Barbara. In any case, Monica would become a Physician's Assistant, get a job and be self-supporting. It was strange to be listening to Barbara's lack of contentiousness. It gave Ida an uneasy feeling, as if things were too perfect.

"And your wedding plans are finalized?" Ida asked.

"Everything is in order," said Barbara. "All I have to do is order the flowers two weeks before."

Barbara seemed to have nothing further to discuss. Ida certainly had plenty she could report, but she wouldn't tell her daughter any of it.

"Well, everything's fine here," Ida said.

"I'll call next week," said Barbara, and she hung up.

Immediately the phone rang.

"Arthur Sandowsky here," said the familiar voice.

"Oh, hello, Arthur," Ida said, trying to conceal her dismay.

"I just wanted to let you know that my letter survived your juice spill. In case you were worrying about it," Arthur continued.

Not only had Ida not worried about the letter, she had actually forgotten that missive's purpose—the memory thing?--, so happy was she about her attempted obliteration of it.

"You seemed to have rescued it, as I recall," said Ida, that part of her memory intact.

"Well, I've had confirmation that the building manager received it, so we should be seeing some action soon," Arthur informed her. "I'm personally calling each tenant who signed the list to keep them updated."

"That's very thoughtful of you," Ida told him. Forewarned is forearmed, she reminded herself. "What kind of action can we expect?"

"I'm quite sure the tenant in question will receive a notice of inspection," Arthur explained. "Management will have to be allowed access to that apartment."

"And what will they be looking for?" Ida asked.

"Anything that would indicate a baking business," said Arthur, falling into Ida's trap. "Industrial equipment, appliances, large baking pans. Anything not commensurate with home baking."

"I see," said Ida. "Well, thank you for keeping me up to date."

"I'll call and let you know when there's some action," Arthur told her, and he hung up.

Ida sat down at her kitchen table to think. She would have to alert the China dolls about Arthur's plot against them, but she would not tell anyone. And who was there to tell except Sandy?

"You look like the cat that ate the canary," said Sandy as she entered the room carrying a dust rag and a can of Pledge.

"Oh, I was just thinking," Ida quickly said. "I was picturing myself at my daughter's wedding, wearing that pretty outfit that I wore to your sister's wedding."

"You'd better not tell her that you've already worn it," said Sandy. "She might be insulted."

She certainly might be, Ida thought, especially if Barbara knew she had worn it to the wedding of her cleaning girl.

"You've got that cat ate the canary look again!" Sandy exclaimed. "What's gotten into you today?" You sure you're feeling all right?" Sandy moved closer to Ida and peered at her face.

"I'm perfectly fine," Ida insisted. "I was just thinking about... things."

"What things?" Sandy demanded.

"A new cake recipe," Ida replied, because it was the first thing that popped into her mind to say other than the truth.

Again Sandy looked at her strangely.

"Maybe you should have a check-up," Sandy suggested.

"What I need to check are my recipes," said Ida, going to her bookshelf.

Sandy shrugged and left the kitchen. And soon Ida heard the roar of the vacuum cleaner. She opened a baking book on the table in front of her and pretended to be reading while she was actually thinking of how she could foil Arthur Sandowsky's plan.

Chapter 48

Ida looked for the Cheong sisters in the lobby, hoping they would be coming or going with their shopping carts, but had no luck. She spent hours at the kitchen window, trying to catch them. She even tried knocking on Kitty's door, but no one ever answered. The twins seemed to have dropped off the planet. Then one day Ida's doorbell rang. She looked through the peephole and couldn't see anyone, which meant it was the twins.

"*Ni hau*," said Kitty and Lily as Ida ushered them inside. Lily held a napkin-covered plate.

Ida put up water for tea as Lily revealed what was under the napkin.

"Special cookie," Lily announced.

Ida recognized the cookies immediately. They were Martha Stewart's Peanut Butter Whoopie Pies, right out of the purloined Martha Stewart Cookies book. Ida had nearly forgotten about the missing book, taken up as she was with waging war against Arthur's war against Kitty. And now that she remembered her missing book (how could she have forgotten? The memory thing again!) she had a brief second thought about helping the China dolls elude Arthur's machinations. But the moment passed. She thought of poor Lily the household slave to Sven, and her own personal satisfaction in thwarting Arthur. She poured everyone tea and tucked into a whoopee pie. The cakey chocolate cookie was moist and rich, the peanut butter filling surprisingly delicate.

"Not use peanut butter," said Kitty, seeing Ida's expression. "Use sesame butter."

"I think I actually prefer it," Ida told her.

"Birthday party very success," said Kitty after several Whoopie Pies had been consumed. "Now have many order special cake. Have new stove, two oven, can bake more easy."

"Many day we try new oven," explained Lily. "So understand. Now expert."

So that was where the twins had been, Ida thought. Holed up in Kitty's kitchen with the new stove. She supposed it was like trying a new recipe on the old stove you knew, just the reverse, which she found more daunting. Decades ago, she, Irwin and Barbara had moved to a new apartment and a new stove. It was quite different from her previous stove, and had taken several weeks to get used to. Overcooked and undercooked vegetables and burnt roasts and bleeding chickens had resulted. Not to mention fallen cakes and dried-up cookies. She imagined the twins working through the night, timing the baked goods to the nanosecond so the bakers could get them perfectly right.

"So I guess you'll be very busy," Ida remarked, eying but refraining from eating the last whoopee pie.

"Very busy," Lily nodded.

Kitty reached into her pocket and removed an envelope.

"This put under door. Please you tell say what. I cannot read English." She held out the envelope.

Ida took it. It had been opened and the contents put back inside. Ida removed a letter. The letterhead was that of the apartment building's management company. Ida quickly read the letter.

"This letter says there's been a complaint against you," Ida told Kitty. "It says you are disturbing your neighbors by creating a bad cooking odor at night, that is keeping tenants awake."

Lily looked puzzled.

"What is odor?" asked Kitty.

"A smell," said Ida. "Like perfume. Or garbage."

The twins looked at each other.

"We just bake," said Kitty. "Cake not smell like garbage."

"Well, apparently several people in the building don't like the cake smell." Ida was going to add "especially the peanut butter" but as this was not in the letter she decided against it. "And it says you are running an illegal business from your apartment."

"But is my apartment!" Kitty protested. "I can do I want."

"Not exactly," Ida tried to explain. "In the United States we have laws. In New York City we have laws. You can't have a commercial business out of a rental apartment. At least not a baking business."

"No?" said Lily.

"If you prepare and sell food, you need a license from the Health Department," said Ida.

"My cake clean!" said Kitty indignantly.

Ida realized no amount of explanation would get her point across: they could not do what they were doing. She returned to the letter.

"The building manager is going to send an inspector to your apartment," Ida told Kitty. "You'll have to let them in."

"Inspect what?" Kitty asked.

"Taste cake, see if good?" asked Lily with a giggle.

Ida was temporarily distracted by the idea of an inspector looking for evidence of an illegal baking business and being offered a piece of cake. Or a cupcake. Or perhaps they would be offered an entire cake as a bribe. She brought herself back to the letter.

"They'll be looking for evidence that you're baking more than an ordinary tenant," Ida said.

A look of comprehension crossed Lily's face.

"New stove," said Lily. "Freezer," she added.

"No problem," said Kitty. "I ask Super put new stove basement, put old stove my apartment. Put freezer basement."

"Cake pan," said Lily. "Too many. Put basement."

"When inspector come?" Kitty asked.

Ida looked at the letter.

"July fourteenth," Ida said. "So you had better move everything quickly."

"Inspector come, we show no problem," Kitty said confidently.

Ida said nothing. She imagined they would move the appliances in the middle of the night to avoid being seen. Of course, the sound of a loaded hand truck or dolly rumbling down the hall and into the elevator would present another problem. But the problem was not Ida's.

"Cannot bake many thing in old stove," said Lily. "Oven too small."

"Now have many order," said Kitty. She stared across the room at Ida's stove.

Ida realized where this conversation was going. The China dolls wanted to move their baking operation into her kitchen. Such a favor was too much to ask.

"I'm afraid my stove hasn't been working properly," she lied, crossing her fingers in her lap. She had told more lies in the last month than she had in the last several decades. "I've got to ask the Super to call the stove repairman."

The twins' faces fell.

"What about Lily's stove?" Ida suggested.

"Sven not like, said Lily.

"We move new stove just one day," Kitty decided. "After inspector, move back. No problem."

"Can keep cake in freezer in basement," said Lily. "Ask Super plug in freezer."

Ida wondered how well the twins would have to grease the Super's palm to accomplish their scheme. She had never had the need for anything out of the ordinary from the roster of Supers who had worked in the building since she'd moved in. Years ago, Arthur's mother had told her of strange goings-on in the building, people who broke their lease and moved out in the middle of the night, assisted by the reigning Super. There had been stories of new bathroom fixtures purchased by management and meant to be installed before new tenants moved in, but which the Super had instead sold and pocketed the money. There had also been a young hunk of a Super who made his way into female tenants' beds when he went to their apartments to make repairs. So she supposed moving stoves in and out was not that unusual.

The twins slurped up the last of their tea and stood up to leave.

"Thank you for help," said Kitty.

After they were gone, Ida cleared away the tea dishes. There was still one Whoopie Pie on Lily's plate. She decided it would be perfect for the next morning's breakfast, wrapped it up and put it away.

Chapter 49

Ida reached into her mailbox and was surprised when her fingers encountered a large thick envelope. The usual contents of her mailbox were thin junk mail. Dr. Barbara had long ago arranged for most of Ida's bills to be paid automatically from her bank account. The front of the envelope appeared to have been hand written in fancy calligraphy. She turned the missive over and saw the identity of the sender—Dr. Barbara Rappaport—and realized it was the wedding invitation. It was, after all, mid-July, and people usually sent out such invitations six weeks in advance. She hurried back to her apartment and went into the living room to read the contents. She always found it best to be reclining against her sofa cushions when reading correspondence from her daughter.

On closer inspection, the outer envelope appeared to be made of a thick velum. Carefully, she pried it open and extracted yet another envelope with her name written on it. She recalled the purpose of such an envelope: at weddings with multiple receptions, not all guests were invited to everything. So each inner envelope was stuffed with the appropriate invitations. Judging by the thickness of her inner envelope, she was being invited to the full spectrum of events. She pulled out the largest embossed card and read it.

You are cordially invited to attend the wedding of

Dr. Barbara Rappaport

And
Dr. Steven Rasmussen
Saturday September 9th
Twelve Noon
Luncheon to Follow

This was followed by the address of a resort which Ida assumed was in the vicinity of Los Angeles.

So the fiancé had a name! Ida wondered what his specialty was. Might he be a prostate surgeon? It seemed to be a popular specialty these days. There were television advertisements for prostate treatments, which would have been unheard of decades ago. But then this Dr. Rasmussen might not be such a doctor. He would be Barbara's age. More likely a cardiologist. It would be Monica who would be likely to marry a prostate surgeon.

And now she recalled Barbara's dreadful luncheon menu. No doubt she could eat a hearty breakfast at her hotel. Surely Barbara would put her in a hotel, too busy for houseguests. But maybe Ida should bring some emergency rations with her, just in case. Dr. Barbara was gluten free and Ida could be stuck in the house without any decent bread. She liked toast for breakfast. Gluten-free was not like Kosher, where you couldn't bring a forbidden item into a person's house. Although she had read somewhere that certain gluten free people had celiac disease, a wheat allergy, and were so sensitive that even a whiff of wheat flour could set them off. She didn't know if Barbara had celiac disease and wouldn't ask. The question could lead to a diatribe against Ida for serving her daughter all that wheat-based bread, cake, and noodles years ago. Ida could eat her bread in the guest bedroom if necessary. She would look in the supermarket for little packets of jelly.

She reached into the large envelope, which seemed to contain several more embossed cards, and pulled out the top one. This was a "wedding supper" at a restaurant. Hopefully, regular food would be available. The next card was an invitation to a Friday night dinner the night before the wedding. And the last was a Sunday brunch, after which Ida supposed the guests were expected to leave, having gained several pounds. She took the four invitations and laid them out on her coffee table as if she were playing Solitaire, and studied each one. A new problem presented itself. She would need a different outfit for each event. She already had the two-piece for the wedding itself. She pictured the contents of her closet, trolling for other suitable garments. Nothing came to mind. She would have to enlist Sandy to buy more clothes. Years ago, in the Bronx, there was a neighbor, Mrs. Bolognese, who had a way with her sewing machine. Dresses, skirts and blouses could be made to order; all you had to do was pick out the fabric and style. Mrs. Bolognese's forte was making copies of high-priced designer garments. Dr. Barbara's sweet sixteen dress was procured in this manner, as were several of the fancy outfits Ida had needed for family occasions. And Ida would need luggage in which to carry this new wardrobe. Why couldn't Barbara just elope, Ida wondered, but she knew that was not her daughter's style.

Ida scooped up the embossed invitations and began to return them to the envelope when she paused and peered into the envelope again. She shook it but nothing further appeared. Something was missing, the small r.s.v.p. note and stamped return envelope. Ida returned the invitation card to the coffee table. She leaned back against the sofa cushions, not knowing what to think. Was the omission an accident? Or did her daughter simply assume her mother would attend? But surely some assistant at Barbara's end, because Barbara was too busy for these mundane tasks, would be taking a count of responses and would be one short if he or she didn't have Ida's r.s.v.p. Ida imagined arriving at the first event, not finding her little place card, and causing a to-do when there was no place for her to sit. It would not be her fault, but embarrassing nonetheless.

For a moment she entertained the thought of calling Barbara to rectify the mistake. But she couldn't consider this an emergency. And suppose Barbara was at another thyroid conference in Hawaii? She would be doubly annoyed with Ida for calling about such a trivial matter. Although a person's marriage could never be considered trivial.

Ida went to the kitchen to make herself a cup of tea, but she couldn't stop thinking about the missing r.s.v.p. card. Was this Barbara's subconscious way of telling Ida she didn't really want her at the wedding? Ida had learned about the subconscious from Barbara herself when she was in college and studied psychology. One day Barbara had come home and, over dinner (meat loaf, baked potato, creamed spinach, Ida recalled—how did she remember that?) explained that sometimes people's behavior was a manifestation of something they felt on a deep level but did not want to admit to themselves. Like leaving their chemistry book on the bus presumably by accident, because they really hated chemistry and didn't want to have to do the homework. Ida had been skeptical of this concept, as she had always observed people's behavior to be quite obvious. But now that she gave it some thought, it was possible that no one's subconscious desires had been directed at her before. And all these years later (forty?), the very person who had enlightened Ida about the subconscious had directed their own subconscious behavior at her! Maybe. Or maybe it was just an ordinary mistake. Ida would ask Dr. Barbara about the missing r.s.v.p. card the next time she spoke to her. If she remembered.

Chapter 50

The night before the inspection of Kitty Cheong's apartment, Ida was awakened by a loud bang. This was followed by another loud bang, and her bed seemed to vibrate. She turned on the bedside lamp and looked at the clock: midnight. Then she remembered the inspection. The noise must be the Super moving out the new stove and the freezer. Ida wondered if the inspector would think to look in the basement storage room for evidence, but she was sure they would not. They were simply doing a job, not on a vendetta. And she was certain they could be paid off. And thinking of vendettas, it was lucky that Arthur lived on the other side of the building on the top floor and could not hear the noise. Ida imagined him flinging on his bathrobe, shoving his feet into slippers, and, in his role as president of the tenants association, rushing to the source of the disturbance. There was another crash, followed by the slamming of a door. One of the illegal appliances must be making its way to the elevator. Ida was tempted to put on her own robe and slippers, ring for the elevator, and go down to Kitty's apartment to make sure no one was hurt. But that would make her a witness to a possible crime. She pictured Sandy shaking both her head and her finger, forbidding Ida to leave her bed. Ida wondered how the other tenants were reacting to the noise. She hoped there would not be another notice taped to the lobby wall the next morning.

Realizing there was not much point in trying to get back to sleep until the appliance-moving was finished, she got out of bed and went into the kitchen. She decided a midnight snack was in order. The only midnight snack she had personally experienced was on a New Year's Eve early in her marriage. She and Irwin had gone to a party at which midnight supper had been served. Ida had been brought up on the principle that eating after dinner was unhealthy, a cause of weight gain and insomnia. But she knew people did it anyway. There was even a chef on a television cooking program who routinely raided her refrigerator in semi-darkness wearing a bathrobe.

She fished a decaffeinated tea bag from the cabinet and put up water. Then she peered into the refrigerator. Unlike that of the television chef, Ida's was not packed with succulent morsels of gourmet food. However, there was half a loaf of rye bread, butter, and sliced Swiss cheese. It would have to do. She toasted a slice of bread, slathered it with butter, and topped it with a slice of cheese. The kettle whistled and she quickly made the tea. She sat down to eat and drink.

Half an hour of silence went by. Then the sound of voices penetrated the night. There was another crash from below. What if the old stove was damaged? But she remembered the twins would not be baking on the day of the inspection. Tomorrow night the old stove would be exchanged again for the new one and all would be well. By the time Ida finished her tea and toast, quiet had again descended on 388 Bayside Avenue. She returned to bed but could not get back to sleep. Finally at three a.m. she dozed off, and woke with the sunrise at six. She was quite bleary-eyed when Sandy arrived.

"What happened to you?" Ida's cleaner demanded as she looked Ida up and down.

Ida explained about the inspection and switching of appliances. Sandy shook her head.

"Those twins are something else," she said. "They'd better hope they make enough money to go back to Hong Kong soon, because if they're not careful they'll end up being deported."

Ida had no idea of the China dolls' earnings from the bake sales. But the freezer and new stove must have cost a good bit. Even if those appliances increased the cookie output, it would take an enormous amount of cookies to pay their cost and increase profits.

"What I don't understand," Ida told Sandy, "is why they don't just call their family in Hong Kong and ask them to send the money for the air tickets. It could just be a loan."

"The Chinese have something called 'face,'" Sandy told her. "My ex-boyfriend learned about it when he worked in Chinatown. It's very important to them to not admit they made a mistake. Lily married a foreigner and came to the U.S. to start a great new life. She doesn't want to admit her husband turned out to be abusive."

"But that's ridiculous!" declared Ida.

"To you, yes," Sandy agreed. "But not to Lily." The issue was left hanging by the ring of the telephone: Dr. Barbara.

"Are you all right? Your voice sounds strange," Dr. Barbara said immediately after Ida's hello.

"Of course I'm all right," Ida replied. "It must be a bad connection."

The connection was clear, but Ida was not about to explain her lack of sleep due to the maneuvering of illegal appliances, nor her preoccupation with the China dolls' refusal to admit they had made a mistake.

"I'll have the phone checked," said Barbara, "and you should have yours checked too. It's not safe for you to be without a phone. I wish you would get a cell phone."

Ida's not having a cell phone had been a bone of contention for years. She had pointed out that she spent most of her time in her apartment and it would be silly to pay for something she might never use. Also, she would have to memorize another number, not an easy task for a nonagenarian. She wondered why no one had yet invented a cell phone that could take calls from the same number as one's home phone.

"I'll think about it," Ida told her daughter, trying to close the subject.

"You've been thinking about it for years," Barbara retorted. "I'm going to send you one. A.A.R.P. has one with a large keypad. You can keep it for emergencies."

Ida knew A.A.R.P. was an organization for retired people. She wondered if Barbara was going to retire.

"Everything all right with your job?" Ida probed.

"The reorganization of my department didn't affect me," Barbara said, assuming that was what her mother was referring to. "A few doctors will have to share secretaries was about all that happened."

Ida vaguely recalled something was going on with Barbara's job, and her question had been answered. Dr. Barbara would not have to retire. Even though she had said she would retire to Hawaii, she could always change her mind and come to New York City. Not that Ida did not love her daughter. But the thought of being supervised by Dr. Barbara—well, Ida didn't want to think about it.

"And how is Monica?" Ida asked.

"I'm not in much contact with her," Barbara said, "but you can call her on her cell phone. Do you have her number?"

"Not in much contact" was not the reply Ida expected and she was momentarily stymied.

"Yes, I have her number," she finally said.

"We'll talk next week," said Barbara, and she hung up.

It was not until an hour later that Ida remembered she had forgotten to ask about the r.s.v.p.card.

Chapter 51

That evening, Ida wondered if she should bother to go to bed, as she assumed the China dolls would be doing the dance of the stoves. But she dropped off to sleep at eleven and was surprised to awaken at six in the morning. She decided it best not to pursue the matter. Several more days passed with no late night noise or baking smells. She thought the twins might have returned to Hong Kong after all. Then, at midnight came a loud crash from below. This was immediately followed by screams, followed by a volley of what she assumed was rapid Chinese. Another crash, another scream. After only a moment's hesitation, Ida got out of bed and put on her robe and slippers. At first she considered calling 911, but had second thoughts. The twins had overstayed their visas. Besides, she didn't know what kind of emergency might await an ambulance or the police. Against her own better judgment she left her apartment and rang for the elevator. The hallway was silent. She got off the elevator and hurried to Kitty's apartment, from which no sound could be heard. Were the China dolls dead? Ida pressed her ear to the crack in the door. She heard the faint sound of voices inside, and rang the doorbell.

Of course no one answered. Even if they heard the bell, the twins were probably in the midst of stove work and wouldn't want to be discovered. And Ida didn't want to make enough noise to rouse Kitty's neighbors. She resorted to gentle but steady knocking for several minutes. Finally, a faint voice mouthed the word "who."

"It's Ida," Ida said as loudly as she dared. "Open the door!"

The locks clicked, the door cracked open and Kitty peered out. When she realized it was her elderly neighbor, she quickly opened the door wide enough for Ida to squeeze inside and just as quickly closed and locked it.

The sight that greeted Ida was not what she expected: two stoves and a hand truck in the center of the kitchen, and Lily and Kitty looking sweaty and disheveled.

"I heard screams," said Ida, "so I came to see if you were all right." She eyed the kitchen warily. "Where is the Super?"

"Super go vacation," Kitty said angrily. "Change stove first night, then go, not tell us. We get other Super give key, but not help bring new stove back. So we take hand truck, bring ourself."

"You lifted that stove?" Ida exclaimed.

"Not difficult," explained Kitty. "Put hand truck under, one person lift, one push down on truck, then we go to elevator, bring here."

"I see," said Ida. "But you have to hook the new one back to the gas line."

"We can do," said Kitty, "but Lily say no, too danger."

That accounted for the screams and rapid Chinese, Ida thought. She was surprised that Kitty's downstairs neighbor, whoever it was, had not called the police after the crashes and screams. But New Yorkers were infamous for their non-involvement in other people's lives.

"Do you mind if I sit down?" she asked, sitting at the kitchen table.

She supposed there was no hope of a cup of tea without a working stove. Then she noticed a large plastic contraption on the counter, plugged into an electrical outlet.

"I give you tea," said Lily, taking a cup from the cabinet, throwing in some tea leaves from a metal container and pressing the top of the contraption so that hot water streamed into the cup.

"Sorry, no have cookie," said Lily.

"So you've been without a stove for several days?" Ida asked Kitty.

Kitty nodded.

"I bring Kitty food each day," said Lily. "Cook more, bring before Sven come home."

"I heat in microwave," said Kitty. "Must buy." She pointed to a small new microwave oven on the counter. "Cook rice in rice cooker."

Ida glanced across the room, trying not to be obvious. Kitty's counter was now taken up by the microwave, rice cooker and hot water heater. The Martha Stewart Cookies book was nowhere in sight. She wondered if it might have migrated to Lily's apartment.

"Are you doing the baking in your apartment?" Ida asked Lily.

"We bake some cookie, but must bake fast," said Lily. "If Sven see, very angry."

Sven was not the only person the twins had to hide from, Ida thought. All they needed was for Arthur to run into them in the elevator transporting dozens of cookies. He could snap a photo with his cell phone and use it for evidence.

"When will the Super come back?" Ida asked.

"Two more week," said Kitty. "He go his country. Take long time."

Ida felt sorry for the twins. Yet they had brought their current situation on themselves.

"We put cookie in freezer in basement," Kitty went on. "Have key. But take more time."

The three women sat morosely in silence. Then the doorbell rang. For several moments the women neither spoke nor moved. Ida could feel her heart beating rapidly. She hoped she would not have a heart attack. It would not do to have Dr. Barbara find out her mother had suffered a heart attack in the middle of the night while in the kitchen of two Chinese women with expired visas, two stoves and a hand truck. She realized she had stopped breathing and took a deep breath as quietly as she could. The doorbell rang again. The women remained frozen in place. After several more minutes Kitty got up and crept to the door, then returned to the kitchen.

"I think they go," she reported. "Cannot hear breath. Elevator door close."

They drank more tea. No one spoke.

"I think I'd better go home," Ida finally said. She had no idea of the time. She looked around Kitty's kitchen but saw no clock.

"I also go," said Lily. "If Sven wake up, I not there, be angry."

They stood up to leave.

"Maybe we should take the stairs," Ida suddenly said. "Whoever rang the bell might be waiting in the elevator."

Kitty frowned.

"Maybe hide in stair," Kitty said. "Take elevator more fast, more safe."

"You too old take stair," Lily told Ida.

The twins had an exchange of rapid Chinese.

"We ring elevator, Lily check. I go stair, walk up your floor," Kitty said. "Lily walk your apartment. Then we know you safe."

"Good idea," Ida agreed.

Kitty took her keys and quietly opened the apartment door. Like thieves, the three women crept into the hall, letting Kitty's door close softly behind them. Kitty entered the stairwell while Lily rang for the elevator. Ida noted that it had been waiting on the fifth floor. Whoever had rung Kitty's bell had come from there. But the elevator was empty on arrival. Ida and Lily got in and went quickly to Ida's floor, where Lily saw her safely to her door.

Once inside, Ida turned on the kitchen light. Her clock showed two in the morning. She was glad it was not Friday. She knew she would be bleary-eyed, and she didn't want to have to make up a story for either Sandy or Dr. Barbara.

Chapter 52

It was bad enough, Ida thought, that she did not get back to sleep until two-thirty in the morning. But it was adding insult to injury to be awakened at six-thirty by shouts and screams from her upstairs neighbors: Lily and Sven.

"Where the hell were you last night, you little whore?" Sven shouted in his Nordic-accented English.

"I here in bed with you!" answered Lily in a high-pitched scream.

"Don't lie to me, bitch! I wake up and you're not here!" Sven shouted.

"You just have dream," Lily insisted. "Where I can go?"

Due to the volume of this conversation, Ida could not help listening. What Sven said was true. Lily had not been in his bed all night. Ida could vouch for Lily's whereabouts, but she suspected that Sven would not be pleased to hear about the stoves either.

"Go and make my breakfast!" Sven barked. "And not that Chinese rice shit! I want bacon and eggs. And toast." There was the sound of a door slamming, followed by silence.

There was no point in trying to go back to sleep, Ida decided. Even if she was able to do so, what if Sven didn't like his breakfast and started another shouting match? So she got up and made her own breakfast. Hearing Sven demand eggs, bacon and toast had given her an appetite. While she didn't care for bacon, and didn't have any on hand in any case, she had plenty of eggs and bread. She scrambled two eggs, slathered two pieces of toast with butter, and made tea. All was quiet in the upstairs kitchen. She imagined the tall blond Swede wolfing down his food. Ida usually breakfasted on cereal, but now, eating hot food, she began to think of other hot breakfasts she could have made: French toast or pancakes. She didn't know anything about Chinese breakfast food but assumed French toast was not in the repertoire. Maybe Sandy would know via her ex-boyfriend. Or she could always go to the source: the China dolls. But she would wait until the stove problem was solved.

She passed the morning quietly, watching television, and was beginning to think about lunch, when the telephone rang.

"Hi, Grandma!" Monica said brightly.

A bit too brightly, Ida thought.

"Hello, Monica. How are you?" Ida asked. Her kitchen clock showed twelve noon, which meant it was only nine in the morning on the west coast. And Monica was not an early bird. "Is everything all right?" Ida added before her granddaughter could reply.

"Oh, everything's fine," Monica said in the too-bright tone. "I'm just a bit under the weather."

"Have you gone to the doctor?" Ida asked. She immediately realized the ridiculousness of her question. Monica not only worked with doctors, she was studying to be a physician's assistant.

"No, I haven't gone to the doctor," Monica replied. "I'm sure it's nothing serious."

"How are you feeling, exactly?" Ida probed. She felt like Dr. Barbara conducting one of her inquisitions.

"It's just a bit of stomach trouble," Monica explained. "I've been a bit queasy. I think I'm not used to the kind of food I've been eating."

Ida wondered if Monica was making Magic Celery Chicken every night. Maybe she needed some new recipes.

"I hope you're not eating fast food—you know, burgers and fries," Ida told her. "Remember, when you were in the nunnery you were eating vegetarian food. Your body might not be used to a normal diet."

"Oh, no, I'm not eating fast food," Monica assured her.

"Well, when I'm queasy, I always make cinnamon tea," Ida said. "It's very easy. Just boil water, add some powdered cinnamon, the kind you buy at the supermarket, and wait until it's cool enough to drink. And don't drink it all at once. Just sip it every few minutes until you feel better."

"Thanks, Grandma, I'll try it," said Monica, still too brightly. "I've got to go. I'll call you again soon."

"Take care, dear," said Ida, and she hung up.

As she prepared tuna salad for lunch, Ida thought about the cinnamon tea. She tried to recall where she had heard about it. And when had she ever felt queasy? Then she remembered: when she was pregnant with Dr. Barbara. And now she put all the pieces of the puzzle together. Monica had moved out of her mother's house and in with a friend. The friend had to be a boyfriend. A woman would not bake Light or Dark Rocky Road, or cook Magic Celery Chicken, for just a roommate. Ida concluded that Monica was pregnant. She stared at her tuna salad for several seconds. Then she brought it to the table, sat down, and stared at it again.

Ida assumed Monica knew she was pregnant. Although given her granddaughter's general lack of direction in life, Ida realized she should assume no such thing. But then why had Monica called and mentioned the queasiness? Ida herself had never had a pre-marriage pregnancy scare, but there had been several high school friends who did. She recalled that the first stage was denial of the obvious. Missing a period, morning nausea, they were unmistakable signs, but somehow women just didn't want to believe they were in trouble. Of course, in these modern times an out-of-wedlock pregnancy was not thought of as "in trouble" but just one of those things. Movie stars flaunted their illegitimate pregnancies and married the child's father later on. Sometimes. Ida wondered if the reason for this delay was a maneuver on the mother's part to see what sort of father the father turned out to be. If he was not up to snuff, she could avoid both marriage and divorce. Ida decided she was not going to call Monica and tell her she was pregnant. Her granddaughter was twenty-five years old. She would have to figure things out for herself. Besides, even if Monica decided on abortion, Ida could not be of any help. She thought fleetingly of the China dolls' trip to the Chinese herbalist when Lily thought she was pregnant. Were there Chinese herbalists in Los Angeles?

And then there was the matter of Dr. Barbara. It was certainly not Ida's place to tell Barbara of her own daughter's pregnancy, or even just a hunch of it. So it was best to pretend ignorance and act totally surprised if told of the situation. Ida tried to imagine Dr. Barbara's reaction to the news. She actually couldn't. Given Monica's history, her mother might simply shrug and say "what else?" Or she might have a conniption fit, the pregnancy being the last straw on the pile of communes, pie-baking, and nunnery.

She put Monica's pregnancy aside and applied herself to her lunch. There were just too many complicated situations going on. When she finished the tuna salad she wished she had a good dessert, and realized she hadn't baked anything for herself or anyone else in several weeks. She would have to remedy that. Immediately. She longed for a sugary, buttery pound cake, with a scoop of chocolate ice cream. A check of the refrigerator revealed plenty of butter, eggs and milk. Her dry ingredients were in good supply, and she got to work. While the cake cooled, she could go to the store to buy ice cream.

Chapter 53

The following Friday, when Sandy asked "what's new?" Ida said she had nothing to report. In any case, there were now so many things to report that she probably couldn't remember all of them.

"Have the twins gone back to baking?" Sandy asked.

"I don't think so," Ida replied. "At least I haven't smelled anything at night, and I haven't seen them coming or going with their shopping carts. But I've resumed baking," Ida informed Sandy. "I was feeling a bit down, so I made a pound cake. And then I made a batch of spice cookies. When you're finished cleaning, I'll make tea and we can have some of each."

Ida felt better just talking about the baked goods. The baking process had refreshed her and she was ready to tackle whatever situation occurred. Including Dr. Barbara and the missing wedding invitation r.s.v.p. card. Right on schedule, the telephone rang: Dr. Barbara.

"Before I forget, there's something I have to ask you," Ida said. "It's about the wedding invitation."

"You did get it, didn't you?" Dr. Barbara asked.

"Oh, yes," said Ida. "But something was missing. There was no r.s.v.p. card to let you know I'm coming."

There was a long silence on Barbara's end.

"Yes," Dr. Barbara finally said. "Actually, we forgot to have them printed."

There was now a silence on Ida's end, as Barbara's answer was totally unexpected.

"Well," Ida finally managed, "I suppose you can just call the printer."

"I suppose," said Dr. Barbara.

Ida realized having the r.s.v.p. cards printed now would cause more problems. The cards would have to be mailed to all the invitees, which would necessitate another envelope and postage.

"Actually," Dr. Barbara cut into Ida's thoughts, "several people have already telephoned about the r.s.v.p. cards. So I think we'll just let people call and let us know."

Ida immediately thought of a problem with this system. The invitees wouldn't know by what date they had to r.s.v.p. She pictured Barbara getting calls a night or two before the wedding, invitees announcing they had forgotten to call and say they were coming. Or worse, just showing up with no advance notice.

"We'll call everyone in a few weeks," Barbara cut in again, "and ask them to let us know by August fifteenth." She paused. "So I assume you're coming." It was said more as a command than a question.

"Of course I'm coming," Ida assured her. "You can go ahead and make all my arrangements."

"Will do," said Barbara. "I'll talk to you next week."

Ida hung up the phone and felt the need to sit down. It was not a physical need, rather, her mind was so taken up with working something out that it could not support whatever energy was needed to remain standing. She was trying to remember something—that memory thing!—and finally she did: the subconscious. Somehow the subconscious was related to Barbara's and her fiance's forgetting to order the r.s.v.p.cards. Or whichever of them had been responsible for remembering to do it. Did that person subconsciously deliberately forget them? Because they didn't want the wedding to take place? Ida was pleased with herself for thinking of this theory, and would have liked to propose it to Dr. Barbara, but she couldn't, because what if it were true? She couldn't imagine her daughter not wanting to get married after all, not after the finding the location and the dress, not to mention the work put into the gluten-free menu. On the other hand, she could imagine Barbara's fiancé, Dr. Whatever-his-name (she had completely forgotten it) having a change of heart. Men liked to eat, and the prospect of going gluten-free for the rest of his life, at least in the couple's home, might have proven too much. And if Dr. Barbara didn't get married, what then? Would she still move to Hawaii? Ida made herself a cup of tea and stared into it. She had been so startled by the business of the r.s.v.p. cards that she had completely forgotten about Monica's pregnancy. Which was good, because she might have been tempted to mention it.

"Reading tea leaves?" Sandy asked as she entered the kitchen.

Ida smiled.

"I wish I could," Ida sighed. "I could answer a lot of questions."

"What questions?" Sandy asked.

"Have you heard of the subconscious?" Ida replied.

"Sure," Sandy said. "Psychology 101."

Ida told her about the missing r.s.v.p. cards. Sandy let out a long whistle. Then she sat down.

"I would definitely say there's something going on, and it's not good," Sandy commented. "Do we know who was responsible for ordering the invitations?"

"No," Ida said.

"So it could have been a secretary. Or the printer," Sandy mused.

"I don't think so," Ida told her. "Barbara definitely said 'we forgot to order them.' If it had been a secretary or the printer, she wouldn't have hesitated to blame them."

In fact, now that Ida thought about it, Barbara's failure to assign blame was in itself a sure sign that something was amiss.

"Too bad if they cancel the wedding," Sandy said. "You've got that nice outfit you wore to Charlene's wedding."

"Oh, I forgot to tell you," Ida now told her. "It's not just the wedding and reception. There's a dinner the night before, and a wedding supper the day of the wedding, and a brunch the morning after. I'm going to need a few more outfits."

"That's easy enough," Sandy laughed. "I love to go shopping."

"I don't remember weddings having so many events," Ida said. "You used to just go to the ceremony and then there was a meal. And sometimes a band, and dancing. Like Charlene had. I would think that's enough."

"I agree," Sandy said. "I think what started to happen, people moved all over the place, so when a person got married, the guests traveled a long way to go to the wedding. And the ones getting married felt they had to provide some meals. So there was the rehearsal dinner the night before, and then the brunch the morning after." She paused. "Now they even have destination weddings."

"Destination weddings?" Ida asked.

"Right," Sandy explained. "The couple pick some place—maybe a resort island in the Bahamas, that sort of thing."

"And they expect guests to go there? And pay their own expenses?" Ida was astonished.

"Yes," Sandy confirmed. "I think it's pretty nervy."

"I'll say," Ida agreed.

"But it's become very popular," Sandy went on. "And people feel pressured to go if they're invited."

"Well, if people would put their foot down and refuse, then there wouldn't be any of that nonsense. The couple couldn't get married in the Bahamas if no one would come."

"They could still get married," Sandy corrected her. "But they'd be by themselves. That wouldn't be as much fun."

Ida supposed she should consider herself lucky that she was obliged only to attend several meals in Los Angeles. Dr. Barbara might have decided to get married in Hawaii. Ida tried to picture herself on a beach, wearing a caftan and a lei. It would not do.

"I'll make you some tea," she told Sandy, "and we'll have cake."

Chapter 54

Several days later, Ida was awakened in the middle of the night. There had been a spell of hot weather, and now they were getting a break. She had turned off the air conditioner and opened a window, glad of fresh air. She had wakened from a dream in which she was baking cookies with—who? Her granddaughter? Or a younger child, possibly Monica's child. Ida emerged from the dream confused in the darkened bedroom. The scent of vanilla cookies filled the air. Where was she? Then reality returned. The odor of vanilla cookies was real. And she knew the China dolls were baking again.

Ida tried to remember whether their regular Super was back from his country, and could have reconnected the twins' new double oven stove. But so many things seemed to have happened in the last few weeks that she actually had no idea of how much time had passed. The smell was pleasant and she went back to sleep. In the morning, both the dream and the vanilla scent had vanished.

When she went to the lobby for the mail later in the day, the China dolls were coming in through the service entrance, pushing their shopping carts. The carts were spilling over with baking supplies. Ida could see sacks of flour and sugar, cartons of eggs, and several packages of quarter-pound sticks of butter.

"*Ni hau*!" the twins greeted her in unison.

"*Ni hau*," Ida managed. "I see you've gone back to baking."

"Last night bake many cookie," Lily reported.

"Ten dozen," said Kitty. "Have big order from Mah Jongg lady."

"So the Super came back and connected your stove," Ida commented.

"Super not come back," said Kitty. "Stay his country more time."

"Then who connected the stove for you?" Ida asked.

"I connect," said Kitty proudly.

Lily nodded, as if to verify this fact.

"You?" Ida asked, startled. "But how did you know how to do it?"

"We look on Internet," Kitty explained.

"Sven have laptop computer," Lily said. "We take to library. Have free wi-fi. We look up information."

"See de…" Kitty hesitated.

"Diagram?" Ida supplied.

The twins nodded.

"We see, I connect," Kitty said. "Then turn on stove. Everything work."

"So now can bake," Lily said happily.

"Tonight make sesame cookie," said Kitty. "Many dozen."

Ida was glad to see the China dolls happy, but she had her misgivings about the connection of the stove to the gas line. Dr. Barbara had long ago taken the attitude that many appliance-related tasks were actually quite simple, but men build a macho mystique around them in order to supply themselves with jobs. The idea of a macho mystique, the opposite of the famous Feminine Mystique (Ida had heard of this book but never read it) was an interesting theory. But Ida was not convinced that anyone other than a professional should tinker with a gas line. Not that their Super was exactly a professional. His office had no certificates or diplomas on the wall, and his command of English was dicey.

"Well, just be careful," Ida advised the twins.

"No problem," said Kitty, and the China dolls pushed their carts into the elevator and went upstairs.

"No problem" was precisely the problem, Ida realized when she returned to her apartment. Not that she didn't love and admire the China dolls. After all, they had come to a foreign country to start a new life and were working hard to make their escape. But the casual attitude of "no problem" could land them in serious trouble. The twins seemed oblivious to this possibility. Perhaps, Ida reflected, it was the attitude of youth. Her granddaughter Monica could be said to have a similar attitude, though Ida couldn't recall Monica ever actually saying "no problem." Monica's drift from one unsuitable employment (if they could even be called employments) to another with no thought to her future was no different, really, from the China dolls' attitude. At least now, in the Physician's Assistant program, she was headed in the right direction. Maybe. Ida now remembered Monica's phone call, the queasiness in her stomach that Ida interpreted as morning sickness. If Monica was pregnant, the pregnancy would probably put at least a temporary halt to her career prospects.

But Ida had to admit she liked the idea of having a great-grandchild. Few women lived long enough to achieve such a distinction. Her relationship with a great-grandchild would be short-lived. And regrettably, by the time the child had enough teeth to bite into a cookie, Ida not only might not be baking any longer, she might not be at all. She tried to think of something she could do. She had never learned to knit or crochet. She supposed she could learn at some Senior center in the area, but she envisioned herself entangled in miles of yarn. Sewing was out of the question, as was babysitting. Well, it was something to think about. And then inspiration hit: she would call Monica. Right now. Just to see how she was feeling. Ida fetched her small phone book—actually just a booklet—most people she had known were dead—which was falling apart. She resolved to buy a new one. She found Monica's number and dialed. The phone rang several times. Finally Monica answered.

"Hello?" said Monica, sounding as if she were emerging from a coma.

"It's Grandma!" Ida announced enthusiastically.

"Hi, Grandma," Monica replied with a much smaller degree of enthusiasm.

"I thought I'd see how you are," Ida went on. "I was concerned about your stomach trouble."

"Oh, that," said Monica. She paused. "I have to tell you something. But promise you won't tell my mother."

"Of course," Ida assured her.

"I don't think I'm sick. I think I'm pregnant," Monica told her.

"Oh?" Ida asked, trying not to sound hopeful.

"I've missed two periods," Monica explained. "That's never happened before."

"Have you gone to the doctor?" Ida asked.

"Not yet," Monica said. "I did one of those home pregnancy tests. It was positive."

Ida had seen those home tests advertised in a women's magazine. Back in her day, those tests hadn't existed. You just went to the doctor for confirmation.

"You should go to the doctor right away," Ida instructed her. "So you know for sure. You'll need prenatal care." She suddenly felt the need to advocate for this possible great-grandchild. "What you should eat," Ida went on, thinking of Dark Rocky Road and Magic Celery Chicken. "A healthy diet."

"I know," Monica sighed. "I'll call tomorrow and make an appointment."

"Please do that," Ida pressed. "And get some rest."

"You won't tell my mother?" Monica repeated. "I mean, I know I'll have to tell her eventually but I want to be sure."

"It will be our secret," Ida said. "I'll call you in a few days to see how you are."

"Thanks, Grandma," Monica said, and hung up.

Ida sat down and contemplated her future great-grandchild. She hoped it would be a girl, who would inherit the baking gene. Of course, a boy could be a proficient pastry chef, and she shouldn't have a gender bias. She had seen magazine articles about gender bias. It was the modern term for pigeonholing women into housework. She smiled at the thought of her baking gene being passed on. Until she remembered that Kitty Cheong had reconnected her own stove. Ida didn't think she would sleep easily until the building's Super returned and checked things out.

Chapter 55

Despite being awakened by the smell of sesame cookies at two in the morning, Ida was relieved to have passed the night without hearing an explosion from Kitty's kitchen. But she knew there was trouble ahead. Other tenants, the same as those that had previously posted comments on the lobby wall, had surely smelled the China dolls' baking, and would doubtless be up in arms again. When her telephone rang shortly after breakfast, she was tempted to just let it ring without answering it. But she thought it might be Monica, and on the sixth ring she snatched the receiver from its cradle.

"Ida, I have to talk to you," Arthur Sandowsky practically shouted. "I have to talk to you right away! Can you come upstairs?" he demanded.

Ida stood in her nightgown and bathrobe. She looked at the kitchen clock. It was only nine-thirty, too early to deal with anything, let alone Arthur.

"I can come up in half an hour," she said sweetly. "Shall we say ten o'clock? I'm not dressed yet."

Just as she had hoped, there was a moment of silence on Arthur's end while he contemplated the sight of a ninety-one year old woman in her nightclothes.

"Fine, ten o'clock," he snapped, and hung up.

Ida knew the subject of her meeting with Arthur: the China dolls' baking. She didn't understand why he was bothering her. She was neither the building manager nor the Health Department inspector. But she decided this would be her final meeting with him about the China dolls or anything else. Promptly at ten, dressed in her best summer housedress, she rang his bell. Arthur immediately flung the door open, as if he had been lying in wait behind it.

"I've already had calls from three tenants," he told Ida as he shut the door, "complaining of that peanut-butter cookie smell last night. Do you know anything about it?" He stood with hands on hips, glaring at her.

"Do you mind if we sit down?" Ida asked.

Arthur marched into the man cave and motioned to one of his uncomfortable chairs.

"Well?" he said, perching on the edge of the leather sofa.

Ida frowned.

"Why would I know anything about it? I'm just a tenant in this building, like everyone else," Ida said.

"Did you smell peanut-butter cookies last night?" Arthur demanded.

"What I smell or don't smell is my own business," Ida told him. "Unless I smell gas or smoke, in which case I would call the fire department."

"Ida, I know you're friends with those women," Arthur persisted. "What did they do, pay off the health inspector? It's obvious they're operating a commercial business out of that apartment. I can't believe they haven't been issued a summons."

"Arthur, I'm sorry you're upset, but I really don't know anything about it," Ida told him as sincerely as she could. This was probably the biggest lie she had ever told, she reflected, thinking of the stoves going to and from the basement and the hidden baking pans. She didn't bother to cross her fingers. She didn't care. "Just because I'm friendly with the twins doesn't mean I know all their business."

"Well, you'd damn well better find out!" Arthur exclaimed. "What am I going to tell the people who are calling me demanding an explanation? They signed a petition! They want action!"

That's what you get for being president of the Tenants Association, Ida thought to herself.

"Why don't you call the Health Department, or the building management, and make an inquiry?" she said. "Surely your position as president of the Tenants Association allows you to do that?"

"I've already done that," Arthur admitted. "The Health Department said the Tenants Association isn't a legal entity, and they can't give me any information. And the building management just said they'd have to get back to me."

"Then you'll have to wait and see," Ida suggested. She was beginning to contemplate heaving herself out of her chair and leaving.

"Don't you understand what this means?" Arthur continued insistently. "If the tenants think I'm brushing them off, they could vote me out of my position as president!"

So this was not just about revenge on Kitty Cheong, Ida thought. It might have started out that way, but it had mushroomed into a bigger attack on Arthur's ego. And it would serve him right if he was voted out. But she was sure he had nothing to worry about. No one would be interested in taking Arthur's job. In fact, until the baking smell situation, no one had been terribly interested in the Tenants Association at all.

"Arthur, you've done everything you possibly could," Ida told him. "You called in the Health department, and they're the final authority."

"Can't you talk to the Cheong sisters? Please, please," Arthur now begged.

Ida couldn't stand men who begged.

"Talk to them about what?" she asked, hauling herself out of her chair.

"Ask them to stop baking at night, and do it during the day when most people aren't home," Arthur pleaded.

"Why don't you ask them yourself?" Ida suggested.

For a moment Arthur was silent.

"I just can't," he said.

Ida realized that of course he couldn't. Not after he had undertaken a vendetta against them. What he should have done, what any sensible person would have done, was to have gone to the China dolls when the problem started and asked them to stop baking at night. Not that they would have agreed. But at least he would have made a civilized attempt.

"I'm not telling anybody what to do in their own apartment," Ida said firmly. "Anyway, the baking isn't bothering me." She had worked her way into Arthur's foyer. "Arthur, I've got to go," she said. "I'm sorry I can't help you."

"Those twins haven't heard the last of this," he said, and his door closed sharply as Ida hurried down the hall.

Ida returned to her apartment, Arthur's parting words ringing in her ears. She sat down and debated what had become the usual: should she alert the twins to the current situation? But the fact was there was no current situation. The Health Department had come and gone with no results. Maybe Arthur thought that because he was a lawyer, he could sue the China dolls. But for what? He himself was not the victim of the baking smells. Or maybe he would offer to represent the other tenants who complained of the odors. Ida was sure those tenants would not want to pay Arthur for a lawsuit over peanut butter cookies. Anyway, it was already the beginning of August. By the time anything got to court, if it ever did, the weather would have cooled off and the China dolls would have resumed baking during the day, or at least have closed their windows. So she was finished with Arthur and the baking smells, whether Arthur was finished or not.

She glanced at her shelf of baking books and smiled. She would send some cookies to Monica, as it didn't sound as if Monica was feeling up to baking herself. Ida tried to think what kind of cookie a woman with morning sickness might enjoy. Probably something plain, like shortbread. She checked her supplies and made a shopping list.

Chapter 56

When nine-thirty came and went on Friday morning, Ida began to worry. Sandy usually arrived by nine-fifteen at the latest. So when the phone rang at nine-thirty-five, Ida assumed it was Sandy reporting that she was delayed. But to Ida's surprise, the caller was Dr. Barbara, who always called at ten.

"You're early," Ida said. "Is everything all right?"

"Of course everything's all right," Dr. Barbara snapped. "I've just got a busy schedule today, so I thought I'd..."

Just get the call out of the way, Ida thought but didn't say. Actually, she could well imagine Dr. Barbara's being busy. There were always thyroids to attend to, not to mention goings-on at the hospital. Ida knew about these from her General Hospital soap opera days. And then there was the wedding, only a month away. On the other hand, her daughter could have the sense to keep her impatience to herself. But that was not Barbara.

"So everything's all right, then," Ida said pleasantly.

"Well, more or less," Dr. Barbara finally replied. "I'm sort of rethinking my retirement plans."

"You mean Hawaii?" Ida asked.

"No, but I just might not retire as soon as I thought," Barbara explained.

Ida wondered if Barbara knew about Monica's pregnancy. She could not picture her daughter as a doting grandmother and Barbara might decide to keep working rather than be called upon for babysitting. Of course, if she moved to Hawaii, she would be safely out of range.

"You certainly could keep working," Ida agreed.

"I know," Barbara said sharply. "Have you spoken to Monica lately?"

"As a matter of fact, I have," Ida nattered on. "She called me the other day."

"Oh?" Barbara sounded surprised.

"Just to say hello," Ida reported. She realized she was about to embark on a new series of lies. If she kept it up, she could be in the Guinness book of records.

"Monica has been calling in sick to her classes and her clinic hours," Dr. Barbara informed Ida. "One of my doctor friends at the hospital called and gave me a heads-up."

Now here was something neither Ida nor Monica had thought of, Ida realized. She and Monica might keep a secret, but Barbara was part of the medical community.

"Maybe she has the flu," Ida suggested. "Or something."

"Or something," Barbara agreed.

"Well, I'm sure she'll get over it soon," Ida replied, knowing it would probably take another seven months. "She certainly has enough doctors at her disposal."

"Right," said Dr. Barbara with an edge of sarcasm.

Ida could see Barbara's probable point of view. Monica had had twenty-five years of failure to become a responsible adult. Even as a child, she had drifted from one activity to another, plunging in and then giving up and moving on to something else: girl scouts, piano lessons, ice skating, tennis. She tried everything and then threw everything aside. It was a miracle, Ida reflected, that Monica had completed all her mandatory schooling, and with decent grades at that. And now, just when it looked like her granddaughter had finally put her act together, Monica had reverted to being Monica. Ida didn't know what to say.

In the silence she heard the lock click on her apartment door and knew Sandy had arrived.

"I've got to go. My cleaning girl is here," Ida told Dr. Barbara. "I'm sure Monica will be fine."

The door opened and Sandy appeared but something was amiss. At first Ida couldn't put her finger on it. But further scrutiny as Sandy closed the door revealed disheveled clothes, smeared make-up, and sweat trickling down her neck. Even in the hot weather, Sandy was always perfectly turned out.

"What's happened to you?" Ida exclaimed. "Come and sit down."

"There was a little riot on the subway," Sandy explained, sitting in a kitchen chair.

Ida brought a roll of paper towels and Sandy mopped her face and neck.

"The train was stalled in the tunnel, and a fight broke out at one end of my subway car," Sandy elaborated. "So everyone ran to the other end of the car. But I'm perfectly all right," she assured Ida. "And I have news."

"News?" Ida asked. She put a glass of water on the table in front of Sandy.

"It's about Charlene," Sandy said. She picked up the glass of water and took a long drink.

In the chaos of everything that had been going on lately, Ida had actually forgotten about Charlene and the possibility that she might want her job back. Ida abruptly leaned forward in her chair.

"What about Charlene? Is she going to have a baby?" Ida asked hopefully.

"Well, not yet," Sandy said. "But she's going back to work. She's going to start a business."

"A business?" Ida leaned back. She thought of the twins and their cookie business. "What kind of business?" she asked warily.

"A cleaning business," Sandy told her. "She's going to hire other people to do the actual cleaning, but she'll get the clients and workers and match them up. That way," Sandy continued, "she and Charles can adopt a baby and she can run the business from home and be with the baby."

Ida nodded. So Charlene wouldn't want to clean Ida's apartment.

"So I'll still be your cleaner," Sandy said. "I'll just be working for Charlene, instead of directly for you."

Ida took a moment to grasp this.

"Will I have to pay more?" she asked.

Sandy shook her head.

"No," she told Ida. "You'll just stay at the current rate. In fact, you'll be her first official client."

Ida liked the sound of that. It wasn't often that you got to be the first at anything.

Sandy drained her water glass.

"So I guess I'd better get to cleaning," she grinned. Then she paused. "Anything happen with the twin bakers?"

Ida reported on the connecting of the new stove, the resumption of baking odors, and her latest encounter with Arthur.

"I don't like the sound of all this," Sandy shook her head. "Especially the stove."

"I know," Ida agreed. "But it's already been more than a week, and nothing has happened, so I suppose we're safe."

"Maybe," Sandy agreed. "But I hope those girls will have the regular Super check it out when he comes back."

Ida was sure the China dolls would do no such thing. If the stove worked, they would assume it was fine. And the Super was already a few weeks overdue. Maybe he wouldn't come back at all.

"I'm actually more worried about Arthur," Ida admitted. "He's still out to get back at Kitty."

"Men!" Sandy shook her head. "And they talk about scorned women! But you see it in the news all the time—men shooting or knifing their wives or their girlfriends."

"I don't think Arthur wants to kill Kitty," Ida quickly said. "Just punish her."

"Well, I would hope he doesn't want to kill her," Sandy finally got up from the table. "But if he ends up in jail, promise me you won't visit him and bring him cookies."

"Oh, I'd bring him cookies," Ida countered, "made with arsenic."

The women looked at each other and burst out laughing.

Chapter 57

Ida fell asleep easily that night. She was greatly relieved that Sandy would continue to clean for her. It was one sure thing in the midst of the other uncertain situations. She was in such a deep sleep that when she was awakened, and later on tried to describe the sequence of events, she could not be sure of their proper order.

The night was mild and her window was open. When she was awoken by a smell, at first it seemed to be just a smell—she had by now become used to the baking odors. But quickly she realized this was not the scent of cookies. Then she heard screams, and an exchange of what must have been loud, rapid Chinese. This only served to confuse her, but finally she realized the odor in her bedroom was acrid. Something was burning!

What first occurred to her was that the China dolls were baking and accidentally left a batch of cookies in the oven too long. Or in the process of putting the raw cookies into the oven they had accidentally tipped the tray, causing dough to land on the bottom of the oven and burn to a crisp. Both situations had happened to Ida from time to time over the years. The air would soon clear. But when it seemed not to be clearing, and even getting worse, she sat up in bed and realized what she smelled was smoke.

She immediately got out of bed and went to her bedroom window. Should she close all the windows to prevent the smoke from coming in? It would certainly block the flow, but would also block the air which she needed to breathe. Or should she simply leave the apartment? While she debated this, her smoke alarm went off. At least she assumed it was the smoke alarm. She also had a carbon monoxide alarm, but now recalled carbon monoxide had no odor. Ida was pleased with herself for remembering to change the smoke alarm's battery. What to do? She decided to throw on some clothes and leave, and she hurried into a housedress and slippers. But leaving presented its own problem. She recalled you were not supposed to use the elevator in the event of a fire, and Ida was unstable on stairs. Besides, the hallway staircase was on the far side of the elevator. If the fire was below her in Kitty's kitchen, it might be dangerous to take that route. The only alternative was the fire escape at the living room window. It was far from the fire, but Ida could not see herself managing that even in daylight, let alone darkness. She could picture the China dolls scampering down the fire escape like monkeys. But there was quite a drop from the last fire escape rung to the ground, and the ground was cement. Who would catch them?

Then she realized she had not heard a fire engine siren. The China dolls (assuming the smoke was coming from their apartment, but she could not be certain) most likely didn't know they were supposed to call 911, or even that the number existed. Ida hurried to her phone and called.

"There's smoke pouring in," she told the operator. "Send the fire department!" She gave the address. "It might be coming from the third floor front," she added.

"Ma'am, leave the building immediately," the operator told her.

Although she knew she should not stop to take anything with her, Ida grabbed her purse. Then she looked at her kitchen bookshelf. Would the baking books go up in smoke? She took a shopping bag from the cabinet, thinking she would fill it with books. But she realized carrying a heavy bag would only impede her progress out of the building. And what if she dropped them and they were scattered? They would be safer left behind.

She opened her apartment door to a hall filled with smoke and quickly shut it. Wet towel, she thought, she had seen it on television. She hurried to the kitchen, grabbed a dishtowel and ran it under the faucet. Without bothering to wring it out, she draped it over her head and face. It would be difficult to see where she was going, but she couldn't see much in the smoke anyway. Taking her purse and positioning the strap firmly over her shoulder and the purse under her arm, she opened her door, stepped into the hall, and closed the door behind her. She didn't bother to lock it, thinking the fire department might need to get in.

Slowly, she made her way down the hall, guided by touching the wall. Luckily, she had lived in the building for so many years, Ida thought as she crept along. She knew the layout by heart. The wet towel prevented the smoke from entering her lungs, though if anyone saw her through the fog they might think they were seeing a ghost or a monster. The hall was strangely quiet. Hadn't the other tenants woken up? If they had their windows shut and their air conditioners on, as many people did during the summer regardless of the outside temperature, they might not yet be aware of the smoke. As she passed each apartment, she rang the bell and pounded on the door several times, but did not linger. Finally she made out the large red Exit sign over the stairwell.

Thanks to the fire door, the stairwell was not yet filled with smoke and Ida managed to slowly climb down. As she approached the third floor she began to hear a banging sound which became louder as she reached the landing. Worried that someone might be trapped in their apartment, Ida opened the stairwell door and peered down the smoky hallway. The sound was coming from the vicinity of Kitty's apartment. Then Ida made out the figure of a man.

"Kitty! Kitty!" she heard him shout and he banged on the door again.

It was Arthur, holding a white handkerchief to his mouth and nose.

Ida gasped. He was trying to save Kitty! He loved her after all! But this was no time for romance.

"Arthur!" Ida shrieked as loudly as she could. "Arthur, you have to get out! Now!"

Arthur gave the door one more series of bangs and came lurching down the hall and into the stairwell, and Ida shut the door firmly behind him. He seemed startled when he looked at Ida. She realized her kitchen towel was draped over her face and she lifted it up.

"Ida! What are you doing here?" Arthur exclaimed. Tears were streaming from his eyes, either from the smoke or for fear for Kitty.

"I'm trying to escape the fire," Ida said, exasperated. Surely Arthur couldn't be that dense. "Let's go," she commanded, and turned to the stairs. They had only two more flights to reach the lobby.

"But Kitty..." Arthur whined, pointing back to the hallway.

"I'm sure Kitty has left," Ida told him, though she was not sure of anything. "She's young and moves quickly. She'll be waiting for us outside."

Arthur followed Ida and they reached the second floor landing. Ida paused to catch her breath. Only one more flight to go, she told herself. But then she seemed to collapse onto the floor. She had the sensation of being scooped up and carried. Outside, blinding red and white lights flashed in the dark and there was shouting and crying. Then everything went blank.

Chapter 58

Ida did not know where she was or why. There were sounds and shapes coming and going. Then the fog cleared. She was aware that she was not in her own bedroom. There were no flowered curtains. And she knew she had not died and gone to heaven, because a woman with a familiar face sat beside the bed: Dr. Barbara.

"Barbara!" Ida exclaimed.

"Oh, you're awake," Barbara said, putting down her newspaper. "How are you feeling? Do you know you escaped from a fire?"

Barbara's tone was relieved and attentive, but Ida immediately realized her daughter was probably giving the hospital hell: the room, medication, attention. But maybe this was a good thing, Ida decided. She would get the best care.

"Yes, I remember now," Ida said, the night of the fire coming back to her. "I must have fainted and a man carried me out."

"He said you actually saved his life," Barbara reported. "He was hanging back, trying to reach someone who had already left, and you persuaded him to come with you. Who was he?"

Ida tried to think.

"It was the president of the Tenants Association," Ida finally got out. "But..." She was about to confess that she had not actually known that Kitty had left, but held her tongue. "Did everyone escape?" she asked instead.

"Yes, amazingly enough, everyone got out unharmed," Barbara assured her. "Even you. You just fainted—probably from lack of oxygen or overexertion on the stairs. The doctor said you'll be fine. You can go home in another day or two."

"I hope I can still go to your wedding," Ida said, wondering if her clothes had been ruined by the smoke.

Barbara seemed to be debating with herself.

"Actually, my wedding has been postponed," she finally said.

"Oh?" For a moment Ida was startled, and yet she wasn't. "That's too bad," she said. "All those lovely plans. Will you get a refund from the country club?"

"Well, there will be a wedding," Barbara told her. "Monica is getting married, so we'll just have it there instead of mine."

"Monica getting married!" Ida tried to pretend delighted surprise. "How wonderful!"

Dr. Barbara frowned.

"Monica is pregnant," Barbara said.

"So is the fiancé a doctor or some other medical person?" Ida asked, letting the pregnancy slip past as if it were nothing out of the ordinary.

"He's a motorcycle mechanic," Barbara said, tight-lipped.

Ida was puzzled.

"How did she meet a motorcycle mechanic?" she asked.

"He cut his hand fixing a motorcycle, and he went to the clinic emergency room," Barbara explained. "It happened to be Monica's day to observe. And the rest is history." Barbara let out a resigned sigh. "We'll have to change the menu for the wedding reception," she went on. "The fiancé and his family are devoted carnivores. We'll have to serve steak." She winced.

"I'm sure it will be lovely," Ida insisted.

"Yes, I'm sure," Barbara agreed sarcastically.

Ida knew how Barbara felt about Monica. But Barbara was still Monica's mother and should be accepting of her daughter, regardless of Monica's faults. Just as Ida herself had to accept Barbara.

"You know, Barbara," Ida said, "you shouldn't be so hard on Monica. Life isn't easy, and not everyone is cut out for a high end career. At least she's marrying a man with a skill and I'm sure he makes a decent living." And Monica could easily have married someone as flighty as herself, Ida thought.

Barbara took this in.

"True," she admitted.

A nurse entered the room, saw Dr. Barbara, and left.

"I have to fly home tomorrow," Barbara said. "I had to reschedule several surgeries and I can't keep postponing them. And everything seems to be under control here. A woman named Sandy will take you home when you're ready. She's been here several times, but you were asleep. She said she's your cleaner?" Barbara phrased it as a question.

"She's more than my cleaner," Ida said. "She's my good friend."

"She seemed quite capable, and she knew so much about you, she convinced me that she could handle everything," Barbara concluded.

Sandy could even handle Dr. Barbara, Ida reflected.

"I was thinking," Barbara went on casually, "it might be time for you to consider Assisted Living."

"Assisted Living? What on earth for?" Ida protested. That would mean no kitchen. No oven. No baking! It was out of the question. "I will not even consider it!" Ida declared.

Barbara didn't press the issue. She promised to call Ida daily, and left to pack for her return to Los Angeles.

Two days later, Sandy arrived with Ida's clothes.

"You scared me nearly to death!" Sandy cried out.

"You should have known better," Ida admonished her. "I would never let something like a fire get me."

"I guess you're right," Sandy agreed.

"Is my apartment all right?" Ida asked.

"You were lucky," Sandy told her. "And smart. You closed all of your windows before you left, and that kept most of the smoke out."

Ida had no recollection of closing the windows—that memory thing!

"The kitchen was a bit grimy, though," Sandy continued, "but I got that cleaned up."

"What has happened to the twins? Are they still there?" Ida asked. Barbara had assured her that all the tenants had escaped, but she wanted more concrete knowledge.

"I didn't see them when I went back," Sandy said. "But sometimes you could go weeks without seeing them. In any case, I'm sure Kitty's apartment isn't livable. That's where the fire started, apparently. You can tell by looking at her windows."

Then the China dolls must have gone, Ida thought sadly. Kitty would definitely not move in with Lily and Sven, and Lily wouldn't stay without Kitty.

Sandy helped Ida get dressed and they left the hospital in a taxi. The apartment building on Bayside Avenue looked the same, except for the soot-blackened window of Kitty's kitchen and an extra-large pile of trash out on the sidewalk.

"I guess they're still cleaning out Kitty's apartment," Sandy remarked, nodding at the burned mess.

As they walked past the trash, something caught Ida's eye. It was a book. The cover was a bit singed at the edges, but the size and shape were familiar.

"Sandy, look," Ida pointed. "Over there. Could you grab that book?"

Sandy reached over, snatched the book, and held it up: the Martha Stewart Cookies book!

Ida beamed as Sandy handed it to her. She opened it and flipped through the pages. Sure enough, there were her hand-written notes scribbled in the margins. And now she wondered: was it possible she had agreed to lend the book to the twins, and forgotten?

"It's a miracle that book survived!" Sandy exclaimed. "It should have been burned to a crisp."

Ida tucked the book under her arm and they continued to the lobby.

Up in her apartment, everything seemed just as she had left it. She noted the bookshelf and the gap where the Martha Stewart Cookies book had been. Now the gap could be filled.

"If you make a list, I'll go to the store," Sandy offered.

Ida jotted down a few items, including eggs and butter, and Sandy left.

Ida was glad to be home, yet there was an emptiness, knowing the China dolls were gone. But never being one to brood, she began to look through her Martha Stewart Cookies book, trying to decide what she would bake next.

Epilogue

Ida attended Monica's wedding a month later. She found the groom very handsome, and met his friends, all of whom rode motorcycles. When she returned home, she baked and sent the happy couple large batches of cookies (Sandy brought the packages to the Post Office) which, Monica reported, were well received, especially by the bikers.

Arthur became devoted to Ida, which she took as a mixed blessing.

"If you need anything, just call and I'll come immediately," he assured her.

She occasionally left a plate of cookies at his door, but managed to avoid another visit to the man cave.

That December, as a few snowflakes drifted from the sky, Ida looked out her kitchen window and recalled how one year ago the China dolls had arrived. A few days later she reached into her mailbox and took out a postcard. There was foreign postage on it and she couldn't imagine who might have sent it. Then she made out the scribbled message:

"Dear Ida, we now have cookie shop in Hong Kong! Please come to visit! Kitty and Lily"

The China dolls! She turned the card over and looked at the picture of a storefront. The sign was in English and Chinese: Good

Fortune Cookie Company. So the twins had gone into the baking business in Hong Kong. Ida puffed up with pride. After all, she had been their teacher.

For a moment she actually contemplated going to Hong Kong for a surprise visit. She had survived the trip to Los Angeles. But then she reminded herself that she had recently passed her ninety-second birthday, and Hong Kong was much farther away than California. So she folded a piece of plastic wrap around the postcard to keep it clean, and propped it on the kitchen counter, and whenever she baked, she thought of the China dolls and the fun they had together.

Acknowledgements

Many thanks to Iris Lee and Lina Zeldovich for their continued moral support of my writing and to Iris Lee for her editorial assistance.